"Come with me," Buckingham said. "Come back to England with me and I will make you my wife."

"But I am already married."

"He will divorce you, if you come with me, and I will make sure that Richelieu does nothing to interfere."

Anne shivered. She knew Richelieu too well, and the thought of what he might do to stop her chilled the marrow of her being.

Buckingham held her tightly. "I will not let anyone or anything keep us apart," he promised. But he was unaware that the diabolic Richelieu himself had made the identical vow for the same woman....

THE
PASSION

AND THE
RAGE

Elizabeth Godwin

FAWCETT GOLD MEDAL • **NEW YORK**

THE PASSION AND THE RAGE

© 1980 Elizabeth Godwin

Published by Fawcett Gold Medal Books, a unit of CBS Publications, the Consumer Publishing Division of CBS Inc.

ISBN: 0-449-14320-1

Printed in the United States of America

First Fawcett Gold Medal printing: February 1980

10 9 8 7 6 5 4 3 2 1

ONE

      A messenger had come the previous evening, ordering him to present himself to the king with all possible haste. But he had stayed with his host, Sir Anthony Midmay, until he had taken dinner with the old gentleman and had spent a pleasant few hours giving him a full account of the latest happenings at court. It had been nigh midnight when he had finally left to answer the urgent summons of Charles, the King of England.

"Let his highness wait," he had told his host. "I have little enough time that I might call my own." There had been more than a trace of haughtiness in his rich bass voice. He might have added that he had known why the king had suddenly summoned him back to Whitehall Palace. But he had not. His years at court had taught him that even dear old friends could not always be trusted.

"The matter, I am sure," he had said with a smile that brought boyish dimples to his manly face, "will not lose one jot of its urgency if I tarry here awhile longer. For by God's own truth, even an hour away from the court is a good physic for the weariness of the place. If it were not for my coming here to Apethorpe from time to time, I might truly perish."

His host had laughed, and shaking his bony forefinger at him, had declared him to be "a most persuasive liar, probably equal to the Prince of Liars, the very Devil himself." Sir Anthony's green eyes had twinkled merrily as he had spoken to George Villiers, the first Duke of Buckingham. And now, hours later, Buckingham sat wrapped in his sable-trimmed cloak, chilled to the very bone, as his coach jounced its way through the darkened streets of London. The journey from Apethorpe in Northamptonshire had swallowed what remained of the night. Along the way, he had dozed intermittently. But as soon as the coach entered the city, he awakened and gave orders to his coachman to head for the docks below London Bridge. He intended to go to Whitehall by wherry. Not because he preferred the long, light rowboat to any other mode of transportation, but rather because he knew the king would expect him to arrive at the palace by coach, or perhaps astride some snorting stallion, breathless from a long hard ride. To do the unexpected, when the ordinary would suffice, had always been his hallmark, and he saw no reason to change.

A cold mizzling rain was falling when the coach came to a halt. The footman hastened to open the door for him.

In the east the sky was a gray wash. The smell of the sea mingled with the stink of the river. The tide was out, and many of the larger ships rested hull-down in the mud of the riverbed.

He turned to the footman and, adjusting his sword,

said, "My compliments to Lady Buckingham. Tell her I was called by the king from Apethorpe and I will return to her as soon as I am finished with the king's business."

"Yes, milord," the man answered respectfully.

Buckingham nodded and, gathering his cloak more securely around him, walked down the rickety wooden steps and onto the floating platform, where the wherrymen were waiting like so many sleeping birds of prey.

As soon as they saw him the many rose as one and in a single voice called out, "Hoars, sir, hoars, will you 'ave my hoars t'is mornin'?"

The duke slowed his pace. In the ever-graying light of the coming dawn, he cast his eyes over the lot of them.

They were hard-looking men, with broad chests, bent backs, and arms thickly corded with muscles from a lifetime of pulling at the oars.

"You there," Buckingham called to a man with cornsilk hair and an enormous pair of hands. "A shilling to take me to Whitehall before the sun is full up."

"I'll take ye to Whitehall, but none in London will see the sun today," he said, gesturing up toward the sky. "An' maybe not tomorrow either, if'n the clouds an' rain stay."

Buckingham smiled: the man's answer was more sensible than his offer. "The shilling is yours for the journey no matter if the sun comes full up or remains hidden," he said.

"Done!" the wherryman replied, offering his hand to help the aristocratic-looking gentleman down into the wherry. He was surprised by the strength of his passenger's grip; it was easily the equal of his own.

As soon as the duke had settled himself on the bow thwart, the wherryman pushed away from the landing stage and began to row. Many of his fellow wherrymen good-naturedly shouted obscenities after him, which he volleyed back with foul-mouthed

7

curses that brought a smile to Buckingham's finely shaped lips.

"It be all in fun," the wherryman explained, as he guided the small craft toward the middle of the Thames. "They be good lads...known 'em most of me life. A few of the ol' ones knew me father an' mother."

"It's good to have friends of long standing," the duke said, though he was quite sure the wherryman did not expect him to answer. Men in his station seldom spoke to those beneath them, unless to give them an order. And any extended conversation was unthinkable. The working classes existed for the sole purpose of serving their betters. It had always been so and so it would always be...at least that was generally the way people believed. Even the duke served a master, though his, by the grace of God, happened to be the king.

"'Cept fer grub, a warm dry place to sleep an' a woman to lay wid, a man's friends is all he has that's worth anythin'."

"Yes, I suspect you are right," Buckingham replied.

The wherry was almost in midstream now, and though nothing of the sun was seen, the sky had become perceptibly lighter. The dark shadows of night were, before the duke's very eyes, giving way to variegated shades of gray.

In the pearly light, much more of the river and the life on it were being etched. Other wherries were moving within hailing distance of the one he was on. Downriver there was a veritable forest of masts, to say nothing of the hoys heavily loaded with everything from coal to foodstuffs for the eager buyers in London. Much of the wealth that came into the country from distant places entered by way of the docks that crowded both banks of the river below London Bridge.

"Tide comin' in," the wherryman said, glancing over his shoulder at the gentleman who had hired his craft. "Be changin' 'bout the time we reach the bridge. Best hold fast to the gun'ls—t'e river gets to be very fast there."

Buckingham thanked him for his concern and assured him he had gone upstream with the tide many times before.

Mist along the banks of the river thickened, obscuring most of the structures or making them appear so insubstantial that they might easily be mistaken for the contents of some strange dream, or even an illusion on a river that in gathering fog appeared to be lost, having no beginning and no end.

The duke suddenly felt the surge of the incoming tide. It lifted the wherry and moved it forward with incredible swiftness.

The wherryman laughed and sang out, "I'll let the river do me work fer a bit." And he lay back on the oars, using one or another of them to keep the craft from moving too far to the right or left.

The wherryman knew his trade. Buckingham enjoyed watching him, as he enjoyed watching anything done with a high degree of skill. It was said of him at court that he was as wont to dally at a blacksmith's forge or a potter's wheel as to take part in the afternoon's social functions.

"Hark ye!" the wherryman exclaimed. "You can hear the water growlin' at the bridge. I can let you off on this side an' pick you up at the O'd Swan on the other. Save ye from a good washin'."

"A good dousing will wake me up and make me fit company when I come before the king," the duke answered.

"Aye, so it be his majesty ya be goin' to see. I was wonderin' what takes a man to Whitehall so early in the day."

"I assure you, my good man, none but a summons from the king would bring me there." Buckingham laughed.

The roar of the water pouring through narrow arches became much louder and more turbulent.

The wherryman dug his oars in the rushing tide.

He fought to keep his craft from being caught up by the surging water and spun around. Now and then he looked over his shoulder at the bridge that began to rise darkly out of the water.

The bridge itself was no more than a street with houses thrown across it and nineteen stone piers supporting it. Where the channel was very deep, a drawbridge permitted smaller ships to make their way to the upper reaches of the river.

Buckingham now turned to the bow. The wherry was so close to the bridge that not only was the yellow glow of many lanterns visible, but the structure itself loomed up. Within moments, the frail craft was hurtling toward one of the black openings of the arches. Its bow was suddenly deep in the white rush of the water.

The duke tightened his hold on the gunwale. A shower of water rose up and then rained down on him. The roar of the water was deafening. The wherry pitched and rolled violently. The bow suddenly leaped up and moments later slammed down. It was almost as if they were suddenly caught by a giant hand. All at once they were plunged into the total darkness of the archway.

The river hurled itself at the stone piers and in turn was thrown back. The water rushed forward, taking the wherry with it.

Suddenly they broke free of the darkness: they were on the other side of the bridge, where the river was considerably calmer.

Buckingham used a handkerchief to wipe the water from his face.

"It be easy from here," the wherryman said, as he began to row in a steady, easy stroke. "If'n there'd be sun today, you'd be at Whitehall before it be full up."

The duke laughed and agreed he would. Then he did something that even for him was unusual: he asked the man his name.

"Ed," the wherryman answered. "Me name be Ed.... An' wot be yours?"

"Buckingham," the duke replied. "I am Buckingham."

"I'd shake yer hand, milord." Ed laughed. "But I'd have to stop rowin'."

After they had exchanged names, each of them lapsed into silence. Convention would not permit either man to press the conversation. Besides, Ed was already breathing hard from pulling at the oars, and the duke was becoming immersed in his thoughts.

Buckingham looked meditatively toward Whitehall, which was just beginning to show itself through the mist. From his own sources of information in France, he had already learned that Lord Kensington had concluded, but a few days before, the necessary arrangements that would enable King Charles to marry Henrietta Maria, the fourteen-year-old sister of Louis XIII, the King of France.

His summons by the king was, he was certain, for him to be personally apprised of the forthcoming nuptials and to discuss the various items Cardinal Richelieu had managed to make part of the marriage contract. Charles had already given his guarantee to allow English Roman Catholics freedom of worship. But Richelieu must have asked for considerably more before he would permit Louis to agree to the marriage.

The cardinal, the duke knew, was the power behind the French throne—even more than he, himself, was in England. Each of them served weak masters. Richelieu was Louis' minister. Buckingham, in addition to all his official titles, was the king's favorite. The duke was determined not to allow Charles to give away anything that might make England suffer in any way in the present or the future, regardless of how much the king wanted a queen at his side or in bed.

"We're here, milord," Ed announced, shipping his oars as he brought the wherry smoothly alongside the stone landing.

Buckingham sprang up and leaped onto the quay.

He was a tall man with good shoulders, a narrow waist, light-blue eyes, a well-tended beard, and long black hair, which he refused to cover with a wig. The wavering light of the torches made him look taller and cast his shadow over the wherry. Though he was in his mid-thirties, he looked much younger.

"Two shillings," he said, taking the coins from his purse. "One for swiftness and a second for the pleasure of your company." He tossed the coins to the wherryman.

Ed caught them and asked if he should wait.

"I cannot say how long I will be," Buckingham answered. "But if ever I need a wherry and I find myself where I found you, rest assured I shall seek you out."

"Thank ye, milord, thank ye. And God bless ye!"

Buckingham waved, pushed back his cloak, and with his right hand resting easily on the golden hilt of his sword, he strode up to the palace entrance.

Immediately the two palace guards crossed their halberds in front of him, blocking his way.

"The Duke of Buckingham is here to answer the king's summons," he said in a tone of authority. "Call your captain so I might not keep the king waiting any longer than is necessary."

One of the men shouted for the officer of the guards. As soon as he showed himself, the duke was admitted into the interior of the palace, receiving from the captain of the guards a profound apology for the delay.

"I would have been more annoyed," the duke told the officer, "if I had not been challenged." And having managed to mollify the captain's fear that his men might have unwittingly insulted him, he hurried on his way, making the huge rooms echo with his footfalls.

While Buckingham walked toward the king's apartment, various servants ran ahead to announce his arrival. As the duke passed from one chamber to another the doors opened. Most of the rooms were dimly lit with a few candles. The members of the court were still abed and would not be stirring for several hours.

The duke knew that though he was answering his master's call, his master was waiting for him. Halfway through the palace, he slowed his pace and turned right. As he approached a huge oak door, it swung open, allowing him to enter the king's private study, and a servant announced him.

The king was on his feet. He wore a blue silk dressing gown with the Stuart coat of arms embroidered in gold over his heart. Physically, Charles was a small man. His forehead was very high, his hair light brown, and his slightly prominent eyes had a perpetual look of sadness in them.

The duke dropped to his knee and said, "I am here, your grace, in answer to your urgent summons."

Charles motioned him to stand. "But how did you come here?" he questioned. And before the duke could answer, he said, "We told the guards at the gate—"

"Excuse me, your grace," the duke interrupted, "but I did not come through the main gate."

The king looked up at him questioningly.

"I came by wherry," the duke explained.

"On the river? At this ungodly time?"

"Oh, I assure you my journey was quite rapid. I and the incoming tide reached the palace landing at about the same time."

A light came into Charles' sad eyes; his lips drew apart into a smile.

"Upon my word, Buckingham," he said, laughing, "we should have expected you to do something like that. Next time you will be coming down the chimney."

"If it would mean I might attend your grace more rapidly, then I would at least make a try of it, though I would have to be quite sure there would be no fire below."

The king laughed heartily. Then, clapping his hands, he ordered the door to the room closed. As soon as they were alone much of the formality between them vanished.

The duke flung his cloak over the back of a leather chair and moved to the fire to warm himself, stretching his hands out toward the flames.

"Well, Steenie," the king began, using the name his father had given to Buckingham, "Kensington has finally arranged for us to have our queen."

The duke turned from the hearth and, feigning complete surprise, expressed delight over the turn of events. "Your grace," he said, "I always knew Louis would see the sense of such a union. It most definitely draws our two nations closer together. I was sure that Kensington would win over Richelieu."

The king moved off to a corner of the room and without looking at the duke said, "She will be allowed to continue her faith, and our children will be entrusted to her keeping until they reach the age of thirteen. She will have her own chapels and chaplains. All her private attendants will be French and Catholic. She will come here with a bishop and twenty-eight priests." He turned slowly. "It is little to give," he added somewhat pleadingly, "when you consider what is being given in return."

"Thirteen years is a long time," the duke said, "to have a child's head filled with popish ideas."

"I have agreed to those conditions," Charles said, suddenly launching himself out of the corner.

"As you wish, your grace," the duke responded. "But the questions I raise are not to deny your grace his queen."

"Once she is here," Charles answered, "matters could very well take a different turn."

The duke nodded. There was some truth in that.

"We will be married by proxy. The Duc de Chevreuse will stand for me. And I want you to go to France and bring my wife back to England."

"I am deeply honored," the duke answered in a suitable tone of voice, though he would have much preferred the honor to have been placed on some other courtier's shoulders.

"I can trust you, Steenie," Charles said.

The duke did not feel a response was necessary.

"And while you are there," the king said more buoyantly, "I have two other tasks for you to attend to for me." He smiled and added, "But we will speak of them another time. Now you must ready yourself for your journey to France."

Charles moved rapidly around the room. "I think this marriage will have far-reaching consequences for all of Europe," he said. "France and England together will be able to do what neither nation could do alone." He spoke with passionate conviction. "With Louis as my brother-in-law I'll be in an excellent position to look after the well-being of my country and my family." He stopped in front of a huge window overlooking a small garden that in a few months would be filled with red and yellow roses, but now was as bare and gray as a gravestone. For a long time, the king looked silently out on the garden.

The duke eased himself back to the hearth. Two years had passed since he had last been in France. He shook his head, as if to drive away whatever unpleasant memories might have been called up by his impending trip abroad.

"And I know I can depend on you to be discreet in your personal relationships," the king said, slowly turning from the window. "I have already sent word to Kensington that you are coming."

With a sardonic smile, the duke said, "You can be sure the cardinal will make every effort to see that I am more than discreet."

"Have you had any communication from Anne?" the king asked.

"A brief letter now and then."

The king nodded and moved his hand over his thin beard several times before he spoke. "How much of your *affaire de coeur* does Katherine know about?" he asked.

"I have never spoken about it with her," the Duke answered. "I had no cause to either hurt her or give her insult. But she must know at least as much as everyone else at court."

Suddenly the king's mood changed, and with a burst of high-pitched laughter he said, "Now tell me honestly, Buckingham, whether you want to go or not."

"But I thought the matter was settled."

The king gestured to the writing table. "I have but to affix my signature to those papers and speed them on their way and the matter will be settled."

"Then—"

The king came up to Buckingham and, reaching up, clapped him on the back. "It is my duty, nay my right, to sound out those to whom I entrust great missions of state. Will you go and fetch my bride?"

"I will go, your grace," the duke answered, making a sweeping bow from the waist. "But," he added, "your surprise was far greater than mine."

"How so?" The king laughed.

"I only came to your grace's presence by way of the river gate, but you are sending me from my wife to fetch yours and see the woman I love."

"Are you angry with me, Steenie?"

"Only with myself," the duke responded, "for not having found the way to whistle myself down your chimney."

The two men laughed comfortably.

By the time Buckingham left the king's apartment, the morning was well advanced and many of the courtiers were about, readying themselves for whatever activities the day brought. The duke walked swiftly through the huge rooms, now illuminated by countless lamps and hundreds of candles in an effort to dispel the grayness of the day. He was in a foul mood and only nodded to those who hailed him with the expectation of holding a conversation.

Anyone seeking a royal favor stood a far better chance of having it granted if the petition was put before the king by the Duke of Buckingham. He held that much power; yet he himself was powerless to deny the king anything. Change his royal mind, yes. But never was it possible for him to say *no,* regardless of the nature of the request.

The duke charged out of the palace. He hurried past the gate, ignoring the cries of coachmen who knew him and were anxious to have him as a passenger.

The rain was steady and driven by an east wind. The busy roadways around the palace were already turned to mud. A stream of wagons, riders, and people afoot moved along the city's streets. Vendors shouted their wares, hawking everything from food to Spanish blades.

The duke shouldered his way through the crowds. His first thought was to go home and sleep, but he changed his mind. His humor was too black for him to get any rest, and he had no desire to make Katherine suffer because of his anger. She was a good woman and a fine mother to his daughter.

Buckingham slowed his pace. Realizing his audience with the king had given him a thirst, he stopped at the Laughing Crow, an inn known more for the roughnecks to be found there any hour of the day or night than for the quality of its drink and food. The duke had visited it and others like it many times with several of the more adventurous members of the court.

Buckingham entered the inn. Despite the hour it was crowded and noisy and smelled heavily of sweat, sour beer, and roasted meat. Several of the men close to the door stopped talking when they saw him.

The duke looked at them. His pale-blue eyes, which women thought pleasing and men found either inscrutable or devoid of any warmth, like the blue ice found in the frozen parts of the sea, forced them to turn away.

A short, bald-headed man in a greasy apron came pushing through the crowd. "Milord," he wheezed, "how might Michael Dodds serve you this dreadful morning?"

Buckingham was suddenly undecided about his choice of drinking place. He was alone, and though he was an excellent swordsman, he would be no match for three or four well-armed men.

"I remember you, milord," Dodds said. "You came here a fortnight or so ago with two or three other gentlemen."

"I did," Buckingham answered.

Dodds grinned. "You're not an easy one to forget," he said. "Not too many gentlemen who come here are as generous as yourself."

Buckingham thanked him for the compliment and remarked that the place was too crowded for his liking.

"I have a pleasant closet," Dodds said, "where a gentleman can be alone, or share his time and drink with a wench, if that be his pleasure."

"Alone," Buckingham said sharply.

"As you wish, milord," Dodds answered with a slight bow.

Buckingham followed the innkeeper to the other side of the room, where they mounted a narrow flight of steps and entered an ill-lit hallway.

"The rooms here," Dodds explained with a gesture of his hand, "are for the use of my customers. Some take them by the night, some by the week, and some even by the hour."

Buckingham's room was next to the last. It was small, furnished with a bed, a table, two chairs, and a stand for a pewter basin and ewer of water. A small grime-covered window looked out on a narrow, dirty alleyway.

18

"Be extra threepence for candles," Dodds said. "Five more for clean linen on the bed."

Buckingham went to the door and examined the lock.

"You'll be safe enough in here, milord," Dodds assured him.

Buckingham paid for the candles and the clean linen. "The rest you will have when I leave here," he said, dropping his cloak over one of the chairs. "Now send me up your best Madeira, bread and —"

"I have some fine roasted mutton, capons, an' squabs," the innkeeper told him.

"A brace of squabs," Buckingham said.

"Are you sure that you don't want a wench?"

"If I change my mind," Buckingham replied, "I will tell you."

"See that rope there," Dodds said with a twinkle in his brown eyes, "the one above the head of the bed? You just pull on it three times and before you know it a wench will be at your service. Those that are here are some of the best-lookin' ones in London, and clean, too. I have a surgeon look at them every so often for the pox, or I does it myself." He grinned broadly. "There's a bit of fun in doing that. Now if you want to—"

"My food and drink, Master Dodds!" Buckingham ordered.

"Yes, milord," Dodds answered with a bow, as he slowly backed out of the room.

Buckingham closed the door and went to the window. He tried to open it, only to discover it was nailed shut—a precaution taken, no doubt, to prevent a guest from leaving before paying his score.

Buckingham removed his sword but slipped the blade halfway out of its scabbard and placed it against the wall, within easy reach of his right hand should he have to draw it. He sat down on the edge of the bed and pulled off his boots, opened his short jacket, and loosened the lace around his neck. He was very weary. With a deep sigh, he stretched out on the bed and placed his hands behind his head.

Directly above him was one of the half-dozen raw wood beams that supported the ceiling. Even in the grayness of the room he could see several star-shaped spiderwebs suspended along the length of the beam and the calcimined surface of the ceiling. His eyes moved from wall to wall. They were bare and streaked with filth.

He wondered whether, as some claimed, the walls retained the memories of events that happened in the room. If they did, then surely they must have been witness to all manner of human passions and crimes.

He pursed his lips; it was not something that anyone could know with any degree of certainty, and because it could not be easily demonstrated, he was oddly thankful. He closed his eyes.

In a room not much different from the one he now occupied he had first held Anne of Austria, the Queen of France, in his arms... nay, he first made love to her!

The inn, Les Trois Cygnes, was on the Rue St. Jacques, on the north side of Paris. The meeting had been arranged for him by the Duchesse de Chevreuse, a lady in waiting to the queen. The assignation had taken place in the early evening of a bitter-cold November day, with the sky full of rushing dark clouds and the smell of snow heavy on the air.

He had arrived at the inn some two hours before the hour set for their tryst. Under the name of M. Cordeaux, he had engaged the room for the night and ordered food and drink. Because his command of the French language was flawless, he was sure his real nationality would not be discovered. And in a conversation with the innkeeper, a thin man with a jolly laugh, he had nonchalantly informed him he would be expecting a guest. The innkeeper had nodded and with a chuckle had offered another bottle of wine for the lady, saying he would be sure not to disturb them.

"Oh Anne...Anne," Buckingham said aloud, looking again at the bare walls. "I have been only half alive these past two years...only half alive!"

With a ragged sigh, he closed his eyes again and allowed himself the luxury of recalling the sweet memory of his assignation with the queen....

Except for the flickering yellow light from a single candle and the reddish glow spread out around the small hearth, the room had been quite dark. The arrangement agreed upon between them was for him to wait in the room.

When the time grew nigh to her arrival, he began to pace, pausing now and then to look out at the dark street. He as anxious as an untried man.

A dozen unforeseen situations might have prevented Anne from joining him. The king could have asked for her company, though that was something he seldom did. The queen mother, Marie de' Medici, might have become suspicious of the sudden light in her daughter-in-law's black eyes.

But neither the king nor the queen mother caused him as much concern as Richelieu. For several days, Buckingham had been aware that the cardinal's men were following him, though he was quite sure he had skillfully managed to elude them before arriving at the inn. The cardinal was as much his adversary as if he had raised a sword against him. Buckingham would have preferred to face Richelieu that way than to have to counterplot against his plots.

Then suddenly his thoughts were interrupted by the sound of several horses outside the inn. He rushed to the window. His breath quickly fogged the glass. He hastily wiped it clear with his handkerchief.

There were two women wearing black cloaks, and four musketeers. The two women hurriedly entered the inn, while one of the musketeers led the horses to the stable behind the inn and the other three men took up positions in the street. One remained in sight of the inn, but the other two were lost in the darkness. Before he turned from the window, Buckingham realized that sometime during the evening it had begun to snow.

He faced the door. His heart beat so loudly he was sure the sound filled the room. He heard the steps creak, then light footfalls in the passageway.

She stopped.

He took a deep breath.

She knocked softly.

In a trice, Buckingham was at the door. His impulse was to fling it open, but instead he moved it slowly until she stood fully before him. The upper portion of her face was concealed by a black domino. Though she was completely cloaked, the rapid rise and fall of her breasts was clearly visible.

Neither of them spoke.

Buckingham stepped back into the room and, with a gesture of his hand, bade her enter. As soon as she was across the threshold, he closed the door and slipped the bolt into place. His heart was still hammering. The words he wanted to say did not seem right for the situation, and so he remained silent.

The queen stood close to the bed. She ran her black-gloved hand over the edge of the eiderdown quilt.

Buckingham stood with his back against the door. Once before he had been wildly in love, but that had been years ago. James had been on the throne, and he himself had just become the old king's favorite. He had been foolish enough to let his heart loose to the daughter of Sir Roger Aston, master of the robes. But for all his feelings, the relationship had no chance of ever coming to anything more than a love affair between two young and very beautiful people. Neither she nor he had a fortune. And he had been told by her father, Sir Roger, and his own parents that a good dowry, rather than love, should guide him into wedlock. He had followed their advice and had eventually married Katherine Manners, the daughter of the Earl of Rutland.

The queen faced him. She pushed the hood from her head. "We came here by a circuitous route," she told him in a small, uncertain voice.

"I was afraid you would not come," Buckingham said, realizing his voice was as uncertain as hers.

She untied the string of her cloak.

Buckingham rushed forward, took the garment from her hands, and set it over the back of a chair. He did the same with her long gloves when she gave them to him. Finally, she removed the domino.

She wore a blue taffeta gown, with small puffed sleeves trimmed with white lace.

Her face was flushed. Her eyes were alive with green fire. Between her breasts she wore a simple cross of gold. The queen was twenty-four years old. She stood very straight. Her mouth was small, with a lower lip slightly behind the upper one. Her skin was very white. She wore her chestnut hair curled plainly on the top of her head.

Buckingham could no longer contain himself. Sweeping her into his arms, he pressed his hungry lips against hers. They devoured each other with kisses. Her lips tasted of cherries, and the floral perfume she wore filled his brain with marvelous bursts of yellows.

"Oh, Anne," he whispered, "I have prayed for this moment."

"And I have longed for it," she told him in a voice choked with emotion. "I have dreamed of it."

Buckingham kissed that place between her neck and shoulder that pulsed with the surge of blood. His hand glided gently over her breasts.

She trembled and in a low tremulous voice, she said, "If I am backward with the ways of love, please, I beg you to be patient with me. Though I am married, I have known neither love nor pleasure."

"I will be patient," he assured Anne, holding her fiercely to him.

They kissed again; this time Buckingham moved his tongue against hers, while his hand undid the top three buttons of her gown. He freed one breast, put his lips to its full-budded nipple, and—

The door to his room suddenly burst open! Buckingham was flung out of his reverie. He opened his eyes.

Two men with clubs in their hands came at him.

He rolled off the bed and at the same time grabbed his sword, freeing it from the scabbard with one swift motion.

The two assailants rushed at him.

Before he could scramble to his feet, the duke took a sharp blow across his left arm. But the moment he was standing, he drove his blade into the chest of one man and with lightning swiftness parried a blow by the second man, who, realizing he was no match for the agile duke, dropped his cudgel and fled from the room.

Buckingham went after him, chasing the man down the narrow flight of steps and into the main room of the inn. But the man pushed his way through the crowd of drinkers, ran through the door and into the street.

"One did not escape," Buckingham announced, looking at the bloodstained point of his weapon. He turned and retreated up the steps.

The innkeeper came hurrying after him.

"Recognize him?" Buckingham asked, pointing to the dead man with his sword.

Dodds shook his head.

Buckingham went through the dead man's pockets. He found nothing that could identify him.

"They must have followed you here, milord," Dodds offered.

Buckingham shrugged but did not answer. He had many enemies. Any of them might have hired the two men to kill him.

"At least," the duke said, "they got more than they bargained for—especially the one in there. You can be sure he did not come here expecting to be killed. To be the killer, yes...but to be the one who is killed, absolutely not." He reached down and began to put on his boots.

"Then you'll not be staying to eat and drink what you ordered?" the innkeeper asked.

Standing up, Buckingham said, "I think not, Master Dodds, I think not." He placed several shillings on the table. "That should more than pay for the wine, bread, and squabs. Today," he commented, "I seem to be under the influence of an evil star. I think I would be wise if I went straight home."

A short while later, Buckingham left the inn. It was still raining. He hired a litter and told the men to take him to Wallingford House, in Westminster.

TWO

From the window in the sitting room of her apartment, Anne of Austria, Queen of France, looked out at the bare gardens that stretched away from the Louvre for a considerable distance before they came to an abrupt halt at the edge of the Seine. As far as she could see an early-spring snow covered every-thing white. The cold was so intense that ice had formed along the banks of the river the previous night.

"And to think," the queen said, "just two days ago, I saw buds on some of the bushes in the garden. Signs of spring were everywhere. There was that certain delicious feeling of warmth in the air . . . Now there is snow, a wind that howls like a mad wolf and—did you hear that yesterday several wolves were seen to the north of the city?"

She turned toward her lady in waiting, Marie de Rohan-Montbazon, Duchesse de Chevreuse, a beautiful woman of thirty-two, who continued her needlepoint, despite the fact that the queen had asked her a question.

"Louis says this change in the weather is a bad omen," Anne continued, moving from the window to stand before the hearth, where a roaring fire made the air considerably warmer than it had been near the window. "And this time, I will not take issue with him. It is a sign from God that many things will go awry in the seasons to come."

Mme. de Chevreuse looked up from her work, and with her dark-blue eyes fixed on the queen, she said, "I will wager that your signs are very different from the king's. His future may be black as night, but yours will be filled with glorious sunshine."

"Do you really think so?" Anne asked, the tone of her voice betraying her hopefulness.

"I believe it, or I would not say it," the queen's lady-in-waiting answered, adjusting her blond hair with her right hand.

Anne pirouetted three times, and crossing her arms over her breasts, she said, "If only...if only...if only..."

"If only what?"

"If only I could believe my fortune will change, and will be bright with sunshine, then I would look forward to the coming of each new day with delight and not the heavy heart that burdens me so."

Mme. de Chevreuse clicked her tongue sympathetically. "There are so many young men at court who would be only too eager to please your highness," she said. "Several would risk all to serve you."

"And they would lose all, if they were found out," Anne answered. She faced the hearth and watched the flames devour one of the huge logs that lay across the brass andirons. After a long pause, she said in a low voice, "It is not easy, Marie, for a woman, even though she be a queen, to know she is unloved by her husband."

Again Mme. de Chevreuse clicked her tongue. She knew, as everyone else at court did, that Louis was too caught up in the constricting coils of his faith to allow himself to enjoy the pleasure of a woman's embrace.

"As Queen of France," Anne commented bitterly, "I have all a woman might desire. But..." As she spoke, she once again turned to her lady-in-waiting. "I do not have, nor will I ever have, the love of the man to whom I was joined until death us do part. It is a harsh sentence for one whose only crime was to have been born a woman."

Marie moved aside her needlepoint frame and stood up. She was a statuesque woman, with full, high breasts and flaring hips. Her own husband, the Duc de Chevreuse, the youngest son of the house of Lorraine, was much more interested in other young men than he was in his wife. At court, in each other's company, they were courteous and amicable. But they scarcely spent one night together under the same roof, let alone in the same bed. She agreed not to interfere with his way of life, and because he was a gentleman, he offered her the same arrangement.

Marie moved closer to the queen. "My own situation," she said, "gives me some knowledge—nay, insight—into your sadness. It is much like my own. But for the experience of my previous marriage, I too would never have known the full measure of joy that love, physical love, can bring."

Anne flushed.

"May I speak frankly?" Mme. de Chevreuse asked.

In the light of the intimacy of their relationship, the question was asked more for effect than from actual need. There were few things that were not discussed between them.

Marie had even been instrumental in arranging the meeting between the queen and Buckingham at the inn on the Rue St. Jacques. She had accompanied her there and had waited in the room below while she and the duke had given free rein to their passion for each other. Even Louis complained that Anne was too close to Mme. de Chevreuse, that she would do well to be less open with her lady-in-waiting, or failing that, then she should consider changing her.

"We would be nothing if we could not speak frankly to each other," the queen replied.

"Then I say to you," Mme. de Chevreuse told her, "that it is time you took another lover."

Anne shook her head. "There is no one I want," she replied.

"But there are those who want you," Mme. de Chevreuse told her. "The letters from Buckingham, though they satisfy the needs of your heart, cannot satisfy the needs of your flesh. It takes other flesh to do that."

Anne wrung her hands.

"You must understand, my lady, our lives are so arranged that our feelings are never considered when we are sent to the marriage bed; indeed, it is only later that we come to understand that we have any feelings about sex at all. Oh yes, there are a few lucky women whom God has blessed with a spouse who loves them in the spiritual as well as the physical sense of the word. But these are few, and neither you or I are among them. We must seek satisfaction in a bed other than the one into which we were put by our marriage. And if we are fortunate we might even come to experience love, or some feeling close to it, while we satisfy a more urgent need."

The log that lay across the andirons suddenly broke apart, sending up a shower of sparks.

Anne unclasped her hands and glanced over her shoulder at the hearth.

"The king's own brother, Gaston, is ready to serve you," Mme. de Chevreuse said, before the queen could turn to her again. "And he is not the only one."

Anne repeated Gaston's name and, facing her lady-in-waiting, she told her, "Because he makes me laugh, that does not mean I want him between my thighs." She waved her right hand. "I think it is time for Gaston to be married, or take a new mistress. I will not have him for a lover."

Mme. de Chevreuse nodded silently. She had not mentioned Gaston's name without purpose. It was the beginning of a scheme that could, if successful, put Gaston on the throne of France. Having brought forth his name once, she would not hesitate to bring it up again whenever the conversation between herself and the queen touched upon the subject of love.

"I think it is time to have some of the lamps and candles lit," Anne said.

Without hesitation, Mme. de Chevreuse opened the door and summoned several of the servants. "The queen," she said, "wishes to have the lamps and candles lit. See that it is done immediately."

On the other side of the Louvre in a room with two windows that looked out on a snow-covered park, Cardinal Richelieu, the king's principal minister, received the sealed leather pouch from a courier's hand and set the bag down on his writing table. "When did these arrive?" he asked.

"Early yesterday afternoon," the courier answered. "They came to Calais."

Richelieu nodded and stood up. He was a man of middle height, slender, with a haughty air, very dark piercing eyes, a large brow, and a thin face whose length was accentuated by a pair of royal mustaches. Though he was no more than thirty-seven years old, his hair, beard, and mustaches were already flecked with gray. His bearing was military and his mode of dress resembled that of the men under his command, known as the Cardinal's Guard.

"To the fire," the cardinal said, with a quick gesture of his right hand, "and warm yourself."

"Thank you, your eminence," the man said, stretching hands out toward the flames.

"How is the sea?"

"Raging from a gale when I left," the man answered.

"Then there is no chance of another courier coming."

"Not until the storm blows itself out."

Richelieu went to the window. Snow was still falling, though not quite so heavily, it seemed to him, as before. He turned and saw the courier's eyes move around the room, pausing now and then to linger on one of the many exquisite swords, knives, and other weapons decorating the walls of his office.

"Some of them," the cardinal said, calling the man's attention to himself, "some all the way from the Holy Land. There are a few that are the only ones of their kind."

The courier nodded appreciatively.

"You say no ship sails until the storm blows out?" he questioned again. He did not enjoy being without his sources of information. He had organized an elaborate network of spies and couriers to keep him informed of what was happening in all the courts of Europe. Dispatches came to him every day, but he would have had them come every hour of the day and night, seven days a week, if he could have.

"Yes, your eminence."

The cardinal dismissed the courier, telling him to present himself to M. Suret, the quartermaster of his guards, for the night's food and lodging. He waited until he was alone before he sat down at his writing table and, using a special key, opened the lock that secured the narrow link chain to the pouch.

Quickly he riffled through the various papers that had been sent to him from London until he found the one he wanted. It had been dated two days before. There was only one line on it: *"The apple has not yet been plucked."* And it was signed "Giroux."

Richelieu stared at the dispatch with mounting anger that suddenly was expressed in a violent thump on the table with the balled fist of his right hand.

"By the living God," he said aloud, "that Buckingham has a charmed life!" In the past two years, he had secretly financed three different attempts on the duke's life, and not one of them had come anywhere near succeeding.

He reached to his left and poured some wine from a decanter into a lovely green glass, sipped at the liquid, and set the glass down. He pushed Giroux's message aside and began reading the other dispatches. Some were about the condition of the English navy; it was ridden with corruption on all levels and its ships were in a deplorable state of disrepair. Other messages told him about what was happening at court and in the city of London. Richelieu was as interested in the price of food as he was in the movement of soldiers along the roads of England.

More than an hour passed as he read the dispatches. When he finished with the last one, he was somewhat astonished to find that most of the room was filled with the dark gray of twilight and that the candles on his desk had been reduced to mere stubs.

He rubbed his eyes, reached for the glass at his left, and drank the remainder of wine. Then he picked up the message from Giroux, read it again, and, shaking his head with a combination of disgust and disbelief, put the paper in his pocket to show to Father Joseph later in the evening.

Gathering the rest of the dispatches into his hands, he carried them to the hearth and one by one committed them to the flames. He had no need to keep them. Anything that was worth remembering he had memorized, even as he had read the dispatch.

Later that night he would return and draft a message to Giroux. Not only for the king's peace of mind—as much as he, or anyone might speak for it— but also for his own, Buckingham had to be killed.

Louis XIII was a frail man, with sad brown eyes, a scraggly black beard that could not hide his weak chin, and long delicate hands. He had been a sickly child, and now, in his twenty-fifth year, his health had not improved to any great extent. Even as he accepted the obeisance of his first minister, Cardinal Richelieu, in the small dining room, where he and Anne, with the queen mother, Marie de' Medici, and his sister, Henrietta Maria, usually took their supper, he was suffering from a bad cold, brought on by the sudden change in the weather.

Richelieu offered his salutations to the three women at the table, and each returned his greeting with cold formality.

"Would you join us for coffee and pastries?" Louis offered, after blowing his nose loudly.

"You are most kind," Richelieu replied with a nod and took his place at the table. His eyes went to Anne, and for a moment he allowed himself the pleasure of looking at her lovely face, her long, graceful neck, and the white tops of her breasts.

"Anything of interest in your dispatches?" Louis asked, toying with a silver spoon. He began the question without any expression on his face, but when he finished it, there was a hint of a smile on his lips.

"Just routine reports," the cardinal answered, moving his eyes to the king. For some time now, he had been aware that Louis had organized something of a network of informers within the court. Distrust and suspicion were very much a part of Louis' character, and if he were to continue to serve his king, Richelieu knew he would have to accept them as he had so many other things that were offensive to his sensibilities. "If you wish, I will send you a digest of them in the morning."

"I leave the necessity of doing that to your good judgment," the king said, his smile broadening.

Servants in white livery poured coffee into small gilt-edged cups and set before them a golden tray piled high with enough delicious pastries to satisfy ten times their number. Each of the three women ate two, Louis indulged himself with five, and Richelieu ate half of one. But he did drink several cups of coffee.

Much of their conversation consisted of small talk about court activities.

Louis complained that his mother and his wife never told him any of the more important gossip of the court. "We are always the very last to know the latest court scandal. We are the last to know anything," he sulked.

"Your majesty," Richelieu responded with an equanimity that even his bitter enemy, the queen mother, had come to respect, "for you to bother yourself about the trivialities of the court would take you away from the more pressing business of the state. Your attention must be focused on our more serious problems."

Louis nodded and glanced at his wife. He had hoped she would take some measure of pride in Richelieu's words. But as always, she seemed not to have been listening. The expression on her face was totally devoid of interest. He had considered visiting her later that night. But he now decided to postpone his visit to her bed for another time.

"Soon," Richelieu said, "you will have to send an army against the Huguenots at La Rochelle. They must be destroyed once and for all. France must be a Catholic country."

"We have fought them to a standstill," the king said. "They hold little more than La Rochelle, and once my sister is married and we can be assured of England's neutrality, we will move against them."

"We can never be assured of England's position," the queen mother commented, speaking for the first time since the arrival of the cardinal.

"I agree," Richelieu said. "England is a Protestant nation. The Huguenots are more of their calling than they are of ours."

"We will wait," Louis said. "We do not want to do anything that might undo the delicate negotiations that you and Lord Kensington have so successfully concluded."

"As you wish, your majesty," Richelieu answered. "But I hope we do not wait too long, or at least not so long as to give their leaders an opportunity to obtain help from foreign sources." He glanced at Anne, wondering if she guessed he was alluding to Buckingham.

The king drew back in his chair.

Richelieu understood the movement well enough. The destruction of the Huguenots was no longer a subject for discussion. If he were to pursue it, the king would remain silent, or close his eyes and pretend to be asleep.

"I was told earlier," the cardinal said, "by the courier who brought my dispatches, that all the channel ports have been closed by the storm." The king smiled and asked if he thought the snow would soon end.

The cardinal waited for a respectable period of time to pass before he courteously asked to be allowed to take his leave. As soon as he was out of the dining room, Richelieu hurried along the brilliantly illuminated hallways of the palace, nodding to those courtiers he passed, but not stopping to pass a moment or two in idle chatter with any of them.

Louis' attitude toward the Huguenots was, in his opinion, far too lenient. True, the king had brought them to their knees in the field. And for all his childish pettiness, Louis had proved himself a brave soldier. But now when the Calvinist heretics were reduced to holding La Rochelle and they could be utterly destroyed with either one massive attack against their fortifications or a determined siege, the king suspended his attack until after the marriage of his sister. Had the cardinal the power to order a fresh army into the field, he would have done so weeks ago.

At the far end of the palace, where the halls became much narrower and the cut-glass chandeliers gave way to simple wrought-iron fixtures suspended from the ceiling by huge chains, Richelieu's feeling of exasperation with Louis' attitude toward the Huguenots abated. Sooner or later, he knew that he would have his way and Louis would march against the heretics.

The light now in the hallways was reduced to torches, placed along the wall of the passageway at irregular intervals with large spaces of stygian blackness between them. This was the oldest section of the palace, used now for storerooms, stables, and Father Joseph's austere accommodations.

The Capuchin monk was more than Richelieu's strong right hand; he was also the cardinal's chief counselor, giving an overall point of view to the plans for the future destiny of France. Joseph was a humanist, a man steeped in history, a man with the unique talent to relate the past to the present for the benefit of France. To bring Father Joseph to his side was, in Richelieu's opinion, a stroke of sagacity that went unnoticed by practically everyone, including the king. Nevertheless, he was certain that several of the foreign emissaries were aware of Father Joseph's value—including Lord Kensington, who pretended to be a fool. But as the cardinal had learned, during the negotiations for the marriage of Charles and Henrietta, the English lord was indeed a very shrewd man.

Richelieu fingered the dispatch in his pocket.

Buckingham, like the Huguenots, was a canker sore that he had to exscind. The cardinal was not so disingenuous with himself as some other men might have been in similar circumstances. Though a member of the church, he did not bridle his passion, as many in his calling did. His nature was far too lusty for him even to contemplate doing that. His most recent paramour, with whom he had also had a previous relationship while she had been a widow, was Marie, the Duchesse de Chevreuse.

He even had a hand, or rather a voice, in her marriage to the Duc de Chevreuse. That marriage was as much for the cardinal's convenience as it was for that of the participants. But of late, he was becoming more and more stirred by the sight of the queen than any man, except the king, had the right to be. During those times he lay with Mme. de Chevreuse, his mind was filled with images of Anne, the queen. That she had chosen Buckingham for her lover—and he knew she had from Mme. de Chevreuse—rankled him almost beyond endurance.

Richelieu hated Buckingham not only because he was an Englishman and a Protestant but also because the duke had possessed the woman with whom he had fallen in love. "Buckingham...Buckingham...Buckingham," the cardinal intoned. "I will strike you down yet. I swear by the most precious blood of our Savior, Jesus Christ, I will bring you down!"

Another dozen steps brought Richelieu to a place along the wall where the yellow wavering light from a torch rippled over recessed doorway. He stopped and rapped twice on the door. Before anyone on the other side could answer, the cardinal announced himself.

The bolt was slipped and the door swung open, admitting Richelieu to Father Joseph's rooms.

The Capuchin monk was dressed in the habit of his order. He nodded and stepped aside to allow the cardinal to enter. Then he closed the door and shot the bolt. He was a smallish man, with broad shoulders and a barrel-like chest. His face was round, and his eyes were small and gray. As if unaware of the cold and the snow, he wore simple leather sandals on his stockingless feet.

Despite the fire in the hearth, there was enough chill in the room to make Richelieu tremble. He had often offered Joseph better rooms in the newer portion of the palace, and just as often the monk refused them with a wave of his pudgy hand or shake of his head. Sometimes he even said that he had no need for anything better than he had, or that he would only be in the way of the king and his courtiers, especially during their revels, for which he would have no choice but to denounce them in the name of God.

"Wine?" the father offered, gesturing to the carafe on the plain wooden table.

"I have just come from the king," Richelieu said, with a wave of his hand to reject the offer.

"Then at least sit down. Take the chair by the fire."

The cardinal settled down in a large dark wood rocking chair and looked at the hearth. There were only two logs on the andirons, and they were almost all turned to ash. Had Joseph been anyone else, he would have said something about the size of the fire. But anything he might say would elicit a wide-eyed questioning look, which would then require a tedious explanation to satisfy. Richelieu decided to forgo one in order to be spared the other.

The monk poured himself a cup of wine and sat down at the table, facing his guest. Richelieu withdrew the message he had received from London and read it.

"All we can hope," Joseph said with a shrug, "is that the next try will be successful."

"We must find a way to ensure its success," Richelieu responded with fervor. "That man is ten times more dangerous to France than an army."

"I will make additional inquiries," Joseph said. "There must be some person close to him who would be willing to—"

"Many would be willing to kill him. Many have good cause. But because of his standing with Charles, they all know the terrible penalty they would have to pay. It is one thing for a man to die, but to die with agonizing slowness is something else entirely . . . Some of Somerset's supporters would still like to see Buckingham out of the way. Perhaps among them there is one whose hand we might buy?"

"I will look into it," the monk answered.

Richelieu nodded and said, "Whatever we have to pay will be far less than what it will cost France if Buckingham should decide to take up the cause of the Huguenots in Charles' court."

Joseph agreed, and before he poured more wine for himself, he again asked the cardinal if he wanted some.

This time Richelieu accepted, not because he wanted the wine but because the chill had gotten worse and he needed something to warm him. He drank slowly.

"I have gotten word," Father Joseph said, "that the queen is exceedingly restless."

Richelieu nodded.

"She would be less so if the king went to her more often."

The cardinal stood up and set the cup down on the table. "Louis has no affinity for women," he said.

"Have him beget a child and for a while the queen will be occupied."

Richelieu stepped in front of the fire and turned his back on Joseph. He stared at the small fire and saw in it the form and face of the frail king.

"For the future of France," Joseph said, "the child must not be a bastard. The throne must be secure."

"Yes," Richelieu answered, "the throne must be secure."

THREE

Buckingham awoke late in the afternoon.
With the curtains drawn across the two windows, the room was steeped in darkness. Making no effort to rise, he looked at the elaborately decorated canopy above him. His sleep had been full of nightmares, each more gruesome than the one before.

Twice during the night his dreams had made him witness to the grisly spectacle of some wretch slowly dying on the executioner's scaffold. He had stood with the ladies and lords of the court, laughing and drinking not more than a few dozen paces from the spot where a man was having his entrails pulled from the bloody opening in his stomach.

Though Buckingham could not see the man's face, there had been something familiar about him. His laughter had left him, and he had lost his taste for the wine that had flowed so copiously from an unseen source.

The repetition of the horrible event had varied in only one detail: a spray of blood had leaped across the distance that had separated the duke from the scaffold, staining his white satin coat and breeches with red drops. The accident had made the lords and ladies laugh even harder. But it had so disgusted Buckingham that he had fled from the place.

Dreams, as the duke well knew, provided an understanding of some past event, or a view of something in the future. Whether it was one or the other could only be told by fortuneteller. But finding the right fortuneteller was a problem. So many of them were, like other men, rogues and charlatans.

"It's the way of the world," Buckingham said aloud. "And I claim no exception to that way."

He had no doubt that the attempt to assassinate him had contributed certain elements to the nightmare. Added to that possibility was the king's errand, which would once again take him to France and place him near his beloved Anne. The position would be fraught with tremendous danger for himself, as well as for her.

The duke could live with the knowledge that danger was close to him. Indeed, he had had to learn to live with it for the many years since he had become the favorite of James and subsequently the favorite of the old king's son, Charles.

For Buckingham to have maintained his position at court had required more than a passing familiarity with danger and a keen ability to deal with it, whether it came in the form of calumny or from the steely point of a rapier in the hand of an enemy at court or in the field. But he could not tolerate even the slightest possibility that Anne might be in danger because of his presence, and he knew it would be so, once he was in France. She would no more be able to stay away from him than he from her. By their passion for each other, they would be inexorably drawn together.

"The danger to the two of us," he mused, "is Richelieu." Suddenly he wondered if the cardinal's hand was the one that had tried to strike him down in the inn.

Buckingham weighed the thought. It was possible. But the duke also realized that he did not have to go to France to look for enemies who would be willing to see him dead. There were many of them in and out of court.

He rose and went to the window. Drawing aside the curtain to view the gardens below and the street beyond the gate, he was surprised not only to find the ground blanketed with snow but to see that snow was still falling. A late-spring snow, despite its beauty, could become a source of great hardship, especially if it was accompanied by a prolonged cold spell that killed the early planting of rye and barley. With a shake of his head, the duke let the curtain drop and summoned his manservant, Tobias Hoff.

The door opened and Tobias entered the room. He was a small, thin man in his middle years. His hair was white, and his left hand was badly scared from once having been bitten by a Spanish blade during some wild encounter at sea.

"How long has it been snowing?" Buckingham asked.

"It began shortly after you arrived home this morning, my lord ... and from the looks, it will go on for a while yet."

"What hour is it?"

"Going to three, my lord."

"Has there been any message from court?" Buckingham asked.

"None."

Buckingham told the man to fetch a pitcher of hot water and basin and then to lay out his dark-green breeches and jacket. "And please tell my lady I will attend her in the library, or her sitting room, if she prefers, as soon as I am dressed."

Bowing slightly from the waist, Tobias hastened out of the room.

Buckingham returned to the window. Once again he parted the curtains. The first time he had looked out at the snow he had not realized how windy it was. But now it seemed to him that more snow was being whirled about by the wind than was actually falling. Suddenly he thought about the wherryman who had rowed him to Whitehall early that morning.

"Ed," he said aloud, recalling the man's name. The duke smiled broadly.

The door opened and Tobias entered the room, carrying a beautiful rose-decorated ewer of steaming hot water and a large basin that was also decorated with roses. He put them down on a small table and, turning to the duke, said, "Her ladyship will await you in her sitting room."

Buckingham made no reply. Quickly he stripped off his night clothes and began his morning ablution. That done, he dried himself thoroughly and then permitted Tobias to dress him. Rather than wear his silver-buckled shoes, he decided it would be wiser, considering the weather, to put on his high, turned-down brown calfskin boots. When he was completely attired, he stepped in front of an elliptically shaped mirror and studied himself for a long time. His position at court demanded a nonpareil mode of dress, surpassing even that of the king himself. His style was nothing less than elegant.

Buckingham cast a questioning glance at Tobias. It was part of a ritual that had evolved between them over the years that the older man dressed the younger one.

Tobias took one step forward and said, "I think a slight adjustment of lace at the neck would be right, my lord."

The duke turned toward him.

"There, it's done," Tobias told him as he straightened the delicate white lace band around his master's neck.

"Thank you."

The older man stepped back and handed Buckingham his sword.

"Came in good use earlier today," the duke commented, as he buckled the weapon to his waist. "Remind me, and I will tell you about it."

"A good story, I hope?"

Buckingham threw back his head and laughed. "Good indeed that I am here to tell it and the one who would have dispatched me from this lovely world was himself separated from it and sent hurriedly into the next. But sorry to say, his helpmate fled, or the first villain would have had the company of the second ... Ah, I have told you the heart of the story; the rest of it is no more than details."

"I would still enjoy listening to it," Tobias replied.

"You shall—but another time," the duke said, moving toward the door. "Oh, I want you to send one of the house servants to the quay below London Bridge and have him fetch to the house a young, fair-haired wherryman by the name of Ed. Have him wait until I return and be sure he is fed and has a place near a good fire while he is waiting for me."

"I will see that it is properly done, my lord," Tobias answered, preceding Buckingham to the door and opening it for him.

The duke left the room and hurried down a long flight of highly polished steps that led to a central foyer on the lower floor.

The scent of freshly baking bread made his mouth water. He had not eaten anything since the food he had taken with Sir Anthony Midmay, before the king's messenger had arrived at Apethorpe.

The duke stopped one of the house maids and told the woman to have a tray of food brought to his lady's sitting room. "See that the cook sends a bowl of soup with whatever meats are available and some fresh bread. And have the wine steward open a bottle of sherry." Without waiting for a response, he went off into the east wing to see his wife.

A roaring fire in the hearth made the sitting room cozy. Buckingham ate and drank with gusto. He was far hungrier than he had thought, and the presence of food increased his appetite greatly. Now and then he paused to chat either with his wife, Katherine, whom in the intimacy of his house he addressed as Kate, or with his young daughter, Mary, who he took great pleasure in calling Little Mall.

"Father," Mary began, her voice rising in pitch, "nurse says that winter has stolen spring?"

"Oh, I do not think so," the duke answered. "Winter is reluctant to go but must sooner or later pass on. It is the way of things. Then spring will give way to summer...summer to fall...and winter will come again."

"I will tell nurse exactly what you said," Mary responded gleefully.

"I'm sure you will. Now be a good girl and run along and play," Buckingham said.

"Will you come to see me before you leave for court?"

"I will indeed," the duke answered and, sweeping the child into his arms, he hugged her fiercely to him. "Now go!"

A few moments later he and Kate were alone.

"Her face brightens when she is close to you," Kate commented with obvious pleasure. She was a big-boned woman with an open face and a mellow voice.

"Ah, but she looks like you," the duke told her. "More and more, each day. She was made in your image...the same upturned nose and green eyes. Even her hair has the same reddish color as yours."

Kate laughed and said, touching the side of her head with the forefinger of her right hand, "Up here she is more you than me."

Buckingham cast his eyes toward the door. "She will make some lord a fine wife," he commented. "But I own, it will be difficult to part with her." He set his wineglass down and helped himself to another piece of freshly baked bread.

"I was surprised you returned to London so quickly," Kate said, looking directly at him. She was seated in her favorite chair, backed with a needle-point design of her own making. "I had hoped you would have a few days to rest."

"The king summoned me back," Buckingham replied.

"Nothing serious?" she questioned, lacing her fingers together to prevent her hands from trembling. She constantly feared that her husband's enemies would bring him low.

Buckingham stood up and walked to the hearth.

"It is something serious?" she asked in a quavering voice. "Trouble from—"

"Not the way you think," he said, dismissing whatever she intended to say with a wave of his hand. Then, recalling what had happened at the inn, he added in a subdued voice, "Enemies are a fact of life, and as such they should not be half as important as the weather. We can do nothing about either."

"Pray then," she asked, "tell me what disturbs you so."

Buckingham turned to her. The anxious expression on her round face brought him to her. He took hold of her hand. It was cold, and he said as much to her.

"You have made such a mystery out of whatever is troubling you, I am half frightened to death by it without knowing exactly what it is."

"I am to France, Kate," he told her.

Her lips pressed narrow, but she said nothing.

"The king will marry Louis' sister, and I am being sent to fetch her," Buckingham explained. "Word came yesterday from Kensington that he and Richelieu have concluded the necessary agreements."

She withdrew her hand from his.

"Kate—"

"The king could send another," she told him.

Buckingham shook his head.

Katherine stood up and walked to the window. For a long time, she said nothing. Then when she finally did speak it was in a voice just above a whisper. "This morning when I woke, I was filled with such feelings of melancholy that I nearly wept. I felt I was standing at the very brink of some terrible catastrophe." She faced him. "I am indeed standing on such a brink."

"You are my wife," Buckingham said, as he went toward her.

She held up her hand.

The duke stopped.

"I know what I am to you; you know what I am to you; but only you know what Anne is to you."

Buckingham turned away and, resting his palms on the edge of the mantel, again stared down into the fire.

"You were quite right," she said in a choked voice. "The matter is serious."

"I cannot deny the king."

"The question is whether you can deny yourself," Katherine responded. "Here your philanderings mean nothing. You are expected to have women at your call. I understand that, and when you share my bed, I never allow myself to think about whom you might have been with before coming to me."

"Kate—" he began and started toward her again.

"Stay and hear me out!"

He stopped and nodded.

"Though you may think not," Katherine told him, "the Queen of France is far beyond your reach, and no amount of passion, regardless of how hotly it burns, can ever bridge that gap."

The duke nodded.

"Then beg the king to send another," she pleaded. "Someone who would be less vulnerable than yourself."

"Who else would he send but his favorite?" he

asked, facing her. "Besides, I am the admiral of the fleet. By sending me he bestows on his bride a double honor."

"And takes my honor from me," she replied vehemently.

"Not so!"

"Has it occurred to you," Katherine suggested, "the king might be doing this at the behest of others in the court?"

"Charles is openly proclaiming his trust by giving me this commission."

"Then you will not ask him to send another courtier?"

"No," Buckingham answered. "I will go."

"And if I beg you not to go?"

"I must honor the king's request," he said.

"Then my feelings count for nothing?"

"Nor mine in matters of state," Buckingham answered.

"When will you leave?"

"Not for a while," the duke answered. "There are many preparations that must be made before the escort departs for France."

Silently Katherine faced the window again.

Buckingham came up behind her and, circling her waist, drew her back against himself.

"You see," she said, "the trouble is that I love you. If I did not, it would make everything so much easier."

"Yes, I know," he answered, nuzzling her ear. A moment later, he let go of her and hurried out of the room.

She called after him.

But he pretended not to have heard her. There was nothing he could do to assuage her feelings, short of denying his own, and that he could not do.

Before leaving for court, the duke stopped in the nursery to see his Little Mall, lift the child in his arms, and swing her high over his head.

The Great Hall at Whitehall Palace was crowded with courtiers. The king and two of his councilors were at the far end, standing just in front of the massive oak doors that led to the inner rooms of the royal apartment. Here and there, scattered along the entire length of the hall, were small groups of men and women. The low steady hum of conversation was sometimes broken by the sound of laughter. Because of the dullness of the day, the four huge crystal chandeliers were resplendent with hundreds of candles that illuminated the hall.

As soon as Buckingham entered, the conversation lessened and then completely ceased. He walked boldly toward the king. The eye of every courtier followed him. But he gave no indication that he was aware of any of them.

Charles, for his part, did not wait until the duke reached him. He met Buckingham halfway.

The duke made his obeisance.

"Not now!" the king exclaimed, with an impatient wave of his hand. "Now you must tell us of your adventure in the Laughing Crow. All of London is talking about it."

Buckingham looked around him.

"Yes," the king said, "they know. Not five minutes after you departed, Lord Lindsay paused there to slake his thirst and heard the whole story from the inn's proprietor, a certain Master Dodds . . . And I say bravo to you, sir!" The king applauded him.

Instantly from all sides the courtiers echoed the king's words and actions, making the huge hall resound with their acclamations and clapping.

Buckingham nodded and smiled, and holding up his two hands he turned around several times. His face was flushed with pleasure. He thoroughly enjoyed the praise. Had he not earned it, he would be dead.

When the shouting and the applause dwindled, the king raised his hand and called out for silence. "Now

49

you must tell all of us exactly what happened, my dear duke," Charles told him, "so that we might share in your brilliant adventure."

From all parts of the hall, there were murmurs of agreement.

Buckingham placed his hand on the hilt of his sword. "My lord," he said, addressing the king, "I did no more or less than any honorable gentleman would have done in similar circumstances. After all, I am in God's service and in yours, and to permit some rogue to take my life would deny my love for the Almighty and for you, my lord."

"Well said!" Charles exclaimed with a broad smile. "Well said, indeed."

There was another burst of applause.

Buckingham acknowledged it with a nod.

"Now tell us what happened," the king said.

"After I left you, sire," Buckingham told Charles, "I was in sore need of drink and food. On previous occasions I found the Laughing Crow to provide both, and for a price, a good many other services besides. In truth, my lord, Master Dodds might be an excellent source of provender for your majesty's ships. But to get on with the story, I chose to dine alone and rest awhile before continuing home. I was doing just that when suddenly the door to the room was flung open and I was set upon by two rogues. The rest you must know."

"Yes, yes, but tell us anyway."

"I was left no choice but to fight for my life," Buckingham said with a smile. "I managed to skewer one, and the other, fearful that he might meet the same fate, fled. But I must own that all the excitement did not leave me much time to rest."

The king and his courtiers laughed heartily.

"And," Buckingham continued, "I must also own that I no longer possessed the same hunger or thirst that was my reason for going there. I was anxious to be on my way and safe in my own bed."

The king embraced Buckingham and said, "My lord and ladies, it is because of the duke's gallantry, his devotion to me, and his sense of honor that we have chosen him to escort Henrietta Maria, sister of Louis, from her home in France, where she will be married by proxy to me, and bring her to our country, where she will be my queen."

For a long moment there was absolute silence. Though all of the courtiers knew negotiations were being carried on to effect such a marriage, most of them thought that they would never be concluded, or that the final signing was still many months in the offing.

Seeing the expression on the king's face turn to a frown, Buckingham shouted, "Long live the king and God protect his future queen."

The courtiers immediately echoed the duke's words, and once again the king was smiling.

Buckingham smiled too. But he had no illusions about the feelings of most of the courtiers, or for that matter about the feelings of most of his countrymen: they did not want a French Catholic to be the Queen of England. Though his own wife had been a Catholic, he did not see Henrietta Maria renouncing her faith as Katherine Manners had done. Despite his thoughts, the duke continued to smile.

The king and Buckingham, walking arm in arm, left the Great Hall and entered the library, where they were able to speak to one another about matters of state without fear of being overheard.

As soon as they were alone, the king disengaged himself from the duke's arm and dropped into one of the chairs. With a loud sigh, he said, "If only I could enjoy a small part of your adventures instead of having to be what I am. I tell you, Steenie, I often think of those madcap days we spent together in France and Spain."

"They were indeed a great pleasure," Buckingham

replied. Without waiting for the king's permission, he sat down opposite him.

"You are once again my brightest light," Charles told him.

"But dim, my lord, next to yours," the duke responded.

The king nodded and said, "But my light must be looked at for a longer time to see its true brightness."

"Well put," Buckingham told him.

Charles moved slightly forward and said, "I have written to Lord Kensington, telling him of your forthcoming arrival. I should like the marriage to take place early in May so that I would be able to spend the summer with the queen and so that she would be here to witness my coronation."

"I will attend to it, my lord."

"I wish to impress Louis with my wealth and my power," Charles went on. "I do not want him to think I lack for anything."

Buckingham nodded.

"I am prepared to spend handsomely to assure that end is accomplished," the king told him.

"Have you decided on those lords who will accompany me?" the duke asked.

"I have noted some names," the king answered, withdrawing a folded sheet of paper from his doublet. "I give you leave to add others."

"How many more?" the duke questioned, reaching for the king's list.

"Two dozen, at the very least."

"When I have completed the list," Buckingham told him, "I will bring it to you."

"No need to. I have confidence in your ability to choose those lords who will honor me by their presence."

"Your trust, my lord, is most gratifying," Buckingham responded.

"My trust in you, my dear Steenie, goes even further, as you will soon see. Last night I mentioned there were other matters for you to attend to while you are in France."

"You did mention it, my lord."

"I want you to make contact with Henri, Duc de Rohan, and his brother, Benjamin de Sourbise. Assure these noblemen that I will not permit Louis to destroy the Huguenots at La Rochelle, that I will exercise all of my statecraft on their behalf to stay the hand of Cardinal Richelieu." The king removed a small, exquisitely worked ring from his right index finger. "Give them this token of my commitment to their cause."

Buckingham took the ring, saying, "But sire, the two noblemen are under the watchful eyes of the cardinal's men every hour of the day and night."

"You must find a way," the king said. "I have given much leeway to the Catholics of this realm to gain a queen. Louis must give a similar leeway to the people in his kingdom whose religious beliefs are the same as our own."

"The cardinal will not give way," Buckingham responded, rising to his feet. "He sees the Huguenots as heretics. He and his Father Joseph would burn all of them at the stake, if they could." He walked as he spoke, and now he found himself looking down in the flames of the hearth. "The Holy Mother Church would be pleased if Richelieu succeeded in destroying all of the Huguenots and us as well."

"And that is why we must not allow Richelieu to have his way," the king said. "He must be stopped. Once the marriage is an accomplished fact and Henrietta is here, we will be in a position to make a much stronger petition to Louis on behalf of the Huguenots."

Buckingham faced the king. He knew it would be useless to take issue with him on the subject.

"There, there," Charles said, standing, "do not look so troubled. I assure you our view on the Huguenots will prevail. After all, I will soon be brother-in-law to Louis."

"True, my lord," Buckingham answered. "But you will be here in England and Richelieu will be at Louis' side. Were the positions reversed, I have no doubt that you would indeed prevail."

"I have decided on this course of action," Charles answered somewhat sharply, "because I deem it to be the best for us, for the Huguenots, and for France. Louis is tired of fighting them. He has already shown this by granting them the right by the Treaty of Montpellier to live in the cities of La Rochelle and Montauban. My purpose is to maintain our faith wherever it is."

"I will see the Duc de Rohan and his brother," Buckingham said, giving way to the king's demands.

"Excellent, Steenie," Charles answered.

They remained in the library awhile longer and spoke about the untimely snow.

Buckingham remained at court until almost seven o'clock; then he took his leave of the king and went to the Admiralty, where he usually spent the early hours of the afternoon attending to the affairs of the navy.

He crossed the large courtyard. The snow had stopped and the wind had died down. His footfalls made a crunching sound in the dry snow. He looked up at the sky. It was cloudless and full of stars.

Within a few minutes the duke was in the building that housed his office and others connected with the navy and army. Several armed guards stood at attention along the length of the candlelit corridor. When he entered the office, he found his secretary, John Potter, still at work.

Potter immediately stood up. He was a short man, with a round, red face and carrot-colored hair.

"I am happy to see your lordship is unharmed," Potter told him.

Buckingham stopped and raised his eyebrows questioningly. "Ah, you mean what took place at the Laughing Crow?"

"Most certainly," Potter said. "Everyone knows about it. To cut down five men—"

"Five men?" Buckingham exclaimed with a loud

laugh. "In truth, for a moment they might have looked like five. But there were only two, and of the two, my sword only found one."

"Five, two, or one, it makes little difference," Potter told him. "You are everyone's hero today."

"I have been that before," Buckingham answered quietly. "And I have also been everyone's villain. Let us hope that I remain the former for a little while yet before becoming the latter." He walked into the inner office, and Potter followed him.

"I thought you'd be a day or two more in the country," Potter commented.

Buckingham handed his secretary his large cloak and hat and sat down behind a massive oaken desk. The large room was fitted with bookshelves that went from the floor to the ceiling. Though many of the shelves were lined with books, several were adorned with exquisitely crafted models of naval vessels.

"The *Royal Scepter* has come into Portsmouth for refitting," Potter told him, approaching the desk after he had placed the cloak and hat in its proper place, on a peg next to the door. "Her captain is anxious to put to sea again as soon as possible."

"All of them are anxious to put to sea again," Buckingham commented, scanning the papers on his desk. "How long will it take to refit the *Royal Scepter*?"

"Several months, I'm afraid."

Buckingham ran his hand over his short beard. Many of the navy's ships were old and ill-armed, in want of repair. Yet Parliament would not vote the necessary funds to keep the fleet seaworthy, let alone authorize the building of new ships.

"How many are before the *Royal Scepter*?" the duke asked.

"Seven. And one of them, the *Heroic*, needs replanking on its larboard side and foretopdeck."

Buckingham did not answer. He knew that the king in his present frame of mind would not look favorably on any effort that might appear warlike to

Louis, and above all to Richelieu. The king was placing his faith in the ties between himself and Louis that would result from his forthcoming marriage to Henrietta. To the duke, it was a misplaced faith, at least as long as Richelieu stood firmly at the helm.

"And if my memory serves," Buckingham finally said, "two of the others have to have their mainmasts reset."

"Yes, my lord."

"In the morning, draft a letter to the dockmaster, urging him to get on with the work. I will sign it. Perhaps that will move matters along somewhat."

"It will be ready for your signature when you arrive," Potter answered.

"You may go," Buckingham told him.

Buckingham took up a long-stemmed Dutch pipe, filled it with tobacco, lifted a nearby candle to the bowl, and was soon sending clouds of smoke toward the ceiling. The prospect of seeing Anne filled him with warmth and brought a special tightness to his groin.

He set the pipe down to one side, placed a sheet of paper in front of him, picked up a quill, and dipped the sharpened point into an inkwell. He thought for a few moments, holding the quill high above the paper. And then, dropping his hand, he began to write in flawless French:

My beloved Anne—

I am being sent to France to escort the king's bride from your country to my own. I long to see you once again and hear the dear sound of your voice. I did not think the opportunity to be with you would have come so soon, or at all. I am filled with desire for you.

Your most humble servant
Buckingham

He reread the letter twice before folding it and sealing it in an envelope. Buckingham took the necessary measures to make sure it would first go to M. Balthazar Gerbier, a painter, who would then manage to deliver it to the queen.

On the way out of the office, the duke placed the letter in a diplomatic dispatch case. Knowing that by the next night Anne would have already read his brief note, he smiled.

As soon as Buckingham arrived home, he was informed by Tobias that Ed, the wherryman, was waiting in the kitchen.

"Has he been here long?" the duke asked, moving toward the library.

"Since past five," Tobias answered. "He would not come until he'd earned a day's pay on the river."

Buckingham laughed. "Has he been fed?" he asked.

"As you instructed, my lord."

"Good. Fetch him," the duke said and went directly to the fire to warm himself. He held his hands out toward the flames and rubbed them briskly.

A soft knock at the door brought him around, and he called out, "Come in."

"My Lord," Tobias said, "Ed, the wherryman."

Buckingham moved away from the fire. "I hope you have been comfortable while waiting on me," he said.

Ed held his soiled hat between his two hands. He looked around him with the wide eyes of a man who did not trust his own senses. He shook his head. "I never seed anythin' like it. Never believed there be so many books, an' all in one place."

"Sit down, Ed," Buckingham said.

"If'n you Lordship doesn't mind, I'd rather stand...me clothes bein' none too clean."

"I will come right to the point," the duke said. "How would you like to work for me?"

"Wot?"

57

Buckingham repeated the question.

"You want me to be your wherryman?" Ed asked.

"I want you to be my strong right arm," the duke answered. "I need someone who will be at my side, wherever I go abroad, someone I can trust. In a few weeks I will be going to France. I want you to go with me."

Ed nodded.

"Then it is done," Buckingham said, extending his hand. "But you have not asked about your wages."

"No need to," Ed answered, with a shake of his head. "I trust ye to pay me wot I'm worth, no more an' no less."

The two of them shook hands, and Buckingham called for Tobias. "Ed will be part of the household. He will be my bodyguard. Find a good place for him to sleep, and tomorrow have him fitted for several suits of clothes. And make sure he is well cleaned before he goes to bed tonight."

Tobias left the library with Ed in tow.

Buckingham returned to the hearth, stood there looking at the flames, and clearly remembered how warm Anne's naked body felt against his own....

FOUR

Alone, Anne walked all the way to the edge of the river.

The late-afternoon sun was delightfully warm. The snow had all but disappeared, lingering in those places where the trunk of a stout tree or some other obstacle to the sun's rays created a patch of shade for it. But with the passing of another day, or two at the very most, the embracing warmth of spring would completely eliminate any trace of the snow that had so recently blanketed the ground.

She stopped and gazed down at the swirling muddy waters. After the spring thaw and the floods that usually followed, the river's water would gradually become much clearer, so that by June any fish close inshore would be clearly visible. Sometimes during the summer, she would come here and throw bits of bread into the water, delighting in the way the fish lunged for them, sometimes even jumping clear of the water to grab a piece.

Today she was not there to feed the fish, but at the behest of the cardinal, who had sent word he had reason to speak with her in privacy and had suggested they meet at the far end of the garden at about three in the afternoon. Never before had the cardinal made such a request. He had spoken to her either in front of Louis, or in the same room with her ladies-in-waiting. That he had asked to see her in privacy had been a clear indication of just how important he considered the reason for the meeting.

Anne was still gazing down at the turbid waters when she became aware of the crunching footfalls on the gravel walkway behind her. She turned and saw Richelieu striding briskly toward her.

He was, according to the hour marked on the sundial, exactly on time. He came boldly up to her and, bowing from the waist, said, "I most humbly thank your highness for agreeing to meet me here."

Though his words were correct, the derisive look in his black eyes was not wasted on Anne.

"There is no need to humble yourself, monseigneur," she told him, "when in truth you think yourself superior. I am not Louis."

"Ah, but you are his queen!" Richelieu exclaimed. "I would not want to be guilty of offending him by ignoring my obligations to you."

Anne turned away. "You have no obligations to me," she said testily.

Richelieu came alongside her. For a few moments neither of them spoke.

Richelieu took several deep breaths, letting himself enjoy the marvelous rose scent of her perfume. Few women could wear perfume as effectively as she, and from his experience with others in the court, he knew all the secret places on their bodies where the essence was applied. He did not have to close his eyes to conjure the image of her standing naked before a mirror and slowly applying the scented liquid with the tips of her fingers to the area behind her ears, under her breasts, under her arms, over her flat stomach, and between her naked thighs. That image more than all of the others made him take another deep breath.

"I did not think you asked me to meet you here to look at the river," Anne finally said, breaking the silence between them.

"No," Richelieu answered, regaining his composure. "I am here for a very different matter."

"Then state it!"

The cardinal turned toward her. "France," he told her, "needs an heir to the throne, a male heir that will safeguard it from the many princes who are waiting for some disaster to overtake the king, so that they might lay claim to the throne."

Richelieu's words brought a flush of anger to Anne's cheeks. "There has already been one Immaculate Conception," she responded in a tight voice. "I cannot believe that the Almighty would agree to use my body to beget a son for Louis, the King of France."

Her heightened color made her only more beautiful in his eyes. "Should something happen to the king," he said, "you would be in great danger."

"No doubt," she replied. "But I at least could return to Spain. As for yourself, where would you flee to? Ah, back to the embrace of the church, to some out-of-the-way monastery—it would be a far cry from the power you now wield, a far cry indeed." She shook her head. "I don't believe that you would be happy as a humble brother, especially since humility is not one of your strongest character traits."

He ignored her insults and said, "My concern is for the future of France."

"Admirable," she replied with a nod. "But from what I hear, you are not unfamiliar with the way a mortal man must beget a child. I understand that you are indeed familiar with, if not the actual begetting, then all that preceeds it; all that man might do with a woman, you have done. Those are the things, my learned cardinal, that my husband, the King of France, abstains from doing with me. When he does bring himself to lie between my thighs, he cannot manage to forget God long enough to join his body with mine. And without that joining there cannot be an heir, male or female. He must be a man so that I might be a woman. Convince him of that and you will have proved a master of statecraft, far beyond anyone's imaginings."

"The heir must not be a bastard," Richelieu said.

"You have not listened to me, cardinal."

"The throne must be made secure," he told her.

Anne shook her head and in a low voice she said, "Have you ever looked at me, cardinal, really looked at me?"

He could not answer.

"Men as well as women consider me beautiful," she told him. "I am, so I am told, considered desirable by many men. But I cannot stir the passion of the king. He is without passion for me, perhaps without passion for any woman. Do you know that when we were married, he was forced to consummate the marriage under the watchful eyes of his teacher, the Duc de Lyunes? Can you imagine what that was like? The king was just a boy, and he was forced to be a man in front of a—" Her voice suddenly broke and she began to sob.

Richelieu made an open gesture with his hands. He had heard the story from Mme. de Chevreuse and from several others.

"Now do you understand?" she asked, gaining control of herself again.

"That must not be allowed to stand in the way of begetting an heir," he said.

"Regardless of my feelings," she told him, "I have not shrunk from doing what was expected of me. But unless Louis comes to me, what can I do?"

"Go to him," he answered.

"And have him flee from me?" she asked. "Never. I cannot allow that to happen."

"You must take the risk," he said, moving closer.

Anne shook her head. "You ask too much," she told him.

"I ask nothing more than what must be done to protect the throne and yourself," he responded in a low voice.

Suddenly Anne found herself looking up at him. The mocking tone was gone, and his eyes betrayed the unmistakable passion of a man for a woman.

"What do you care what happens to me?" she asked.

"I care very much," he answered.

And before she could speak, Richelieu swept her into his arms. Unable to control himself, he whispered passionately, "I want you, Anne, I want you more than I ever wanted any woman."

Revolted by the swift turn of events, she struggled to free herself from his embrace.

"I love you, Anne!" he exclaimed.

She broke free and, drawing back, struck him across the face. "I would rather be in hell than in your bed," she told him hotly. Turning, Anne ran back toward the palace.

It was almost midnight, and Richelieu was still awake. He stood with his hands clasped behind him and looked down at the red glowing embers of a dying fire.

Anne's vehement rebuff had wounded him so greatly that earlier he had sent word to the king claiming the press of work was so great that he would not be able to join his majesty at supper, as he usually did. Louis would no doubt sulk and complain that even his most trusted minister was conspiring against him. But regardless of the king's humor, Richelieu had his own sensibilities to protect. He could not bring himself to face Anne's disdainful looks so soon after having been rejected by her.

"I will have her!" he exclaimed, wrenching his hands apart and pounding the fist of one into the palm of the other. "I will have that woman."

He strode across the room to the desk, poured himself a glass of wine, and drank most of it before putting the glass down on the table.

For a few moments, he debated whether he should work for a while or go to bed. At the moment, he had no stomach for looking over the various reports on his desk and then writing the appropriate responses to his subordinates. He glanced at his bed, which was no more than a simple sleeping pallet, and he shook his head. At best, sleep claimed very little of his time, and when he was rankled, as he was now, trying to sleep would only exasperate him more, deepening his anger.

Richelieu realized that neither work nor sleep would assuage his restiveness. He went to the casement window and opened it. Though the day had been filled with the warmth of spring, the night was still held by winter's lingering chill. His eyes went to the windows of Mme. de Chevreuse's apartment. There was still a light in her bedroom.

A sudden tightness came into his groin. And he nodded to acknowledge his need for a woman. He had not visited Marie for almost ten days. Her monthly flow had been responsible for his absence for the first five days, and his growing desire for Anne had robbed him of any inclination to lie with any other woman during the second five days. But now he needed to pour his passion into the body of a woman.

He closed the window and crossed the room. Taking his cloak off of a peg, he threw the garment over his shoulders. Just as he started for the door, several sharp raps against it brought him to halt.

Richelieu quickly removed his cloak and tossed it onto the pallet.

Three more sharp raps broke the stillness of the room.

"Who is it?" Richelieu called out.

"Cahusac," a man answered in a gruff voice.

Richelieu went to the door, opened it, and stepped back to allow his visitor to enter.

"I am sorry for the disturbance, your eminence," Cahusac said, falling to one knee and kissing the ring on the cardinal's right hand.

Richelieu bade him stand and waited for an explanation.

"M. Sequir sent me," Cahusac said, speaking slowly. "He has someone in his custody that he thinks you would want to question."

"At this hour?"

Cahusac nodded. He was a big-boned man, with a bull neck and powerful arms. He was deadly with a sword or a knife. A large scar marked the right side of his face.

"Where?" Richelieu asked.

"The Bastille," Cahusac answered. "I have a horse saddled and waiting outside for your eminence."

Richelieu picked his cloak off the pallet and, gesturing toward the door, said, "Let us go."

A short while later, the two men rode through the dark and winding streets of Paris. Here and there a lamp or a candle shone through a window or a crack at the bottom of a door. But for the most part the houses seemed darker than the night that surrounded them.

By the time they had reached the Bastille, the nightwatch had already cried the first hour of the new day. Two guards at the gate halted them, and impatiently Cahusac upbraided them for not recognizing the cardinal. The men humbly begged Richelieu's pardon, and he readily gave it, anxious to join Sequir and his prisoner.

The cardinal and his escort rode into the large cobblestone courtyard, turned toward a large iron door, and halted their horses in front of it. Another guard came out and took charge of the mounts, while Richelieu and Cahusac hurriedly made their way into the depths of the prison.

The very air smelled of fear. Along the corridor were doors to various cells. Now and then a moan came from the other side of a door to break the heavy stillness.

"This way," Cahusac said.

Richelieu followed him.

They descended a dimly lit, winding stone staircase until they were well below the level of the ground and in the torture chamber. There the lighting was provided by four huge torches, whose reddish flames cast the glow of hell over gray stones. The two hooded, bare-chested torturers were busy heating up the irons.

M. Sequir was standing off to one side. He was of middling height, delicate-looking, with a fine blond beard, thin lips, and sky-blue eyes.

The prisoner was strapped into a chair. His shirt had been torn from his back, and though every few moments his tall, well-built body shook uncontrollably, he was wet with sweat. Fear filled his face and widened his brown eyes.

Richelieu went straight to Sequir and asked, "Who is he?" He turned toward the prisoner to see if he knew him. He did not.

"He claims to be a M. Dupris from Calais," Sequir said with a sigh. "But how could a monsieur from Calais be carrying this?" And he handed an envelope to the cardinal.

Richelieu opened the envelope, withdrew the folded paper, and moved closer to the nearest torch in order to read what had been written. The letter was dated the previous day and it read:

Dear Lord Rich—

I have this day received word that the Duke of Buckingham will soon be in France to conduct the king's business.

Your faithful friend
Peter Paul Rubens

Finding Buckingham mentioned in the letter made the cardinal gnash his teeth in suppressed anger. With two quick strides he returned to where Sequir was standing.

"How came you by this letter?" he asked.

"That man there," Sequir answered, "has been under suspicion for some time. He travels to and from the country around La Rochelle and then to Calais. Always he makes a stop at M. Rubens' house, sometimes at M. Gerbier's house as well. Tonight I thought I might try my luck and see what I came up with after he left M. Rubens."

"Buckingham," the cardinal said, rolling the duke's name off his tongue as though it were a wad of spittle. "And that is indeed something!"

"Perhaps M. Dupris might be persuaded to tell a great deal more," Sequir suggested, moving his eyes toward the torturers and then back to the prisoner. "Many who profess ignorance of other matters have suddenly found how much more they really know after being introduced to my two friends there."

Richelieu nodded.

M. Sequir made a slight motion toward the prisoner with his hand.

One of the hooded men picked up a glowing red iron from the fire and, with his companion, advanced toward the prisoner.

"Your real name?" Sequir asked, as he too moved closer to the man strapped into the chair.

The torturer placed the glowing iron close to the prisoner's face, while his companion grasped hold of the man's head, preventing him from turning away.

He screamed as the fire touched his skin. A small flame leaped out of his beard. The air suddenly smelled of singed hair.

"Your real name?" Sequir repeated.

"I have already told you," the man cried out.

Richelieu suddenly stepped forward and said, "Let him be. I believe him."

Sequir started to object, but a quick look from the cardinal silenced him, and he ordered the torturers to retreat.

"It is not our purpose to harm an innocent man," Richelieu said as he moved closer to the prisoner and untied the leather thongs that held the prisoner in the chair. "And now, M. Dupris, I would like you to think of me as your friend. I am a servant of our king and of our country."

"I know who you are, your eminence," Dupris answered.

"Good," Richelieu exclaimed with several vigorous nods. Then, turning to Sequir, he asked that wine be given to Dupris. And when that was done, the cardinal said, "I have a few questions to ask and then you will be free to go on your way. I hope your answers will be as genuine as your name, M. Dupris?"

"It is a sin against the Almighty to lie," he responded.

"Indeed it is," Richelieu commented. He paused for a moment and looked toward Sequir and then back to Dupris before he asked, "How long have you been in the service of Lord Rich?"

"I am not in his service."

"Oh, I would have thought you are. Well, then, whose service are you in?"

"The Duc de Rohan," Dupris answered.

"And that explains why you spend so much time around La Rochelle?"

"Yes."

"Have you ever met the Duke of Buckingham?" Richelieu asked, riveting his black eyes on the man.

Dupris nodded.

"Here in France?"

"Yes."

"And in England?"

"Yes. I have been sent there many times."

"How many times?" Richelieu asked.

"At least half a dozen."

"Then Buckingham knows you and trusts you?" Dupris nodded.

Richelieu moved back to where Sequir was standing and suggested that some food be brought to the prisoner.

Dupris thanked him.

"It is no more than Christian to act kindly toward others," Richelieu answered.

"Amen!" Dupris exclaimed.

In a very short time, a bowl of hot soup and a thick piece of bread were given to Dupris, who devoured both with great gusto.

The cardinal waited patiently until the last drop was spooned up and the last piece of bread was swallowed before he said, "Now, M. Dupris, I have spared you pain and worse. I have given you food and drink, and now I must ask for something in return."

Dupris nodded.

"Have you a family?" Richelieu asked.

"A wife, a son, and a daughter. My son is but ten and my daughter sixteen."

"And you would like to see them prosper?"

"Most certainly."

"Then if you do what I ask, they most certainly will prosper. I will see that you are given ten thousand in gold and I will also assure you that your son will have a fine education and your daughter will be given a dowry that will make a nobleman interested in having her as his wife."

Dupris' jaw went slack, and he took several huge gulps of air.

"You yourself will be given employment at the court," Richelieu continued. "I will do all that for you, if you will do one thing for me."

"And what might that be?" Dupris managed to stammer.

"I want you to kill the Duke of Buckingham," Richelieu answered, his voice suddenly becoming flat and hard. "Kill Buckingham and you and your family will indeed prosper."

Dupris blanched. His hands began to tremble. He tried to speak, but only meaningless sounds came out of his quivering lips.

"Close to him," Richelieu said, now changing his voice to an almost conversational tone, "it will be easy for you to put a knife into him."

"I would not move three steps before someone thrust a sword into me," Dupris countered.

"Ah," Richelieu said, waving his forefinger at him, "it is for you to find a way to do it and survive. And I will help you. I will give you the necessary impetus for the task. Sequir, have your men bring monsieur's family here to the Bastille."

"Oh God, no!" Dupris cried out.

Richelieu ignored the man. Looking at Sequir, he said, "Keep them here. Should M. Dupris refuse to help me, have his wife turned over to the galley slaves and sell his daughter to a brothel of the lowest kind. And as for his son, well, there are enough men around who prefer boys to women."

"I will see to it," Sequir answered.

Dupris shook his head. Tears streamed down his cheeks. He sobbed openly.

"You see," Richelieu said, "I must have something in return for your life, and if you will not help me destroy an enemy of France, then I must take something else."

"Your eminence," Dupris wept, "let them torture me, let them kill me, but I beg of you to spare my family." Dropping from the chair, he placed his arms around the cardinal's legs. "I humble myself before you." The man wept.

Richelieu ordered Cahusac to pull the man away. When he was free, he said, "M. Dupris, a goodly portion of the night has passed. I am very tired. You have my offer. The choice is yours. Come, Cahusac, let us go."

"Your eminence!" Dupris called out.

But Richelieu never turned to acknowledge the man's cry.

"Do you think he will do it?" Cahusac asked, as they walked toward the massive door.

"In his position, would you?" Richelieu asked.

"Yes. Probably."

With a shrug, Richelieu said, "Whether he does it or not, we must find some way to get at Buckingham. To save his family, Dupris will probably try. If he is lucky, then we will have an end to Buckingham, and if he is not lucky, he will probably be killed."

"If he does kill him and manages to escape, will you give him the gold and—"

"I most certainly will," Richelieu said. "I do not go back on my word. I would even do all that I promised for his family if he killed Buckingham and was himself killed afterwards. I will honor my word to M. Dupris."

There were two visitors in Mme. de Chevreuse's apartment. One was Gaston, the king's brother, and the other was the Comte de Chalais, master of the king's wardrobe. Both men were there to find out if the queen was at all interested in Gaston.

Chalais was a tall, broad-boned young man with full sensual lips and a healthy appetite for women, men, wine, and food. He was miffed with Louis for having taken up with M. de Barras, the son of a petty noble from Brittany, and the idea of having Gaston lie between Anne's thighs appealed to him greatly.

Gaston was also tall and robust. Because Louis and Anne did not have any children, he was heir to the throne. Gaston had little love for his brother but was greatly excited by the possibility of possessing Anne.

"She likes you well enough," Mme. de Chevreuse

told Gaston, "but not so well as to entertain any thought of you becoming her lover. Still, she might agree."

"Not as long as she thinks of Buckingham," Chalais commented.

Gaston agreed and poured himself another glass of wine. He drank it swiftly before he said, "I have been thinking a great deal about this matter, and it seems to me my suit could be pressed with more ardor...I mean, with more than just the joys of the bed as an end."

Mme. de Chevreuse nodded. The scheme to have Gaston become Anne's lover was entirely hers. She saw it as a way to increase her hold on Anne and thereby have the opportunity to increase her own fortunes. For the very same reason she had helped the queen to maintain her liaison with Buckingham the last time he had been in France. She thoroughly enjoyed manipulating other people to her own ends, regardless of whether they were above or below her. The only person she could not move as she willed was Richelieu. He was the one who could move her, who could make her cry out in ecstasy. Tantalizingly, he was always just beyond her.

"I would not hesitate to make her my queen," Gaston said, "if I was on the throne."

"Your brother," Chalais told him, "is not about to die for you."

"There are ways of hurrying that along," Gaston replied.

"You would first have to help Richelieu out of this life," Chalais said, looking straight at Mme. de Chevreuse as he spoke.

She flushed, but with an amazing equanimity she responded, "I am not ready to discuss that particular matter. For the time being, I suggest we bend our efforts to getting Monsieur Gaston to the queen's bed. Once that is done, we will consider what next must be done to advance ourselves."

"There are many others at court and abroad who would like to see Gaston on the throne," Chalais said.

"And would those many others be willing to risk their lives to accomplish it?" she asked hotly.

Chalais did not answer.

With a deep sigh, Gaston said, "If Anne would only give me the chance, I am sure I would be able to make her forget Buckingham. I have been told by many women that I am very good in bed, very good." Chalais began to giggle, while Mme. de Chevreuse yawned broadly to indicate how tired she was.

Except for the red glow emanating from the hearth, Anne's room was steeped in darkness. She lay awake listening to the sound of her own breathing. Now and then she sighed loudly, despairingly.

Richelieu's declaration of passion had surprised and disturbed her. She had never imagined the cardinal, of all men in the court, harbored any feelings toward her, other than disdain. And she had certainly never given him any reason to believe she had any tender feelings for him, especially as he had taken it upon himself to hinder, at every possible turn, her liaison with Buckingham. If she had no other reason to hate him, she hated him with all the fury she could for that alone.

The thought of him touching her chilled her blood and brought prickles to her back. Though she had been told by Mme. de Chevreuse that he was an ardent lover, she could not imagine him in love's most intimate embrace.

Anne shook her head and silently vowed that she would never allow him to touch her. Then she turned away from the hearth, fluffed up the satin-covered pillow, and closed her eyes, hoping that sleep would soon come. But it did not. In minutes her eyes were open again.

She was about to call to one of the women who attended her and ask that a posset be brought when the door separating her room from Louis' opened.

There was more light behind him than in front, and he appeared to be no more than a dark form, a silhouette. Anne lay very still, pretending to be asleep.

Louis took a step forward and stopped. He glanced over his shoulder at his room and uttered a deep sigh of resignation.

She almost believed that Richelieu was in Louis' room, urging him on, but such a possibility was too absurd to entertain.

He called softly to her.

Anne remained silent.

He called again. This time his voice was louder.

She knew he was determined to lie with her, driven not by a man's need or love, but most probably by Richelieu's insistence that an heir to the throne be produced. He was very close to the bed when she finally said, "I am awake."

He cleared his throat and asked, "Did I wake you?"

"Not really," she responded, knowing he would not seek a more concrete answer.

Again he cleared his throat, but he did not speak.

Anne clenched her teeth and held her breath. There was nothing she could do but submit to him. She exhaled.

His silk dressing gown rustled when he took it off. Within moments he was in bed next to her. He did not attempt to kiss or caress her. His breath was ragged, not from passion but from the darkness of some terrible fear.

Earlier in her marriage Anne had wondered if he were so reluctant to do what other men do willingly because it caused him pain. But Mme. de Chevreuse had dispelled that idea by telling her that Louis' difficulty had shown itself long before he had married; and that he had always preferred the company of men to that of women.

After several minutes of silence, Louis said in a tight voice, "I know this is as difficult for you as it is for me."

"I endure," she answered.

Louis took several deep breaths before he said falteringly, "I am limp."

Anne clenched her teeth. It was one thing to fondle the organ of the man she loved, but quite another to do it for a man who disgusted her. When she had caressed Buckingham's penis—indeed, when she had put her lips to it—her delight had come from knowing she had given him so much pleasure that he had uttered deep throaty growls of ecstasy.

The memory of having Buckingham's organ in her mouth was so intense that it completely blotted out the reality of the moment. And only when she heard Louis say, "I can do nothing this way," did she return from her past happiness to the unmerciful truth of the present.

"Even if it is done quickly," Louis told her, "we will have performed our duty."

"Yes," she answered and, reaching down, she took hold of Louis' limp organ. Slowly she coaxed it to life, and when it was rigid, she spread her thighs and said, "The rest is up to you."

"I will be quick about it," Louis responded.

Anne closed her eyes. She felt him enter her.

He hesitated.

"Move," she ordered, "or you will lose it!"

He obeyed and began to push his way into her.

She counted the thrusts. By the fifth, she sensed it would soon be over. At the seventh, he groaned loudly. His fluid spurted into her.

Breathing hard, he rolled off of her.

She brought her naked thighs together.

"I will pray God gives us a son," Louis said, as he left the bed and took up his robe. Nausea took hold of Anne. She knew if she opened her mouth to answer, she would vomit.

"Yes," Louis said, "I will spend the rest of the night in prayer. Goodnight."

Anne watched him walk back to the door, open it, and continue into his own room without looking back. As soon as the door was closed, she left the bed, hurried to the commode, bent over the chamber pot, and began to throw up.

FIVE

Because the day was full of springtime warmth, the streets of London were thronged with people. Hawkers were everywhere and the drivers of drays and coaches shouted obscenities at each other in an effort to make way for their own vehicles in the tangle of wagons and coaches.

Claude Giroux threaded his way through the densely packed streets with marvelous dexterity. He was a tall thin man with heavy-lidded brown eyes, sensual lips, and a strong chin, partially covered by a russet beard.

Across the way from St. Paul's he entered a coffee house and went directly to the rear of the establishment, where a heavyset, well-accoutered man was waiting for him at a table.

"Have you been waiting long?" Giroux asked in flawless English as he sat down. Summoning the waiter, he told him to bring coffee and several hot buns.

"Not too long," the man answered. "I always enjoy watching the activities in a place like this."

Giroux looked around and nodded. "There is a great similarity between it and the café," he said.

His companion nodded.

"I was surprised when I received your message," Giroux commented.

"This time I think I have something that might help you with your problem," the man said.

With a smile Giroux said, "I have so many problems, my dear Sir John, that you would have to be much more specific for me to give you the satisfaction of some sort of positive response."

"Buckingham."

"Yes, he is most definitely a problem whose solution has eluded me. I am told that since his experience at the Laughing Crow he has retained a bull of a man to guard his person."

"I have seen him," Sir John Barrow said. "He presented him to the king."

"And what did Charles do?"

"Bade him guard the duke with his life, gave him several pieces of gold and warned that if anything happened to the duke, his own life would be forfeit. The man was too astounded or too frightened to speak. Perhaps he was both?"

Their conversation was briefly interrupted by the arrival of the waiter with coffee and hot buns. As soon as the man departed, Sir John moved slightly forward and in a low voice he said, "During one of Charles' fall progresses he chanced to spend several days at the manor house of a certain country gentleman by the name of Danton."

"Of French—"

"An old Norman family but by this time very English, I assure you," Sir John explained. "Naturally Buckingham was with the king."

"As he always is," Giroux commented, as he bit into a bun.

"Danton has a niece, a young woman of some twenty years with lovely flaxen hair and sky-blue eyes, who found herself the focal point of the duke's attentions. Needless to say, her prudence was overwhelmed by his passion."

"It would have been more unusual if her prudence had remained the stronger of the two," Giroux commented philosophically. "But prudence, more often than not, gives way before a determined assault by passion."

"Especially when a man like Buckingham is determined to have his way," Barrow said.

"What you are telling me is that yet another woman has been ruined by the duke, and in this particular situation the woman's uncle is angry at Buckingham. My dear Sir John, I dare say that on any given day half the noblemen in England are furious with the duke for one reason or another. But somehow he always manages to survive their wrath."

"True enough," Barrow responded. "But this young woman has a brother who is also an officer in his majesty's navy and has frequently come in contact with Buckingham."

"Interesting," Giroux commented, setting down his coffee cup and leaning slightly forward. "What rank does the irate young man hold?"

"Lieutenant."

"And at present where is he?"

"At the Admiralty, where he is occupied with some minor task having to do with the refitting of ships."

Giroux helped himself to another hot bun. It was much cooler than the first but nonetheless very good.

"Paul is only a half brother to Alva. They share the same father, who seems to have been the black sheep of the family. Spent his share of the family fortune on wine and women and died young."

"But not before he managed to spread his seed around," Giroux said, looking at his companion over the rim of the cup.

"As men of his nature do," Sir John responded, taking another sip of his coffee.

"So Paul is ready to kill the duke?"

"I would not go that far."

"You, my dear lord, do not have to go anywhere," Giroux told him.

"What I mean is that young Paul would like to see Buckingham punished. He has said as much in my presence several times these past few days."

"While in or out of his cups?" Giroux questioned.

"In both conditions."

"I would like to meet him at some future date. Would you be able to arrange it?"

"Most certainly."

"I will tell you where and when," Giroux said. "And now if you will excuse me, I must take my leave."

Sir John Barrow nodded.

Charles, in a towering rage, paced back and forth. His brown wig was slightly askew and his hands moved violently against each other like a pair of equally matched fighting cocks.

Buckingham leaned quietly against the empty hearth. He had been summoned from the Admiralty before noon. The message was in the king's own hand. All it said was: "Come at once. Urgent!" He had obeyed.

The time Buckingham spent watching Charles pace gave him the opportunity to think about what might be the cause of the king's anger. There was the possibility that Louis or Richelieu might have taken some action that would abrogate the marriage agreement. And it was also quite possible that Charles had again received a letter defaming him. Such letters always enraged Charles, as they had his father before him.

Charles suddenly went to his writing table and, stopping there, tapped his forefinger several times against a sheet of paper.

"Do you know what this is?" the king questioned, his voice high-pitched with anger.

Suppressing a sigh, Buckingham drew himself up and answered, "No, sire, I do not."

"It is a communiqué from Vice Admiral Cory, informing us that three English ships have been taken by Spanish men-of-war off Antigua."

Buckingham moved toward the desk.

"Three of our ships, Steenie!" the king raged. "Each carrying a cargo worth some fifty thousand pounds." He balled his fist and pounded the table, shouting, "By Christ, we will make Philip rue the day he told his captains to take our ships."

"It is possible," Buckingham offered, "that they acted without his orders."

"Possible, but not at all probable."

Buckingham asked if he could see the communiqué from Admiral Cory. When it was handed to him, he perused it carefully, noting that the action had taken place some six weeks previous.

Admiral Cory, though an excellent seaman, had never been a supporter of Buckingham, and this letter straight to the king was a clear indication of the man's contempt for the head of the navy. Had the news of the Spanish action come to him first, he would have found a way to minimize its importance to the king. The very worst that would have come out of it would have been a harsh letter sent over Charles' signature to Philip. But now there was a storm, and no man could predict which way it would blow before it blew itself out.

"I will not tolerate Philip's actions," the king shouted, his face going purple with rage.

Buckingham nodded. But he did not speak.

"Philip must think he can do what he pleases with English ships," Charles said. "But I tell you this,

Buckingham, I will make him change his thinking, by the living God, I will!"

The duke set the communiqué from Admiral Cory down on the writing table. He knew that most if not all of the king's anger against Philip had little or nothing to do with the taking of the three ships by Spanish men-of-war. In the Caribbean, English would take French ships, French would take English and Spanish vessels, and the English would prey on the ships of the other two nations whenever the opportunity presented itself. Charles' response was the result of the ill treatment he had received at the Spanish court when he had sought the infanta's hand in marriage.

"I have not forgotten Philip's duplicity," the king said, now walking to the window. "Why, we were practically held prisoners while we were there."

"But we did play some wild tricks on the dons," Buckingham said with a laugh, hoping to divert the king and thereby mollify his anger. "I would say they thought we were in league with the devil."

"They will think that and more before we are through with them," Charles answered.

"May I suggest, your grace, we summon the Spanish ambassador and convey our displeasure."

"We will convey our displeasure in a more meaningful manner," the king said. "Issue orders to all our ships that we would look with favor on any Spanish prizes they might take."

Buckingham frowned. The English navy was not prepared for a sea war with Spain.

"When you are in France, I wish you to approach Richelieu on the prospect of joining us in a war against Spain."

Buckingham was about to protest.

"I do not want any discussion on the matter," Charles said. "France and England will be united, and it would be a perfect opportunity to bring Philip to his knees."

"You are asking two Catholic countries to oppose each other and one of them to do it at the side of a Protestant nation. The cardinal has let his views be known on what he and others in the Catholic Church refer to as the 'Protestant heresy.' If we should make war against anyone it should be against France for their treatment of the Huguenots."

"I have already charged you with a mission regarding the Huguenots," the king told him. "If France and England join together against Spain, then through diplomacy, rather than arms, we will be able to aid these Frenchmen who prefer our Protestant faith to the rule of the pope."

"Your highness," Buckingham replied, "the cardinal is implacable on his stand against the Huguenots. He has vowed to destroy them. He will not—"

"You will do our bidding," the king commanded.

"As you wish, sire," Buckingham answered in a low voice, bowing slightly from the waist. "I will speak to Richelieu and endeavor to enlist his aid against Philip of Spain."

"Excellent!" Charles exclaimed, his humor suddenly brightening. "If anyone can woo the cardinal to our cause, you can."

"Thank you, your grace, for your confidence."

"And now let us drink to your powers of persuasion," Charles said. "Come, I will have some wine and cake sent to us while we present ourselves to the rest of the court."

Buckingham nodded; though he would have much preferred to leave, he had no choice but to accept the king's offer ... no choice but to obey a fool. The duke smiled broadly and said, "Yes, some wine would be a very good thing now. A great deal of wine would even be better...."

The Great Hall of the palace was resplendent with candlelight, and the air was heavy with the sweet scent of many different perfumes. Everywhere men in the livery of the royal household attended the hundreds of members of the court. Along one wall a buffet was laid out on ten huge tables. There were several roasted wild boars, huge chucks of venison, giant salmon from the rivers of the north, grouse and partridges by the hundreds, ducks and rabbits, and great casks of ale and wine.

The ball was being given to celebrate the king's forthcoming marriage to Henrietta and Buckingham's departure within three days for France to bring the new queen to her husband's side. It was the most magnificent entertainment seen at the palace since before the death of James, some few weeks earlier.

Charles walked through the hall, smiling and chatting with various courtiers, while the queen mother, with a dour look on her wrinkled face, remained seated near the king's throne. She had not approved of the marriage when her late husband James had started negotiations for it with Louis, and she had not changed her mind now that it was imminent.

Buckingham was never more than a pace or two from the king, and very often it was the duke who drew Charles' attention to a particular courtier, rather than the other way around. Buckingham was more familiar with the members of the court than the king.

Having made his way from one end of the hall to the other, the king stopped and called for the music to begin. He had previously arranged with the musicians to start the dancing with the "Duke of Buckingham galliard," which the duke had composed himself and took great delight in leading.

Buckingham immediately turned to his wife and led her onto the floor. During the past few weeks she had been in an ill humor, denying him her bed and often being waspish when a genteel nature would have been more welcome by him.

"Is it for my benefit or the court's that you have chosen me?" she asked in a whisper, keeping her lips in a rigid smile.

"I do what I do to please myself," he told her as they began the first steps forward.

She attempted to pull away from him.

Tightening his grip of her hand, he held fast to her. "This is neither the place nor the time," he said, "to show the king and the court any sign of discord between us."

"You ask me to forget I am a wife and woman," she replied.

"No," he answered, "I ask you to remember that the king is our friend and we are his guests."

Katherine nodded.

When the music came to an end, the dancers were applauded by the king and then by the other members of the court.

Buckingham led Katherine toward one of the tables. Handing her a glass of port, and taking one for himself, he said, "You dance well, milady."

"Only when I dance with you," she answered, her green eyes moist with sadness.

"Not so," he told her. "I have seen you dance with others, and—"

She shook her head and turned away.

"Please, Kate," he whispered, stepping close behind her.

"I am sorry," she responded after a moment. "I will have better control of myself."

He turned her to him and, taking her hand in his, began to once again go from group to group, always moving toward the king, who was now seated on the throne, laughing at something Lord Causery said to him.

Buckingham and Katherine were passing a small group of men when one of them said, "And it is to that man we must give thanks for our Catholic queen."

The duke stopped.

"No," the man continued, "I do not care if he heard

me. His hand is in this business more than any other. His own wife was a Catholic, and for all we know, he may be one too."

Buckingham disengaged his hand from Katherine's and slowly turned around. He took several deep breaths before he asked, "Which one of you gentlemen has been so bold as to attack me and my wife?"

"I," answered the youngest of the group, a fair-haired man with gray eyes and good features.

"Your name, sir?"

"William Felton," the man answered.

Buckingham stared at him.

"No, I am not a member of the court."

"Oh?"

"I am a guest of Sir Oliver Potter," Felton said. "We are distantly related."

Buckingham moved his eyes from the young man to owlish-looking Sir Oliver. "I never knew rudeness to be one of your traits," the duke commented in an icy voice. "I pray you, ask your kinsmen to apologize to myself and Lady Buckingham and see that he does not drink any more, for I suspect he has already had too much to drink."

"I have only said," Felton responded, "what practically everyone in England is thinking."

"Please, William!" another man said, stepping slightly forward.

"Who are you?" Buckingham inquired.

"John Felton, his elder brother."

The family resemblance was pronounced. The two brothers differed only in that John's complexion was darker and he had black hair. Each had slate-gray eyes.

"I say only what must be said," William replied in a loud voice that drew the attention of many of the guests who were nearby. "No one I know wants the sister of the French king as our queen."

"You have said too much," Buckingham answered. "I ask you to leave Sir Potter—"

"I will show you how we treat men like you!"

William exclaimed, his hand dropping to the hilt of his sword.

Buckingham swore and, pushing Katherine back, he drew.

Within moments women were screaming and the men had formed a wide circle around the combatants.

The king came running down the length of the hall, but by the time he had pushed his way to the front of the ring of men, steel struck against steel.

William was quick on his feet and an excellent swordsman. He drove straight for Buckingham's heart, and each time the duke parried the thrust.

The men circled each other. Sweat poured down their faces.

"Put up your swords!" the king shouted.

"Sire," Buckingham answered, "I fight for your honor as well as my own."

"And I fight to keep a Catholic queen off the throne of England!" William shouted, lunging hard at Buckingham.

The clash of blades rang in the great hall. The men watched the fight with animal intensity, while the women stared at the two circling men with wide-eyed fascination.

The swordsmen moved like dancers. Sometimes one seemed to hold the advantage; sometimes the other.

Then suddenly William's guard went down, and in that instant Buckingham's blade struck home.

With a cry of pain, William staggered.

When the duke pulled his sword free a gush of blood followed it.

William's blade dropped to the floor. "I am dead!" he cried and fell face forward.

His brother ran to him. Cradling the body in his arms, he wept unashamedly.

Buckingham used his lace handkerchief to wipe the blood from his blade. Breathing hard, he approached the king. "I had no choice, sire, but to accept his challenge."

Charles looked at the weeping man and said, "You have made yourself another enemy, Steenie."

Buckingham nodded. "But this time, before God," he said in a low voice, "I am guiltless."

Giroux went down to Dover to see Buckingham and his entourage depart for France.

The duke and the king rode side by side, leading the procession of lords, knights of great worth, and their servants. Buckingham was gorgeously dressed in silk clothing of white and purple. He rode a high-spirited coal-black Arabian stallion, and he looked more regal than the king. The streets along the way to the quay were crowded with people who hailed their king and the duke with the same exuberance.

Giroux watched the procession from the window of the room in the inn where he was staying. He not only had a clear view of the street and quay at the foot of it, but he could see out into the harbor, where five seventy-two-gun ships were waiting to take the duke and the other members of the escort to Calais.

Giroux was too much a man of the world to be impressed by most things he saw. But the panoply of the duke's party most definitely impressed him, and he knew it would have the same effect on Richelieu and Louis when they saw it.

"Any you say," Giroux questioned, turning from the window to face Sir John Barrow, "that Buckingham spent much of his own money for the clothes of those with him?"

"It is rumored that he put himself in debt," Sir John replied. "But he has said, and I have heard him with my own ears, that whither he goes, so goes England, and England must never be less than great and excellent in the eyes of everyone who sees him."

"If that was his intent," Giroux answered, "then he has most definitely achieved it."

Sir John left his chair and went to the window to stand beside Giroux.

Buckingham and the king reached the quay. They

dismounted and received the blessing of the Bishop of London. Several fanfares sounded, and immediately the vessels in the harbor began to fire a salute to the king and the duke. Puffs of black smoke curled up from the open gunports.

Giroux picked up a telescope and trained it on the quay. Within a moment he was able to hold it on the duke and the king. The two men embraced and then separated. The king stepped back, and Buckingham bowed, turned, and made his way down the stone steps to the longboat waiting to take him to his ship.

"So much for that!" Giroux exclaimed, closing the telescope. "I must say Buckingham fits the role he plays."

"Too well, much too well," Sir John agreed, returning to his chair.

Giroux remained at the window. He did not know Buckingham personally. Indeed, he had nothing against the duke. But he had been ordered by Richelieu to assassinate him, and in attempting to carry out the cardinal's order, he found himself becoming more and more involved in Buckingham's life—past, present, and future.

"Well," Giroux commented, "he has passed out of my hands for a while."

"Perhaps he will not return?" Sir John offered.

Giroux shrugged. Buckingham was a worthy adversary. From his own sense of professionalism, he would much prefer to be responsible for the duke's death than have some other agent accomplish it.

Sir John poured a glass of wine from the decanter on the table and handed it to Giroux.

"No, thank you," Giroux said. "But please do not refrain from drinking yourself."

Sir John nodded and sipped at the wine.

"Tell me," Giroux asked, "why do you hate Buckingham so much that you risk your life by giving information about him?"

"I was wondering when you would come around to asking me," Sir John commented with a smile.

"Of course, you need not answer."

"But I want to," Sir John said. "My enmity for him goes back to the time when Lord Somerset was still the favorite of James. There was a scandal over the death of Sir Thomas Overbury. The details now are unimportant, but Somerset was involved—involved, some people think, as I myself do, by the clever machinations of Buckingham himself, or by those close to him. The end, of course, was to bring Somerset down and raise himself to the king's favorite. And now with Charles on the throne, Buckingham has even more power than he previously had."

"I had heard something about the Somerset affair," Giroux commented. "But I did not think it was as political as you appear to make it."

"It is indeed a political affair. The king's favorite determines a great many things. His friends receive the choicest posts. Through him, one can always have the ear of the king. I assure you, it is a position of great political importance. And Buckingham, for all his dash and foppishness, is a political animal."

"So it would seem," Giroux answered.

Sir John set the empty glass down on the table. "If I were you," he said, "I would make every effort to cultivate the friendship of John Felton."

"Felton, Felton . . . I have heard that name recently," Giroux said.

"I am sure you have. He is the older brother of the man Buckingham killed in a duel."

"Do you know where he can be reached?" Giroux asked.

Sir John nodded.

Giroux faced the window. "The weather is turning," he said. "I doubt if the duke's ships will sail this day."

Within an hour after Buckingham boarded his majesty's ship *Valiant*, the sky filled with dark low scud and a brisk northeast wind thrummed against the vessel's shrouds. As soon as the duke could gracefully withdraw from the noblemen in his immediate party, he went directly to his quarters and motioned Ed and Tobias to follow him.

Tobias helped Buckingham into less formal clothing, while Ed, on the duke's word, looked for the captain to ask that he attend the duke.

There were several dispatches waiting for Buckingham. As soon as he was more comfortably attired he gave his attention to them. Three were from Lord Kensington, advising him of the preparations that had been made by Louis to accommodate him and his entourage at the Louvre. The fourth was from Gerbier, and in it was a brief note from Anne, which read:

My darling,

The day draws near when I will once more see you. I tremble with anticipation. I cannot sleep for thinking about you, and when I do sleep, my slumber is filled with such dreams that on waking the memory of them brings a flush to my cheeks and quickens my breath. Yet if you were here, I would do with you all and more than comes to me in my dreams and I would do it without shame and with infinite pleasure.

Anne

Buckingham reread the letter twice, set it down, and poured himself a glass of wine before reading it a third time. Her words filled him with a great yearning. He carefully folded the missive and placed it inside his portfolio. Then he stood up and went to the transom. With one hand braced on the cross beam, he looked out the stern windows.

The low dark hills on the far side of the harbor were already smeared with rain.

A knock at the door brought Buckingham around. "Come," he called out.

The door opened and Ed said, "The captain's here, your grace."

"Have him come in," Buckingham answered, stepping away from the transom.

The captain entered and removed his hat. He was a ruddy-faced man of middling height with sparse brown hair and brown, slightly protruding eyes.

"Thank you for your quarters, Captain Swite," Buckingham said. "And for answering my summons."

"My pleasure, your grace," Swite answered with a ready smile.

"A glass of wine?" the duke offered.

"Yes, thank you."

Buckingham gestured to Ed to pour the wine.

"To your health," the duke toasted.

"And to the king's future bride," Captain Swite offered.

The two men drank, and then Buckingham asked if the captain thought they would set sail that evening.

"The wind is backed against us," Swite replied. "But even if it were behind us, I would not weigh anchor unless ordered. The Channel is a rough place, even in a light blow, and this is not going to be a light one."

"I will not order you to set sail," the duke said. "The lords and ladies aboard the ships are not used to rough weather at sea."

Swite nodded.

"But can you send a fast cutter to Calais?"

"Most certainly, your grace."

"Excellent!" the duke exclaimed. "Have her ready to go in less than an hour. I have some dispatches to send to our minister in Paris."

"The *Hermes* will be close by," said the captain.

The duke thanked him and told him to have one of his officers come to the cabin in an hour for the dispatch case.

Captain Swite replaced his hat and with a slight

bow asked permission to leave the cabin.

Buckingham nodded and immediately sat down at the writing desk. He composed two letters. The first was to Lord Kensington, advising him to set a time and a place for meeting the Duc de Rohan and any other emissaries from the Huguenots. He also asked the minister to arrange for a private meeting between himself and Cardinal Richelieu. "Both these matters," he wrote, "must be kept in strictest confidence." To give his words more authority, he signed the dispatch "Lord of the Admiralty, George Villiers, the Duke of Buckingham." He was sure his manner of signing would not escape the very alert eyes of Lord Kensington.

The second dispatch went to Lord Rich and then to M. Gerbier and was finally addressed to Anne.

My beloved,

I hoped to sail this afternoon, but a sudden storm has delayed my departure. I too have dreams in which you live and breathe. But unlike you no color rises to my cheeks when I wake with sweet memories of what transpired between us. Yes, my heart beats faster and my longing for you increases a thousandfold. But I promise to do all which would make you privy to my dreams and simultaneously satiate, at least for a few delicious moments, my passion for you, as well as yours for me.

Yours forever,
Buckingham

As soon as the dispatches were sealed and placed in the leather case, Buckingham took it up on deck himself.

The wind was blowing hard, and rain was beginning to fall. The *Hermes* was hove to on the starboard side. Under the expert handling of her captain, the cutter was brought close enough to the *Valiant* for the duke to throw the dispatch case into the waiting arms of a man aboard the small vessel.

"Godspeed!" Buckingham shouted as the *Hermes* drew away.

The captain waved and answered, but the wind tore away the words.

After a few minutes the *Hermes* vanished into the rain. Buckingham drew his cloak more securely around himself and went up to the quarterdeck. Close by lay the other ships that made up the small fleet that would be going to France as soon as the weather cleared. He looked up at the sky. It was now solidly cast over with dark-gray clouds, some of which were already turning black with the coming of night.

The rain and wind continued through the night, all of the following day, and into the next night.

Aboard the *Valiant* there was a great deal of drinking, gaming, and whatever other amusements helped to pass the time away. Several of the men managed to find a place to dally with those ladies who were willing to take pleasure wherever they found it.

For the most part Buckingham remained aloof from whatever amusements went on around him. He did play cards twice. And each time he managed to win well over a thousand pounds, which he quickly distributed to the captain and the crew of the *Valiant*. Such generosity gained him the praises of every seaman aboard the ship.

But by the second night, the duke had become very restive. He was anxious to sail, and he knew from his own experience at sea and what the captain told him that the weather would not change until at least the following day.

Despite the rain and the wind, he prowled the deck and absented himself from the revelries taking place below deck. Finally he could no longer tolerate remaining on board without sailing, and he ordered a longboat launched. With Ed at his side, he was rowed back to the stone quay at the foot of the main street in Dover.

Buckingham went straight into the first inn he saw. It was a mean place, with the strong smell of ale, rough tables and chairs. A few candles in niches along the wall gave a little light. The men were a hard-looking lot, either seamen from merchant ships or fishermen. They stopped talking when he and Ed entered and eyed the strangers suspiciously as they went to a small unoccupied table at the side of the establishment.

The duke called for two tankards of ale and two mutton chops.

"Don't think we're welcome here," Ed whispered.

"Welcome or not," Buckingham answered in a voice loud enough for everyone to hear, "we will stay."

None of the men challenged him, and soon they began to talk to one another again.

Food and drink were brought to the duke's table, and he ate and drank with gusto. He told Ed about the wonders of Paris and playfully cautioned him about becoming involved with a Frenchwoman. They had just about finished eating when a hag came into the inn. She stood in the doorway and offered to tell any man's fortune for twopence.

"Here," Buckingham called, "tell mine and I will give you a shilling."

The woman came straight to the table. She had a humped back and straggly gray hair. One eye was completely covered over with a thin greenish skin. Her other eye was set deep in her skull. Most of her teeth were gone, and those that she had were black with decay.

"A shilling," she cried, "and I'll tell you heaven is hell and hell is heaven."

Her breath was foul.

"Tell me my true fortune," Buckingham said, winking broadly at Ed, "or I will have you whipped."

"'Ow will you know if it be your true fortune?" the hag challenged.

"Let me hear it and I will tell you."

"Hold out yer hand," the old woman told him.

Buckingham extended his hand.

The old woman peered down at it. She looked up at him and then down at his hand again. "Here," she said, tracing his life line on his palm with a dirty fingernail. "Here it ends. Right here."

"What ends?" Buckingham asked.

"Why sir, yer life ends—it be plain as day."

"How does it end?" the duke asked.

The hag shook her head. "I only see that it ends," she told him.

"Don't pay her no mind," Ed said. "She be too blind to see anythin'."

Buckingham gave her a shilling, and she waddled out of the inn, talking to herself about what she had seen in the palm of his hand.

"There be better'n her in tellin' fortunes," Ed commented.

"Not three weeks ago," Buckingham answered, "I was told the same thing by a gypsy woman in London." He held his palm up to Ed. And pointing to the life line, he said, "It is indeed very short. See?"

SIX

Wearing a gray cassock, Cardinal Richelieu stood at the window watching the leaden clouds that lay over Paris lighten with the coming of dawn. Father Joseph was seated at the writing table taking notes as Captain Portez gave his account of how he had come into possession of an English dispatch case containing two letters with Buckingham's signature on them.

"My men and I were north of Calais," the captain explained.

"Why?" Richelieu asked, without moving his eyes from the window.

"Wreckers, your eminence," the captain answered. "We have had reports for some weeks now that a group of wreckers had moved into the vicinity and we wanted to catch them at it."

Father Joseph looked up from the paper in front of him and asked, "What do they wreck, captain?" The yellow candlelight gave the priest's face a jaundiced look.

"Ships," the officer answered.

Father Joseph repeated the word and wrote it down.

"Just how do they do that?" Richelieu questioned, turning to face the officer.

The captain looked questioningly at the cardinal. "It is common knowledge what they do," he said.

"That may be so," Richelieu answered. "But for the sake of our records we would appreciate it if you told us how the wreckers function."

With a nod, Portez said, "They mount lights on the rocks so that a captain of a ship at sea will make for them, thinking that they mark the entrance to a safe harbor."

"And that was done last night?"

"Yes, your eminence."

"You and your men watched them set the lights?"

The captain shifted his weight from one foot to the other. He was a slender man with slightly bowed legs and weatherbeaten face with fine lines around his eyes.

"We must have the exact sequence of events," Richelieu explained, "in case there is any investigation into the matter."

"Other than the captain and two of his officers there were no survivors," Portex said. "Most of those that were not drowned were killed by the wreckers."

"Captain, if you please, tell us the exact sequence of events," the cardinal told him, hardening the tone of his voice sufficiently to let the man know that he would not tolerate any evasiveness. He left the window and moved to the right of Father Joseph.

"We did not reach the rocks until after the ship had struck them," the officer replied.

Richelieu nodded. His eyes moved to the top of the writing table. To the left of Father Joseph was the dispatch case. Next to it were the two letters. One was obviously a love letter. But the name of the recipient had been obliterated by either the sea or the rain. Another letter was addressed to Lord Kensington. Its contents were completely legible and gave added fuel to the cardinal's hate for Buckingham and the Huguenots. But it was the other one that raised a storm of anger in him. He pursed his lips and fought down the desire to take hold of the letter and tear it to shreds.

"Your eminence," Father Joseph called softly, looking up at the man behind him.

"Excuse me," Richelieu lied, "but I was trying to picture the scene you were describing. Will you give me more details?"

"There are high cliffs, a narrow beach, and rocks that extend out into the sea for at least several hundred paces. We did not know the wreckers would be there."

"Could they have been anywhere else?" Father Joseph asked. "Are there other places where the rocks give them a place to set their lights?"

"Many along the coast both to the south and to the north of the harbor."

"Then the ship, the *Hermes,* was already on the rocks by the time you and your men arrived?" Richelieu questioned.

"She was breaking up," Captain Portez said. "Her masts had already snapped—they almost always do as soon as the vessel strikes the rocks. By the time we were on the beach, her timbers were going. When one of them broke, it sounded like the firing of a light cannon."

"What did you and your men do when you reached the beach?"

"The wreckers were just coming off the rocks. They did not have much for their trouble."

"I do not understand," Richelieu admitted.

"The ship was a cutter, a small one at that. She had few things of value aboard her. Some rope, shot, and powder. But she broke up so fast that none of the guns could be taken off her."

Richelieu nodded.

"When the wreckers saw us, it was too late for them to run. We had a pitched battle with them. It was short and swift. When it was done, those we had not killed had been driven into the sea. I lost two men, and four were wounded, but none seriously."

"And how did you come by this?" Richelieu asked, tapping the leather pouch with the forefinger of his right hand.

"It was part of the booty we found after the fight," the captain said. "Since one of the letters was addressed to the English ambassador, I thought it wise to bring the pouch directly to your eminence."

Richelieu moved back to the window. The sun was up, and though the clouds were considerably lighter, the day promised to be dull.

"Did you read the letters?" the cardinal questioned, facing the officer again.

Captain Portez flushed and began to stammer.

"Did you read the letters?" Richelieu asked again.

"Only to discover if they were important, your eminence," the captain said. "There was no other way for me to determine their worth."

"Worth," Richelieu repeated. "You mean how much they might fetch in terms of gold and silver?"

"No, your eminence. I meant worth in terms of their importance."

"Do you consider them important?"

Captain Portez began to sweat. His instinct told him he was in danger, but he could not understand why. "I would consider the one to Lord Kensington important," he replied.

"And the other?" snapped the cardinal.

"An affair of the heart," the captain answered, gesturing broadly to indicate that as a man he understood such things.

Richelieu gnashed his teeth, and for several moments he could not speak. What the captain had so cavalierly described as an affair of the heart was at the very moment filling his mouth with the taste of gall.

"You have no idea who the lady might be?" the cardinal asked in a tight voice.

The captain shook his head. "Her name had already been washed from the letter by the time I opened it," he said.

"And do you know who Buckingham is?" Richelieu questioned.

"An English lord, your eminence."

"An English lord who plots with the enemies of France, with the enemies of the church," Richelieu suddenly roared. "A heretic who should be burned at the stake!"

The captain agreed.

Richelieu returned to the writing table and said, "Each of the letters is worth, as you put it, a great deal. They are very important."

"Thank God then that I brought them to your eminence!" Captain Portez exclaimed, feeling very much relieved.

"These letters are so important," the cardinal said, "that here in France only a very few men should even know they exist."

"I understand," the captain responded. "I give you my word that none will ever hear about them from me."

"Thank you, I appreciate that."

Captain Portez.

"At some future time, when it becomes necessary for me to remember your name, rest assured that I will," Richelieu said.

"Thank you, your eminence," Portez said.

Richelieu walked to where the captain was standing. "You may go," he said, offering him his hand.

Portez knelt, kissed the offered hand, stood up, and retreated from the room, closing the door softly behind him.

Richelieu returned to the table. "Have my guards

detain Captain Portez," he told Father Joseph. "Make him as comfortable as possible. I do not want him about until after..."

"After what?"

"Until Buckingham leaves France or has been killed," Richelieu said. "The captain may in a weak moment speak imprudently, and any mention of the letters might be damaging to our plan. I do not want to alert Buckingham that we know what he intends to do. Can you find me a forger skillful enough to duplicate the writing on these letters?"

"Yes," the priest answered.

"Have him here this afternoon," Richelieu said. "And I also want a skilled leatherworker to mend the dispatch case. We will present Lord Kensington with two very interesting letters. And as for these," the cardinal continued, as he picked up the letters from the writing table, "we will keep these for another purpose."

Father Joseph nodded, but he could not keep the expression of displeasure from his face.

"You disapprove?" Richelieu questioned.

"Only of that which springs from lust and not from love of God and country," the priest answered.

"I will not let Buckingham have her."

"To have her for yourself," Father Joseph warned, "you may well lose France, not to mention losing God."

Richelieu did not answer. He had lost God long before he had started to serve France.

Despite the dullness of the day, Mme. de Chevreuse had herself transported by litter to 15 Rue de La Madeleine, where after three raps with the brass door clapper and a short wait, she was admitted by a mulatto servant of M. Balthazar Gerbier, who asked in a low voice that she follow him. He led her into a small sitting room whose windows overlooked a garden rampant with the brilliant colors of spring flowers.

"My master will join you shortly," the mulatto said

as he withdrew behind a closed door.

Mme. de Chevreuse did not give any indication that she had heard him or was even aware of his presence. She stood by the window and removed her long gloves. After a few moments, she walked slowly around the room, looking at the paintings on the wall, all of which were done by M. Gerbier, who if he had had to live by his talent alone would have starved to death a long time ago. Even to her uncritical eye, his ability, such as it was, would never come anywhere near that of Peter Paul Rubens, who was now painting a portrait of the queen.

She paused in front of a nude and studied it intently, trying to define why M. Gerbier had even bothered to paint the woman. There was nothing terribly unique about the model's face or body. Yet, there was something in the slight twist of the lower portion of the torso that showed the barest hint of the lips of her sex. The more Mme. de Chevreuse looked at the painting, the more erotic she realized it was. She was just about to smile at her discovery when the door opened and M. Gerbier entered, smiling broadly.

He was a small, slight man with long delicate hands. He dressed à la mode, with bursts of lace at his neck and at his sleeves.

"My dear duchesse!" he exclaimed in a deep bass voice that would have seemed more appropriate if it had come from a much larger man. He took her hand and brought it to his lips. "I am pleased to have you in my humble home."

She smiled. He always said the same thing whenever she came to see him.

"Would you care for something to drink? Perhaps coffee or chocolate?"

"Chocolate would be fine," she answered.

Gerbier went to the door, opened it, and spoke to someone she could not see. "I have also told my servant to bring some fruits," he said, coming back to her. "I recall how fond of them you were the last time you were here."

"It is kind of you to remember such a trifling detail," she responded.

With a shrug, he said, "I am in the habit of remembering details."

"I was admiring your paintings," she told him. "To have such a talent is a gift from God."

"He might have been more generous," Gerbier replied with a laugh.

Mme. de Chevreuse chose to remain silent.

"I have had word," Gerbier told her, "from a mutual friend."

She smiled. She had guessed that Buckingham would try to enlist her aid again. No one else at court was as close to the queen as she herself was, and as the duke well knew, no one shared Anne's confidences as she did.

"That pleases you?" he said.

"I will have to wait to hear more before I answer," she said.

"Please sit down," Gerbier offered, gesturing toward a red velvet double chair.

Mme. de Chevreuse eased herself down.

A young serving woman entered the room and set a silver tray with fruit tarts down on a nearby table.

She was immediately followed by the mulatto, who brought another silver tray with fine white china cups and saucers for the hot chocolate, which steamed in a beaker with a silver handle. The serving woman poured the chocolate and then left the room.

"Our mutual friend will be in Paris soon," M. Gerbier said, "and he has directed me to enlist your aid in accomplishing some of his enterprises."

Mme. de Chevreuse sipped at her hot chocolate. "Our mutual friend knows that such help entails a great deal of risk and requires that certain people must be paid."

"He does."

"And is he willing to pay?"

"Certainly," Gerbier answered. "You name the amount."

"Oh," she answered, "I would prefer to leave that

detail for a later time."

"But I can tell him that he may count on your help?"

"Most certainly."

"Excellent!"

Mme. de Chevreuse helped herself to an apple tart and said, "Does our mutual friend realize that nothing can come of his passion, nothing that would bring him and the object of his passion together for anything more than a brief interval of time?"

"I do not know," Gerbier replied with a shake of his head. "He is a man who is used to having his way."

"You may tell him I will make whatever arrangements are necessary," she said, picking up her cup.

"His gratitude will be unbounded."

Mme. de Chevreuse nodded. "I would expect nothing less," she commented.

"More chocolate?"

"No, thank you," Mme. de Chevreuse replied. "I think we have said all that had to be said between us."

M. Gerbier agreed.

Anne dismissed all of her ladies-in-waiting from the boudoir. She wanted to be completely alone. The tension in her during the past few days had grown to enormous proportions. She could think of nothing except the time when she would once more see Buckingham. Even Louis' feeble attack on her body and Richelieu's lust for it faded from her thoughts. She wanted nothing more than to be embraced by the man she loved and who loved her.

For a long while she stared at the underside of the canopy above her. Then she shook her head. The need for some sort of release was beyond endurance. She turned to the small table next to her bed, where a single candle burned. Its flame stood straight up. A small thread of black smoke came off the tip.

She remembered holding Buckingham's phallus in her hand. She remembered how warm it had felt against her lips. Anne closed her eyes. Her heart beat very fast, and her breath became shallow.

"Dear God," she whispered aloud, "is it a sin to want to be loved?"

She could feel her nipples grow hard. She pressed her thighs together. Her head filled with images of herself and Buckingham locked in love's embrace. There was nothing they would not do.

"Forgive me," she whispered, speaking not to God but to her still-distant lover. Almost unconsciously, her left hand slid between her thighs and began to caress the soft, pliant flesh.

A sound at the other end of the room made her open her eyes. She could see nothing in the darkness.

She sat up and started to lift the candle toward where she had heard sound.

"Leave it be," a muffled voice commanded. "Leave it be!"

She was about to scream, but the figure came rushing out of the darkness. In an instant she was overwhelmed and he was between her thighs. Even as he took his way with her, she wrested the covering from his face.

"Richelieu!" she gasped.

"One way or another, I told you I would have you," he growled.

Anne gathered a wad of spittle in her mouth and flung it in his face.

"I love you," Richelieu said passionately.

"Do what you have come to do and then let me alone," she wept. "Let me alone!" And no longer attempting to struggle, she turned her face away....

Richelieu hurried back to his own rooms, using secret passageways that he doubted even the king knew about. They had recently been revealed to him by Father Joseph, who had discovered the original architectural drawings of the palace. And whenever he had had the time, Richelieu had explored the twisting maze. First he used a lamp and noted where he could enter the king's chamber, the queen's, and any of the other rooms where the important members of the court slept. Then he practiced retracing his steps in total darkness until he had no need for any source of light. He kept these activities completely secret.

After a few minutes he reentered his own bedroom through a portion of the wall that opened to the left of the hearth. Immediately he went into his sitting room and poured himself a drink of brandy. His hand shook as he lifted the glass to his lips.

Never before had he forced his will upon a woman. Never before had he wanted to experience love and not just physical pleasure. And never before had he been so totally and uncompromisingly rejected by a woman.

He poured another glass of brandy and quickly drank it.

Had he not been told by the woman who attended the queen that she had been dismissed from the room and that the queen wanted to be alone, he would never have gone to her. But as soon as he had learned that she would be alone, he had to go to her.

Richelieu shut his eyes.

He had expected to find her asleep, and then, he was sure, he would have done no more than look at her. But instead he had come up on her when she had just started to touch herself, and though he had seen other women do the same thing, watching her had robbed him of his reason.

"I had to have her," he exclaimed aloud. In a sudden rage, he crushed the glass in his hand, until the shards cut into his palm and blood flowed.

"I love her," he said, opening his hand to let the bloodstained fragments of glass drop to the floor. "But she . . . she loves Buckingham . . . Buckingham!"

He shook his head. He did not understand what spell the Englishman had cast over Anne, but he was certain that if she were not under a spell, she would have been more than willing to give herself to him.

"I could give her a son," he whispered. "A son who would be the next King of France."

Richelieu dropped to his knees. "Dear God," he whispered, "I do not ask for forgiveness, but only that I might protect the throne of France from English bastardy and that my love for Anne provide France with an heir to the throne. And though my love for Anne be sin in Your eyes and in the eyes of the Holy Mother Church, I am willing to take the consequences for that sin in the life to come."

Richelieu crossed himself and stood up. He had not prayed to God for a very long time. Indeed, he would not have prayed to Him now, if he were not so distraught. But he had to hear himself say the words. There was no one to whom he could speak, to whom he could confess his actions. Not sins!

To love a woman was not a sin.

To protect one's country was not a sin.

To be a man was not a sin.

Long before Richelieu had become Louis' first minister, he had realized that sin was something that man defined and not God. If there was a God, He was mute and possibly blind. In truth, God was no more than an instrument in the hands of the pope and hence the church. God, or rather the fear of His wrath, kept order in the world.

"But I am not afraid," Richelieu said, knowing he had prayed in a moment of weakness and now wanting to reaffirm his own courage.

He looked at his bloody hand and wiped it clean with a handkerchief. More blood flowed. He used the handkerchief as a bandage and tied it securely around his hand.

"I will win her," he said softly. "I will woo her to me."

Suddenly there was a knock at his door.

He was startled but almost immediately regained his composure and called out, "Who is it?"

"Father Joseph," came the answer.

Richelieu went to the door and opened it.

"Word has just come that the British ships are lying off Calais," the priest said.

"Then by sometime tomorrow Buckingham will be on his way to Paris."

Father Joseph nodded. Then, looking at the bloody handkerchief, he asked, "What happened to your hand?"

"Nothing serious," Richelieu answered. "I placed it where I should not have."

The priest gave him a questioning look but did not press the matter.

"Goodnight," Richelieu said. "And thank you for bringing me the news."

"Goodnight," the Capuchin monk said.

Alone again, Richelieu retreated into his bedroom, knowing that the next few weeks would be crucial for him, for France, and for Buckingham.

Richelieu dropped down on his bed and closed his eyes, but he did not sleep. His brain was filled with images of Anne's naked breasts and the feel of her body against his. If ever a woman tormented a man, Anne tormented him. And adding to his agony was the certain knowledge that she would willingly give herself to Buckingham.

SEVEN

By morning the wind had lessened and the British ships made for the harbor of Calais. Buckingham's vessel, the *Valiant*, led the procession. All of the ships were festooned with the Stuarts' heraldic flags and those of the more important lords in the party.

The two French warships fired their guns eleven times to salute the English visitors, and on shore the fleur-de-lis flew above the quay.

"Never thought I'd ever get to see France," Ed commented as he stood alongside of Buckingham.

"Someday," the duke answered, "I will take you to Italy."

"Is that where the pope lives?"

"Yes."

"Then I don't want no part of Eitaly," Ed said resolutely.

Almost as soon as the *Valiant*'s anchor was cut loose, a longboat was lowered away to take Buckingham and Ed to the quay, which was crowded with French courtiers, sent by Louis to greet the English visitors informally. The formal welcoming ceremonies would take place in Paris outside the Louvre, if the weather permitted, or inside the huge state reception room, if it should rain or suddenly turn unseasonably cold again.

Leading the French delegation was the Duc de Chevreuse. Buckingham recognized him before the longboat ground against the side of the stone quay.

The French nobleman was a thin, narrow-shouldered man with sensual lips and heavy-lidded brown eyes. He was elegantly attired in pale-yellow silk breeches and doublet, a high brown wig, and silver-buckled shoes. His cheeks were rouged.

When Buckingham pointed him out to Ed, the former wherryman said, "I got nothin' to say the way God makes a man. But it be strange when a man can't enjoy a woman."

"Strange indeed," Buckingham answered with a laugh. "But then again God does some very strange things."

As soon as the longboat was properly secured, Buckingham leaped out and went forward to meet the Duc de Chevreuse.

The two men embraced, and in flawless French Buckingham thanked the duc and his party for their courtesy.

"And you, my dear Buckingham, and all of the noblemen with you are most welcome to France," the Duc de Chevreuse lisped.

The two men spoke briefly of their respective kings, and then Buckingham, looking back toward the ships, said, "It will take several hours for the members of my entourage to disembark. There are with servants four hundred of us."

"Then I will immediately send word to the king

that you will not begin your journey to Paris until the day after tomorrow," the Duc de Chevreuse replied.

"That will be fine. For the next two nights we will remain in Calais."

"I will make the necessary quartering arrangements. The servants, of course, will have to sleep wherever they can find shelter. But I would suggest they remain aboard the ships until morning."

"It will be attended to," Buckingham answered. "But I will have this man and my valet with me," he said, looking over his shoulder at Ed, who was standing no more than two paces behind him.

"Of course," the Duc de Chevreuse simpered. "I did not mean to suggest that you should be without your servants."

Buckingham nodded.

"The royal family will meet you a few leagues beyond the Porte de Clichy," the Duc de Chevreuse explained.

"I am eager to see his majesty," Buckingham answered.

"If you will follow me," the Duc de Chevreuse said, "I will escort you to the small castle of the Comte de Valois, where you will spend the night. I have a coach waiting just at the beginning of the street off the quay."

"Thank you," Buckingham answered, "but I must respectfully decline the offer. I will remain at the inn here in Calais. I am sure there will be problems during the next few hours that will require my personal intervention."

"But—"

The duke held up his hand. "I must insist that I stay at the inn," he said.

The Duc de Chevreuse reluctantly nodded. "The burden of command," he said, "always denies the commander his rightful pleasures."

Buckingham agreed.

The inn was comfortable, and Buckingham used the large main room for his headquarters. The many lords and ladies in his entourage vied with one another for some sort of preferential treatment from the duke. There were those who, if they could not be quartered for the night in the inn, wanted to be close by. There were others who complained that their particular abode was too mean for their station.

Buckingham listened to all of their complaints and with a laugh, or a drink and even sometimes a stern admonition, he managed to settle the members of his party for the night. Late in the afternoon he again met with the Duc de Chevreuse and planned the order of march.

"I think it will take us six days to reach Paris," Buckingham said.

With a sigh the Duc de Chevreuse had to agree. And he immediately dispatched another messenger to the king, informing him of the change.

Later in the evening the English and French noblemen ate and drank together in the various inns of the city. Each praised the other's king, the beauty of their women, and whatever else they could think of. By midnight many were too drunk to stand.

Before retiring for the night, Buckingham was visited by M. Dupris. The duke received him in a small room at the rear of the inn. Ed remained outside the hallway. There was a table in the room, but no chairs. The duke set a candle down on the table. The two men stood.

"You are very kind, my lord, to see me at this hour," Dupris said with a low bow.

"We are friends," the duke answered, "and we have many friends in common."

Dupris nodded.

"Have you any news from our mutual friends?" Buckingham asked, expecting a written communication to be delivered to him.

"Only to tell you they hope and pray for your success on their behalf. Their situation grows more desperate with each passing day."

"I will do my best to help them," Buckingham

answered, aware of how Dupris was sweating. "The king sends this token of his support." He handed Dupris the gold ring Charles had given him.

"There are many Huguenots who believe England will abandon them because they are French," Dupris remarked. "This ring will be a welcome sign to them. But you must understand it is very difficult to keep one's trust in the face of so much adversity. This forthcoming marriage was a sorry blow to them."

"Yes, I could see where it would be. But it also could provide the very means for alleviating their plight. Louis might be more generous now that his brother-in-law will also be a Protestant."

"That is what they hope for. But they are afraid of Richelieu. His hatred for them knows no bounds. He would willingly send all of them to the fire."

"Perhaps his mind might be changed too," Buckingham said.

"I hope and pray, my lord, you can do it," Dupris answered with a bow. "And now I will leave you to your rest."

Just as Buckingham stepped forward, Dupris drew a knife and thrust at him. In an instant, the duke was fighting for his life. He grappled with Dupris. The two of them fell to the floor.

"I must do it," Dupris cried, trying to free his hand from Buckingham's grip. "I must do it or my family will be destroyed."

The door suddenly burst open. Ed rushed into the room. He drove his foot into the top of Dupris' head. The skull cracked and Dupris died with his mouth open.

Buckingham got to his feet and reclaimed Charles' ring from the dead man's pocket. "He was my friend," he said, and then, without looking at Ed, he left the room.

Lord Kensington was a dark-complexioned, strikingly handsome man. He had summoned Lord Rich to his house as soon as he had received word that

Dupris had attempted to assassinate Buckingham. Dupris had been a trusted member of the intelligence network that he, Lord Rich, and others had worked so hard to establish.

Kensington pursed his lips and looked down at the letter that had come from Buckingham the previous day. He shook his head and moved his eyes to where Lord Rich was seated.

"Cahusac, the cardinal's man, delivered the pouch and said it had been found the night before on the beach, north of Calais," Kensington said.

Rich made several wheezing sounds. He was a corpulent man, with a red face, wispy gray hair, and brown cowlike eyes. He took a pinch of snuff and after two loud sneezes said, "I would not trust anything that came from Richelieu's hand."

"Exactly," Kensington answered. "But he must realize that we would not trust him."

"Then why would he take the trouble to send it?"

Shifting his position, Rich said, "Perhaps he is telling you something?"

"I thought of that," Kensington answered. "My guess is that he knows about the forthcoming meeting between Buckingham and the Duc de Rohan, and now, according to this letter on my table, he also knows that Buckingham has requested a secret meeting with him."

"Nothing else from the duke?"

"Only his usual correspondence with Gerbier," Kensington answered.

Rich made a clicking sound with his tongue but said nothing.

"There are only two ways a dispatch case could have come up on the beach," Kensington said, moving away from the writing table and seating himself opposite Rich. "It could have been thrown overboard, which is unlikely, or the ship carrying it could have sunk. I am inclined to think the ship went down. But we will not know that for a while."

Rich nodded.

"Until we meet with Buckingham," Kensington said, "we will not know whether his letter is real or forged."

"Are you going to send Gerbier—"

"I already have," Kensington answered. "That is not a matter in which I want to become involved. Buckingham, for all his calmness, can become very, very angry when something comes between him and his liaison with Anne."

"I never did understand Buckingham's passion for Anne, when he could have any woman in England, indeed in Europe."

Kensington went to the mantel and removed a Dutch churchwarden pipe, filled it with tobacco, and used a nearby taper to light it. After he was satisfied with the way the pipe was drawing, he said, "Such passions have no rational explanation. I doubt if he himself knows."

"Charles should have chosen some other noble to escort his wife home," Rich said. "He must know that Buckingham and Anne communicate with each other."

"I am sure he does," Kensington answered, blowing a cloud of smoke up toward the high ceiling. "But like James, he too is smitten with Buckingham's charm and his ability to handle certain types of political and social situations."

"I daresay you are probably right," Rich responded. "But now to this matter of Dupris. Why would he want to kill Buckingham?"

"I cannot answer that now," Kensington said, "though I think I can guess."

"Guess, then."

"Several attempts have been made on the duke's life in the last two years. All of them were made by men unknown to the duke. This one—"

"Are you saying that Dupris was paid to kill him?"

"Not perhaps in terms of gold ducats," Kensington answered. "But paid nonetheless."

"If that is so, then tell me how he was paid and by

whom. And then tell me how he could have been foolish enough to believe that once he did injury to the duke he would escape with his own life."

Kensington returned to the chair and said, "I will answer the last question first. He did what he did knowing that successful or not, he would be killed. That leads me to your first question. I do not think Dupris could have been bought for any amount of gold. Whatever the price, it had to have more value than gold."

"And pray what would that be?"

"For a man like Dupris, his religion and his family. Since I know his faith was unshakable, I would have to guess his family was placed in some sort of jeopardy, and that suspicion brings me to your second question. Of all of the men in France, there are only two who have been relentless in their pursuit of the Huguenots. They are Father Joseph and—"

"Richelieu!" Rich exclaimed.

"Yes. One or the other of them, perhaps both," Kensington said. "Neither would hesitate to strike down anyone who might give aid to the Huguenots."

"But to kill Buckingham when he is a guest of Louis seems extreme."

"Not to them. They would consider it God's work," Kensington answered.

"Then you are suggesting that Richelieu knows about our plans?"

"Yes. But I will try through various sources to confirm my suspicions," Kensington said. "In the meantime I have written the cardinal a gracious note of thanks for having sent the dispatch case to me."

"Playing the innocent?" Rich laughed.

"Oh, I do not think so. The cardinal will read between the lines. What I wrote might even lead him to suspect I know more than I actually do."

Rich slapped his fat thigh and said with glee, "By the living God, I believe you really enjoy playing cat and mouse with his gray eminence."

"Only when I am the cat," Kensington answered, as he leaned back and puffed contentedly on the pipe.

It was one of those rare occasions when Anne, Louis, the queen mother, and Henrietta—the bride-to-be—were engaged in animated conversation, punctuated at intervals by the king's high-pitched laughter. They had gathered together in one of the smaller sitting rooms to discuss the last-minute preparations for the arrival of Buckingham, the wedding, and the festivities that would follow.

The four of them sat close to one another, Louis in a high-backed chair of carved fruitwood, Anne and Henrietta occupying similar chairs with red velvet cushions, and the queen mother on a large sofa to herself. The window was open and the scent of freshly cut grass filled the room.

"We have arranged to have three days of celebration following the marriage," Louis said. "And each celebration will be larger and more spectacular than the previous one. On the last night, at the stroke of midnight, there will be a fireworks display such as Paris, or London for the matter, has never before seen. I have sent for Signor Passante from Venice to arrange the fireworks. I'm told he is the most skillful in all of Europe in their use."

"I have heard of him," Anne said. "His name was mentioned several times in my father's court."

"Excellent!" Louis exclaimed.

"Have you spoken to the various stewards to provide our English guests with whatever they wish?" the queen mother asked. "They are prodigious eaters and prefer strong beer and ale to wine."

"I have taken care of that," Anne answered, finding it difficult to keep the edge out of her voice. She resented her mother-in-law's constant interference.

"And did you also speak to them about providing the necessary pleasures for their beds?" Marie de'

Medici questioned, with a scornful smirk. "I should think such a provision would not have escaped your supervision."

Anne flushed. She had never been sure how much the woman knew about her affair with Buckingham. "That was not within my province," she answered in a low voice.

"To see that your guests want for nothing most assuredly is, as you put it, in your province," the queen mother said haughtily.

Louis stood up and said, "We will have Gaston see to it."

"And why should he do what she did not?" the queen mother questioned angrily.

"Because she is my wife and Gaston is already on familiar terms with all of the pimps in Paris," Louis replied. "Besides, it is a task I am sure he would enjoy."

"You do your brother wrong," Marie de' Medici responded.

"Madame," Louis said, "I rather think I employ him at a task which by his own boasting he is best suited for."

"And should he refuse?" the queen mother questioned.

"See that he does not," Louis responded, his voice becoming tight with anger. "Pray, madame, see that Monsieur does not refuse." He was becoming more and more chagrined at his mother. "We will not have these next few weeks spoiled by your son, by you, or by anyone else." He took a deep breath before he asked, "Have I made myself clear?"

"Yes, very," she answered.

"Good. Now we can continue with our conversation," Louis said. "I have arranged on each of the days to distribute food to the poor at various places in the city, and I have also given amnesty to certain prisoners that are being held in the Bastille." He walked to the window and looked out on to the garden. "And I have arranged to bestow on our visitors lavish gifts, which will be presented by several different members of the court."

"Oh, Louis," Henrietta exclaimed, "everyone will remember your generosity!"

He turned and with a smile said, "I wish to please our English guest, but I also wish to please my sister."

Impulsively Henrietta jumped up and embraced him.

"Please," he shouted, as though he were suddenly afraid of being strangled to death. "Let go of me!" Wrenching his sister's arms away from his neck, he stepped back. His face was very white and his breath came in short gasps.

"Forgive me," Henrietta said in a whisper. "I did not mean to offend you."

Not able to find his voice, Louis could only shake his head and with his right hand wave her apology aside.

"Please sit down," Anne said to her sister-in-law. "I am sure he is not angry with you."

The young woman looked at her mother.

"Do not fret about it," the queen mother counseled. "I am sure your brother's newly found generosity extends to his sister as well as to our English visitors and the felons in the Bastille."

"You mock me, madame," Louis said, struggling to get the words out.

"Not in the least," she answered. "You have succeeded in doing that yourself."

Turning toward the garden, Louis pursed his lips. He had hoped that this intimate family gathering would leave everyone laughing. Indeed, there had been some laughter. He had laughed, and so had Henrietta. Perhaps that was all that God would ever allow him to have at any one time, just a bit of laughter! If that was His wish for him, then there was nothing he could do to change it. He would bear it with the absolute certainty that in the life to come, he would be granted more laughter than he had in this world. He sighed deeply and was just about to face the three women again when the door opened. A servant announced that Cardinal Richelieu asked to see him.

"Have him come in," Louis replied.

A few moments later the cardinal entered the room. He bowed to the king and to the women. "Sire," he said, "I have something of utmost importance to discuss with you."

"I will hear it here," Louis said.

Richelieu looked toward the women. He could not help but notice how darkly Anne glared at him. Though he had initially felt contrition for having forced himself on her, he no longer felt any other emotion but an increase of passion for her. He wanted her more now because he had already possessed her. He dreamed of making her writhe with ecstasy, of hearing her call his name as her body gave way to spasms of delight.

Moving his eyes to Louis, the cardinal said, "An attempt was made on the Duke of Buckingham's life."

Louis' jaw went slack.

Richelieu's glance darted to Anne. She was very pale. She seemed to be holding her breath, no doubt waiting to hear if Buckingham was alive or dead.

"An attempt," Louis said, "implies a failure."

"The Duke of Buckingham is alive, sire," Richelieu responded. "I understand the would-be assassin is dead. He was killed by the duke's bodyguard." Even as he spoke, he glanced at Anne.

She had clasped her hands together to keep them from trembling. But her breathing was ragged and she seemed to be unusually stiff.

"Do you know the name of the assassin?" the king asked.

"Dupris. He was, from what I could find out, a Huguenot, possibly in the employ of the English."

"Any clue to why he wanted to kill Buckingham?"

"Your grace," Richelieu answered, "many men

have reason to kill the duke. He has lived the kind of life that breeds enemies the way dunghills breed flies."

Louis wiped beads of perspiration from his forehead. "It would have been a dark day indeed if the attempt had been successful. Our forthcoming bond with England might have been completely destroyed."

"If that was the will of God," Richelieu answered, "it would have happened."

"We must make absolutely certain that nothing harms any of our guests," Louis said firmly.

"I have dispatched my own guards to see that the duke and all the members of his party are safe from harm," Richelieu explained.

"Your majesty," Anne said, speaking slowly to keep the quaver out of her voice, "I think you should dispatch some of M. de Treville's men to protect the English."

"The Musketeers?" the king asked.

"Yes. They have served you faithfully in the past, and you can rely on them to lay down their lives if need be to protect your interests."

Richelieu felt his color rising. The Musketeers and his own men were bitter enemies. On more than one occasion members of his corps and those of the Musketeers had crossed swords, often leaving several men on each side mortally wounded. He uttered a slight cough and said, "The Musketeers have enough to watch over here in Paris."

"Then divide the duty of the Musketeers with those of the Cardinal's Guard," Anne quickly offered. "Send half from the Musketeers and half from the Cardinal's Guard."

"That could be done," Louis said.

"If you think it is a satisfactory arrangement," Richelieu told the king, "then I will write out the necessary orders."

"Do it at once and I will sign them," Louis said. "M. de Treville will be pleased by the assignment."

"I have no doubt he will," Richelieu answered. "And now if your majesty will excuse me, I will attend to the writing of the orders."

Louis nodded.

The two men bowed politely to one another and the cardinal left the room.

"Buckingham," Louis said, "has a reputation for being a great womanizer." Then he shook his head. "It is a pity to see a man waste himself in the pursuit of women, when what they can give has so little value. It is a question that begs for an answer. But I'm afraid there is no answer. And now if you will excuse me, I have several things that must have my attention."

The three women started to stand.

"Please," Louis said, "do not disturb yourselves on my account." He went to the door and moments later was outside of the room.

As soon as he was gone the three women stood up and, without saying a word to each other, went their separate ways.

Anne hurried to her apartment. That Buckingham might have been murdered was too much for her to bear and still maintain any degree of composure. And yet she had been forced to do exactly that, or betray herself to Louis. Silently she thanked God that Louis had agreed to send a contingent of Musketeers to Calais. They would prevent any harm from coming to Buckingham.

With her heart still beating wildly, Anne immediately sent for Mme. de Chevreuse and then went to her writing table in a small room that was called the Queen's Library by her servants and ladies-in-waiting. The dark wood shelves on two of the walls were lined with books. A small casement window opened onto a vista of the Seine and the fields beyond it. A writing table and a chair were close to the window. In the early morning large swaths of sunlight fell over the desk. But now it was well into the afternoon, and though the day was bright with sunshine, the interior of the room was gray.

Anne lit an oil lamp and sat down at the table. She set out a sheet of paper that had been made especially for her in Fabriano, Italy. Her crest was at the top of it. She took time to sharpen a quill, and after dipping it in lamp black ink, she began to write:

My Dear M. de Treville, Captain of the
    King's Musketeers—

On various occasions in the past I have had reason to put my trust in a young and loyal musketeer under your command. I must now ask that he be sent to me immediately and that this request be kept in the strictest confidence, since it concerns matters of state.

The musketeer I request is M. d'Artagnan. When he completes his duty with me, he will immediately be returned to your command. I also request his friends Athos, Porthos, and Aramis be assigned to me for the same period of time as M. d'Artagnan.

To show my gratitude for your service, I shall be very generous in my praise of you and your men to the king and on your behalf ask that he grant whatever suit you have cause to press forward.

                Yours most sincerely,
                Anne of Austria,
                Queen of France

Anne reread the letter and, satisfied that she had expressed herself as well as she possibly could, sprinkled drying powder on the paper to dry the ink and waited a moment before she brushed the white powder off. She folded her letter in thirds, inserted it in an envelope, and applied her seal to the still-soft sealing wax.

A soft knock at the door caused her to call out, "Come in!"

A servant announced Mme. de Chevreuse.

"Yes, yes," Anne said impatiently. "Have her come in." She stood up and moved away from the table.

"Your highness!" Marie said, genuflecting.

"Please," Anne told her, "we can dispense with ceremony."

"For the servants' sake," Marie answered with a laugh. "They must not think our friendship overrules the obedience that I owe you."

"Something very serious has taken place," Anne said. "A certain M. Dupris attempted to kill Buckingham last night."

"Oh my God!" Marie exclaimed.

"God was indeed with him," Anne said. "He was not hurt and the man Dupris is dead."

Marie crossed herself.

"I have written a letter to M. de Treville," Anne told Marie, as she stepped back and picked up the sealed envelope from her writing table. "I want you to deliver it to him as soon as possible."

Marie nodded.

"I have asked for the same musketeers that accompanied me the night I met Buckingham at the inn. I want those men to protect the duke during his stay in France." She paused and, casting her eyes downward, said, "I know of one who would be grateful if the duke had been struck dead, who might even be willing to hire another to strike a blow that he himself dare not."

"Richelieu?" Marie whispered.

"I have been ill used by him," Anne suddenly sobbed. "Ill used!"

Marie ran to the queen and embraced her. "Would that someone would lift his hand against that man and free the rest of us from the grip of his serpentine coils. He and his adviser Father Joseph rule France."

"He would rule me." Anne wept.

"Tell the king," Mme. de Chevreuse said. "Perhaps—"

"If I tell the king," Anne sobbed, "my love for Buckingham will be made known to him. I cannot take that risk. I cannot have the one joy in my life taken away from me. I would rather endure Richelieu's embrace a thousand times than lose the opportunities that now present themselves to me to be with the man I truly love."

Marie gently held the queen to her. She now understood why the cardinal had not come to her bed for the better part of a month. His passion had turned elsewhere.

"In time," Marie said, stroking the queen's back, "perhaps we can do something to rid ourselves of the cardinal."

"If it were possible," Anne responded with a deep sigh, "I would lend my effort to it."

"I think it is possible," Mme. de Chevreuse said. "I think it is very possible to help ourselves and France at the same time...."

EIGHT

Everyone in the Louvre was anxiously awaiting the following day's meeting between the royal family and the Duke of Buckingham just outside of the small village of Char, to the northeast of Paris. All through the day and well into the late-evening hours messengers galloped between the advancing column of English courtiers and Louis, who was anxious to know the hour-by-hour progress of his English guests.

The king's impatience, it seemed to Mme. de Chevreuse and even to Richelieu, though each expressed it to themselves differently, was in large measure the result of the warm welcome that the people of France were giving to Buckingham.

All along the way, from Calais on, the peasants

and the townspeople were cheering the duke and throwing flowers at him. It was also said that some of the young women bared their breasts to him and offered themselves for his pleasure.

Mme. de Chevreuse saw in Louis' chafing a rising jealousy. The people—his people—were showing more love and affection for Buckingham than they ever had for him.

But Richelieu viewed his king's mounting anxiety in the light of his own concerns. The cardinal was certain that Louis, the monarch, would be totally eclipsed when standing side by side with Buckingham. The king, though he sometimes took a childish stance on certain matters, was not a fool. He was becoming more and more disturbed, and with more and more reason.

At five o'clock in the evening, Louis abruptly left the hall, and though the courtiers lingered there for more than an hour, he did not reappear. Eventually one of his personal servants made the announcement that the king was tired and would prefer to have supper with the members of his immediate family.

Mme. de Chevreuse repaired to her own apartment and went about the tasks required for the following day's celebration. She had had several new gowns made for the various balls that would precede and follow Henrietta's marriage, and now, with the aid of her maids, she set about choosing the garment she would wear the next day.

She would be standing to the right and slightly behind the queen. She would have much preferred a position that would have allowed her to view Anne's face and the expression that would come over it when the queen saw Buckingham for the first time in two and a half years. There was no malice in her wish. She was just curious. Though she had had several lovers, she had never experienced for any of them anything near the passion that Anne professed to feel for Buckingham.

It took an inordinate amount of time to try on the

two dozen gowns and their matching shoes. By nine o'clock she had chosen a pale-green silk dress with puffy gold-embroidered sleeves and a deep, rounded décolletage that ended just above her nipples. After a few minutes of deliberation she chose a pair of shoes made of soft Morocco leather and decorated with a buckle of gold shaped like a rose.

Just as she was about to announce that she was ready to sit down for supper, she was informed that Cardinal Richelieu wished to speak with her.

"Tell him," she answered, "that it would be my pleasure to receive him."

"Where, madame?" the man asked.

"Why here, of course," she answered.

A few moments later, Richelieu entered the room. He was dressed as he had been earlier in the clothes of a man of the world rather than those of a prince of the church. Like any true daughter, she knelt and kissed the ring on his finger.

"You may rise," he told her.

There was laughter in her eyes. This man had held her naked body against his; regardless of his rank in the church, he was still a man who groaned with delight when his fluid poured into her. She enjoyed the charade but doubted that he did.

With disdain, Richelieu looked at the other women and at the clothing that was flung over every chair and couch.

"You see," Marie explained, "I am preparing for tomorrow's celebrations." She was pleased that the presence of her maids and the disarray had moment-arily caught him off balance. It was a small victory, but nonetheless a victory.

"And those that will follow, no doubt?"

"Why, yes."

He moved a bit closer to her and said, "I wish to speak with you in private."

Her eyes went wide. A smile tugged at her lips and suppressed laughter flooded her eyes.

"It is a matter of great urgency," he told her.

She nodded and told her servants to be sure that everything would be ready for her in the morning. Then, turning to Richelieu, she said, "If your eminence will follow me, I am sure I can find a more suitable place for a conversation about a matter of great urgency."

He realized she was mocking him, playing on his words, so that they would take on a meaning he had never intended for them.

They crossed a small foyer, went through another room, and finally wound up in her bedroom. "Now," she said, "tell me what this great urgency is."

Richelieu was familiar with the room. He sat down in one of the chairs close to the window and gestured to her to occupy the opposite one.

"I would much prefer to stand," she answered haughtily.

"Suit yourself," he answered with a slight shrug.

For several moments neither one of them spoke.

Marie was unsure of herself. Richelieu had obviously not come to satisfy his lust, which was as great as that of any man she had ever known. Had that been his reason, he already would have had her in bed. He was not a man to waste time when it came time to satisfy his passion. Not that he was a selfish lover. On the contrary, he was thoughtful and tender. He knew all the secret places to touch in order to make of a woman an instrument of pleasure in his hands.

"Have you wine?" he asked.

She nodded and moved to a small table, where there was a cut-glass decanter and several long-stemmed glasses.

"Pour some for yourself," he told her.

She carried his glass to him.

"To the future of France," Richelieu toasted, lifting his glass toward hers.

Marie echoed his words and clinked her glass against his.

"The days ahead of us promise to be extraordinarily interesting," the cardinal commented, after sipping his wine. "You no doubt noticed the king today?"

"It was impossible not to," she replied.

"That is why I am here," Richelieu said.

"He sent you?"

"Oh my dear madame," he responded, "nothing like that. He does not know I am here, and yet I am here on his behalf."

Suddenly Mme. de Chevreuse was frightened. Her conversations with Monsieur, the king's brother, and Chalais were treasonous enough to warrant her imprisonment in the Bastille, at the very least, or even a horrible death. She fought to keep herself from trembling.

Richelieu drank more wine and studied her with quiet thoughtfulness.

Marie managed a coquettish smile, though her feelings were tending much closer to fear. His silent scrutiny was almost unbearable. Her breathing became shallow, making her breasts rise and fall rapidly. He was always partial to them. He especially enjoyed sucking on her nipples. She wished now she could bare them for him to look at.

"The king," Richelieu said quietly, "will need our loyalty now more than ever."

"It is rightfully his," she answered.

Richelieu set the empty wineglass down on a small side table. He stood up and went to the window. "If given a chance," he said, looking out at the garden below, "Louis can be a good king, possibly a great king."

It was a propitious moment for flattery, and seizing it, she said, "Only if you are there to guide him."

Richelieu continued to scan the darkened hedges for several moments before he faced her. "I am no more than his servant," he told her. "But he is the embodiment of France, of all that she could be."

Though he spoke softly, Marie was very much aware of the passion in his voice. If the cardinal loved

God—and in his way she was sure that he did—then he loved his country more, very much more.

He stepped away from the window and returned to the chair. "Marie," he said, using her Christian name to denote an intimacy between them, "a few moments ago I told you I came here on behalf of the king, but that was only part of my reason for coming." He leaned slightly forward and again suggested that she sit down.

She was about to tell him that she still preferred to stand, when she suddenly saw something in his gray eyes—a darkening, perhaps—that made her change her mind. With a sigh, she sat down.

"The other part of my reason for coming to you," Richelieu said, "is you yourself."

"I am greatly flattered," she answered.

"The king is my prime concern, but I also have some small concern for you," he told her, moving his eyes toward the huge canopied bed. "I have not forgotten the time we spent together."

"Nor I," she answered softly.

He reached across the distance that separated them and, taking hold of her hands, said, "Do not involve yourself in matters that can only lead to your disgrace and perhaps have even worse consequences."

Again Marie became agitated. "I have no idea what you are talking about," she responded, trying to draw away.

He held onto her. "I know about your visit to M. Gerbier's house," Richelieu said with a weary nod. "Yes, M. Gerbier is—"

"You had me followed?"

"You were seen by one of my men entering the house," he explained. "M. Gerbier is more of a friend to the Duke of Buckingham than he is to our king."

Her eyes went wide with astonishment.

"That I know such information should not surprise you," he said. "It is my responsibility to know such things."

Marie could not answer.

"If I discover you have done something to injure the king," he said, releasing her hands, "I would not hesitate to punish you. Indeed, it would be my duty to see that you would be punished, and nothing, not even the sweet times we spent together, could save you." Relieved that Richelieu's visit had nothing to do with Monsieur and Chalais, Mme. de Chevreuse regained some of her lost aplomb. "I assure you," she told him, "I do no injury to the king, or anyone else for that matter."

"Do not jest with me. I know how it is between you and the queen."

"Ah, then it is not the king whose interests you have at heart but the queen?"

"They are one and the same," he answered, suddenly springing to his feet.

"Surely you do not believe that?"

"I will put it to you bluntly," he said. "Do not aid Anne in her thoughtless escapade with Buckingham or I will—"

"Do not threaten me, Armand," she told him, using his Christian name for the same reason he had used hers earlier. "Do not speak of protecting Louis when you want his wife. Do not—"

Before she could finish, the cardinal struck her across the face, turned, and left her bedroom.

The following morning was filled with bright, warm sunshine. The sky was very blue and spotted with puffs of fleecy white clouds.

Directly to the northeast of the village of Char was a huge expanse of flat, open fields. The Duc de Chevreuse pointed it out to Buckingham when they reached the top of a gentle rise that was still several leagues away.

"The royal family must be there," Buckingham said, scanning the area with his glass. "I see the King's standard." And he handed the telescope to the duc.

"It is his standard," the Duc de Chevreuse affirmed. And then with a sly laugh he added, "He is seldom on time to any state function, much less early. I think he must be eager to marry off his sister, or perhaps to see you, my dear Buckingham."

"See me he shall," the duke laughed, and, turning in the saddle, he shouted to the rest of his entourage that the King of France was waiting for them.

A cheer rose from the long column that stretched out behind him. Buckingham was dressed in a suit of purple satin embroidered with hundreds of pearls. He rode a magnificent white Arabian stallion. He moved ahead of the other riders. The musketeers were close behind him, and Ed followed them. The entire length of the column was studded with magnificent heraldic banners and flags.

Not more than an hour before, Louis had decided to remain seated on his portable throne rather than meet Buckingham in the open field. He was not going to allow himself to be diminished by the duke's superior height, or even his charm. He was king and he meant to exercise his puissance to his court, to his subjects, and to the English. Through his own glass Louis saw Buckingham and the Duc de Chevreuse the moment the two of them crested the hill. He tightened his lips and said nothing.

Then suddenly one of his generals shouted, "I see them . . . I see them." He turned to the queen mother and offered her his telescope.

"I shall see them when they arrive," she answered.

Anne forced herself to sit very still. She wore a robe of green satin, embroidered with gold, having wide pendant sleeves looped up with bouquets of diamonds. Her neck was encircled by a ruff of fine Flemish lace. Her hair fell in ringlets, and she wore a small coquettish hat of green satin, looped with strings of pearls and adorned by a heron's plume.

Cardinal Richelieu wore his ceremonial vestments. He stood close to Louis' throne and from time to time shifted his weight from one foot to the other.

Spread out on either side of the king were the most powerful nobles in France, and above their respective places flew their heraldic flags. Soldiers were everywhere, especially along the perimeter of the fields, to keep the peasants from coming too close to the king and his courtiers.

Louis touched Richelieu's sleeve, and when the cardinal bent close to him, he asked, "Has Buckingham been informed of the change of plans?"

"No," the cardinal answered, "I thought it better to let him be taken by surprise."

Louis nodded and bit his lower lip.

The column of Englishmen slowly moved across the open field. Now and then trumpets sounded a fanfare and were answered by those on the French side.

Anne's eyes were riveted on the figures at the head of the procession. Slowly they began to emerge. Then suddenly she realized that for several moments she had been looking at Buckingham. Her heart skipped a beat and began to race. Color quickly suffused her cheeks and neck. She moved slightly forward.

She found him as stunningly handsome as she had remembered. The horse he rode was something of a prancer, and Buckingham seemed to enjoy the animal's capering with the confidence of a man who knew that if need should suddenly arise, in an instant, he could bring the horse completely under his domination. On all sides of her, courtiers were whispering about how superbly the duke rode.

Even as she looked at him, Anne longed to have his muscular body press down on her, to have his hands on her breasts. The very thought of it charged her nipples with tingling excitement. Her whole being tightened with sexual need. She pressed her thighs together.

"They are slowing down," Richelieu said.

"I think Buckingham understands what you expect him to do," the cardinal said. "He is speaking to Chevreuse."

Buckingham gestured toward the seated king and asked, "Were you notified of the change?"

"No, my lord," the duc answered. "Had I been told, I would have informed you."

Buckingham accepted the duc's explanation without comment. For a while now, his eyes had been on Anne. He wanted to race up to her, lift her into the saddle, and then gallop off to a place where they could forget who they were and give vent to their passion. Despite the distance separating them, he was very much aware of the rapid movement of her breasts and knew that her desires and needs were identical to his own. For several moments, he was so engrossed in thinking about Anne that he was barely aware of his surroundings. Then, realizing his companion was waiting for his reply, he wrenched his thoughts back to the scene before him.

"We were supposed to meet on the field," the duke said. "I as the representative of my king and Louis as—but you know all that."

"Yes," the duc responded unhappily. "It was to be a grand gesture of friendship between our two countries."

To prevent anything from endangering the forth-coming marriage of Charles and Henrietta, Buckingham would have to bend his knee to Louis, while the king remained seated on his throne.

"It appears that it might well turn out to be something that is considerably less," Buckingham answered.

"I pray not," the duc responded.

Buckingham had not expected to be treated in a manner one jot less than would have been due Charles had he come to claim his bride himself. He was angry at Louis' lack of courtesy toward his king and himself. But being well schooled in the ways of kings, he realized that any display of anger, or even chagrin, would be injurious to Charles, and he would do nothing to endanger the forthcoming marriage between his king and Louis' sister. Buckingham understood that he had no choice but to bend his knee to Louis, if that was what his majesty wanted.

Almost as soon as he made the decision, he saw the king suddenly stand.

"We changed our mind. We will meet him as was originally planned," Louis said to Richelieu.

"But sire, I am sure he would come to you."

"We will meet him on foot," Louis responded sharply.

The whispering stopped. Every eye was on the king.

Louis made his way down the four steps and started to walk slowly across the field. His back was very straight and his head high. He tried to affect a calmness, but he was perspiring profusely, and his knees seemed to have lost their ability to support the rest of his body. A huge black fly suddenly buzzed around his face, attempting to find a place to land. For fear he would look ridiculous, he dared not raise his hand to brush it away.

"All will go well," the Duc de Chevreuse said with a broad smile as he watched the king cross the field.

Buckingham leaped from his horse and called Ed to take the reins. "Hold him steady," he said, "or he will go charging after me."

"Don't ya worry none," Ed answered.

Buckingham patted his mount on the muzzle.

The animal responded with a gentle snort.

"We will see about getting a lovely French mare," Buckingham told the horse.

"Aye," Ed answered, "I was thinkin' I'll try one of those lovely frog ladies meself."

Buckingham nodded and said, "Be sure to pick one that is unattached, or at least one that has some sort of understanding with her husband." Then he turned and walked nonchalantly toward the king. But his eyes went beyond him, to where Anne was.

She had moved slightly forward, as if she could not restrain her body from bending to his. With her lips parted, she gazed as intently on him as he on her.

Though Richelieu watched the two men approach each other, he was very much aware of what was happening between Anne and Buckingham. It was as if each held the other's eyes by the exercise of some powerful unseen force such as that strange power that drives a compass to see and hold a north-south line regardless of which way the ship would turn. To see her better, he moved his head slightly to the left. She was indeed beautiful! And once more his brain filled with the image of her in his arms. Though he had ravaged her, he was certain that if Buckingham did not exist he would be able to teach her to love him. He closed his eyes and let his memory once again savor the softness of her body.

A sudden cry of dismay went up around him. He opened his eyes and saw that Louis had somehow lost his footing. The king would have fallen but for Buckingham, who moved quickly to help him.

"Your majesty!" Buckingham exclaimed, helping the king to stay on his feet.

"We most earnestly thank you," Louis said in a choked voice, looking up at the handsome face above him.

Responding to Buckingham's gallantry, the French courtiers rose as one and applauded him.

"Your grace, are you able to walk?" the duke asked.

"We are," Louis said. "Shall we proceed? We are anxious for you to meet the rest of the family."

"It will be my pleasure," Buckingham answered.

The two men turned toward the French courtiers. For several moments neither of them spoke. Then Buckingham said, "On behalf of my sovereign, King Charles of England, I offer you his, as well as my own, greetings. He is most anxious to receive his bride and take you to his heart as the brother of his wife and his esteemed friend."

"We offer greetings and salutations to your king and hope that his marriage to our sister will serve to bring our two countries closer together," Louis replied.

Buckingham nodded. So much for the formal statements between them, at least for the moment. Louis was less robust than he remembered.

"We trust your journey from Calais to Paris has not been too taxing?" the king said.

Before he answered, Buckingham looked behind him. Already the column had begun to move forward. Ed had dropped back into his assigned place, and two of the other noblemen had moved forward alongside the Duc de Chevreuse.

"Your people have been most gracious to us," the duke answered. "But I might have made better progress if my entourage was not so large."

"We have heard of its size and splendor," Louis said. He did not appreciate Buckingham's reference to the graciousness of his people.

To the blare of trumpets, Louis mounted the steps, and the duke followed.

"We wish to present you to our queen," Louis said.

Buckingham genuflected before Anne. "It gives me great pleasure to see your highness once again," he said, taking her hand in his and fervently pressing the back of it to his lips. For a moment, he looked straight into her dark eyes. They were filled with fire.

"We are most pleased to welcome you and your entourage to France," she responded, haltingly.

"No more than we are pleased to be here," Buckingham said, feeling her hand quiver in his before he released it. In quick succession he was introduced to the queen mother, Monsieur, and the bride to-be, and finally he found himself facing Richelieu.

The cardinal offered his hand, expecting Buckingham to kneel and kiss his ring.

"Your eminence," the duke said, "it is a pleasure to see you again." And instead of kneeling, he took hold of Richelieu's hand and shook it vigorously.

The cardinal was too surprised to show his displeasure, and withdrew his hand.

"You must excuse me," Buckingham said in English, knowing Richelieu understood and spoke the language fluently, "but it would go against the dictates of my faith and my king for me to kneel to a representative of the pope."

The cardinal's gray eyes went to slits. "Yes, I understand," he said stiffly.

"I was sure you would," the duke answered, and with a smile he let go of Richelieu's hand.

Louis asked what the exchange between them was all about.

"A difference of customs," Richelieu answered.

"An excellent description!" Buckingham seconded with a laugh.

Even before the column of English noblemen and their ladies reached the platform, Louis declared he wanted to return to the Louvre. "We would be honored," he said to Buckingham, "if you rode in our coach."

"It would indeed be an honor," the duke answered. A short time later he was seated opposite Anne and alongside Monsieur for the long ride back to the palace.

Louis spoke of the winter's harshness and asked if the weather had also been a problem in England.

"It was a very hard winter," Buckingham said, keeping his eyes on the king, when in truth he wanted to look at Anne. "We had snow late in April."

"Ah, so did we!" Louis responded.

"But why speak of the past, when the present is here?" Monsieur offered. "I never let the past trouble me."

"That is very true," Louis commented, "which we often think is a grave shortcoming."

Though the words were mild enough, Buckingham realized Louis had rebuked his brother.

Chagrined, Monsieur turned his face toward the window and said nothing more.

"I pray to God," Louis said, "the summer will be good and our harvest abundant."

"Amen to that," Buckingham answered.

A strained silence settled down inside the coach. Buckingham listened to the creaking of the springs and the sounds made by the wheels as they rolled over the uneven roadway. For him to be so close to Anne and not be able to touch her was almost unendurable. From time to time his eyes locked with hers, and he understood that she was as tormented by the situation as he.

The coach rolled into Paris through a massive gate and bumped along a cobblestone street.

"Tonight," Louis suddenly said, "we are going to have a masquerade."

"I am sure it will provide diversion for everyone," Buckingham commented, flicking his eyes to Anne, who answered with an imperceptible nod.

Shortly after Buckingham was installed in his rooms, he was visited by Kensington and Rich. The duke led them into a small room with an oriel window overlooking the Seine and walls finished with dark oak wainscot.

"Please, my lords," the duke said, "sit down." He looked around for a decanter of wine and quickly found it on a lovely carved sideboard that stood in one of the corners. He offered his guests wine.

Both of the men declined. Lord Kensington asked after Charles' health.

"Tolerably well," Buckingham answered, pouring himself a glass of wine and moving to the center of the room. "But anxious to be bedded down with his wife, as would any man be whose experience with women has been limited." And then he lifted his glass and toasted the king. "May his marriage be happy and fruitful," he said.

"I will drink to that." Lord Rich laughed.

Buckingham lost no time in pouring two more glasses of wine and presented one to each of his guests. Each man offered a toast to Charles, and several were made to the queen-to-be.

"Now tell me, worthy lords," Buckingham asked, "what brings you to my room, looking so grave and woebegone?"

Lord Rich eyed Kensington, who was the appointed ambassador to the French court.

Buckingham clicked his tongue and commented, "As serious as all that, eh?"

Kensington nodded and said, "He is not the kind of man to—"

"If you mean my refusal to bend my knee and kiss his popish ring?"

"It was an act of defiance that might make your negotiations with him, whatever they might be about, more difficult."

"Surely even he would respect the integrity of my motive," Buckingham responded. "To kneel to him would have meant denying my own faith and king. I told him no more than that."

"Your letters to me did not come in the usual manner," Lord Kensington said, and he went on to explain how he came by the diplomatic pouch.

"And there were no survivors from the *Hermes*?" Buckingham questioned with obvious concern.

"If there were, we were not informed," Lord Rich answered.

Buckingham went to the sideboard and poured himself another glass of wine. "I did not realize the sea was so rough when I sent her out of the harbor," he said in a low voice as though he were talking to himself. "I did not know the captain, but I saw him on deck when the pouch was thrown aboard. He was a young man." He pursed his lips and for several moments said nothing.

"You cannot hold yourself responsible for an act of God," Kensington said.

Buckingham did not answer. But he decided to investigate the matter as much as was possible to discover if there were any survivors and if there were, why the French authorities had not notified Lord Kensington. He refrained from mentioning anything about his intentions, and with a sigh he told his two guests that he would personally thank Richelieu for forwarding the pouch to the proper recipient.

The two lords looked questioningly at each other and then at him.

"You are not concerned that Richelieu knows of your correspondence with his queen?" Lord Kensington asked.

"No," Buckingham answered. "He has known about it for some time now."

"And should he take the matter to the king, what will happen to the marriage and your plans to speak with Richelieu about matters concerning our country and France?"

"He will not mention it to Louis," Buckingham answered.

"Are you absolutely sure?"

"I am never absolutely sure of anything," Buckingham answered. "But the cardinal has no wish to make a public spectacle out of his sovereign's private life. He did not keep the letter; therefore, I am led to conclude that he did not have a specific need for it. And Anne destroys each letter after she reads it. She is _fully_ aware of her responsibility in the matter."

"Be very careful," Rich cautioned. "The cardinal is no ordinary man. His enemies say of him that he is more possessed by the Devil than by Christ."

"And what do his friends say?"

"He has none," Lord Kensington answered.

"Not even Louis?"

"He needs him and therefore is forced to abide him."

"Though he is friendless," Lord Rich said, "never forget he is the most powerful man in France."

Buckingham nodded. He would have liked to say, "Then, my Lords, the cardinal and I are well matched." But instead he thanked them for their concern and said he hoped to see them that night at the masquerade.

"Not if my costume is effective," Lord Rich answered.

"I might just come as myself," Buckingham said, "and astound everyone."

His guests thought his remark extraordinarily

droll and laughed until their eyes began to tear.

"I will have to remember that and tell it at court when I return," Lord Kensington said, still laughing.

As soon as Richelieu reached the Louvre, he hurried to Father Joseph's room.

"I tell you," the cardinal stormed, "the man had more audacity than any ten men. He even had the effrontery to tell me that to make any sort of obeisance to me would be against his faith and an act against his king—and he said that in English, knowing full well that Louis, who was close by, does not understand a word of that language." He paced back and forth, striking the palm of his left hand with the fist of his right.

The Capuchin listened without showing any emotion. He sat at his writing table. The two candles on either side of him cast a yellow light over his parchmentlike skin. He knew Richelieu was in a rage and was, for the present, incapable of thinking logically. But once the cardinal's emotions had burned themselves out, he would once again be the most reasonable of men.

"I am seriously considering going to the king," Richelieu said. "I have the letters from the diplomatic pouch. The one to Anne would be enough to end the marriage and send Buckingham back to England in chains—French chains!"

"And risk a war?" Father Joseph asked.

"I tell you it will come to that in the end," Richelieu said, striking the top of the Capuchin's writing table with such force the pot of ink on it and several quills jumped.

"Rather than war," Father Joseph counseled, "follow the dictum of our Lord and turn the other cheek, at least for now."

Richelieu was about to say he was not without his human shortcomings, but for him to tell his friend that would serve no purpose. If any man knew his strengths and weaknesses, Joseph did.

"I am calmer now," he said.

"With Buckingham here in our midst," the Capuchin told him, "we must be circumspect about our future plans. We must smile and be gracious to our guests without ever forgetting they are also our enemies."

The cardinal nodded.

"And above all we must find a way to prevent an alliance between the Huguenots and the English, so that when it comes time for us to destroy the heretics we will not be hampered by English intervention."

"I will turn the other cheek," Richelieu responded.

"It is the only way," Father Joseph said, "when you become involved with someone like Buckingham."

"There is no one else like Buckingham," Richelieu answered. "Believe me when I tell you that."

Father Joseph shrugged but did not reply.

Anne was ecstatic. She hugged herself as she practically danced around her sitting room. "I cannot tell you," she said to Mme. de Chevreuse, "how I feel. I am full of joy, so very full of joy." Reaching down, she grabbed hold of Marie's hands and pulled her lady-in-waiting to her feet. "Did you see him?" she laughed. "Did you see him?" And not waiting for an answer, she said, "He looked like a god, a Greek or Roman god." And releasing Marie, she again whirled around the room.

"He is an extraordinarily handsome man," her lady-in-waiting said.

"I stared so hard at him I was afraid my eyes would pop out of my head," Anne told her.

"And from what I could see," Marie responded, "he could not take his eyes off you."

"After two and a half years," Anne said, "I want to feast on him."

"I am sure you will, as he will feast on you," she answered.

Anne looked at her. Suddenly the two women began to laugh. "I will feast and he will feast," Anne shouted with glee, "and neither of us will ever consume a morsel of food. Such feasting, such feasting was made for lovers."

"You must be very careful," Marie cautioned. "The cardinal will have his spies everywhere."

"Yes, I know," Anne replied. "But even with all his spies he will not keep me from a happiness that is mine."

"I will do all I am able to help you," Marie told her.

"Dear friend!" Anne exclaimed, throwing her arms around her lady-in-waiting and embracing her. "I trust you with my life."

"And I give you mine."

"Then I know I shall be safe from Richelieu," Anne said. "Safe from the one man I hate more than any other." She released Marie and walked to the empty hearth. "How could you ever have loved him?"

"Lust, not passion, drove me to his arms," Mme. de Chevreuse explained. "His desire for me was beyond my strength to deny."

Suddenly Anne burst into tears. Running to her confidante, she threw her arms around the woman and sobbed.

Mme. de Chevreuse patted Anne gently on the back and in a soft voice said, "What is it? Tell me what is making you so unhappy."

"What will I do if I am with his child?"

"Do not think about such a possibility, and pray to God it has not happened," she answered in a whisper.

"Buckingham must never know," Anne pleaded.

"He will never hear about it from my lips. I will swear by all I hold sacred your secret is safe with me."

Once more the two women embraced and passionately reiterated their bonds of friendship for one another. But Mme. de Chevreuse reminded herself that she never again need fear Richelieu, because what she knew about the cardinal probably made her the most powerful woman in all of France.

The masquerade was magnificent. The huge hall of the Louvre was filled with hundreds of French and English courtiers. The great crystal chandeliers were illuminated with hundreds of candles. Everywhere servants in white livery decorated with silver buttons attended the costumed guests.

Red and white wine from every region of France flowed in enormous quantities. The amount of food was stupendous. There were a dozen different varieties of fowl, fish, and meats to fit every taste. Here and there a servant lightly sprinkled perfumed water over the guests with a small dipper of gold. Flower petals were strewn over the floor. And musicians played dance after dance, to the delight of the masked guests.

Buckingham was dressed as a pirate. He wore a black patch over one eye and a red silk kerchief around his head. Nearby stood Lord Rich in the accouterments of a Roman senator. Together they had come from Buckingham's rooms.

"It will soon become terribly hot in here," Buckingham observed, "if they do not open the doors and let some cool air in."

"The French are not partial to night air," Lord Rich responded.

"Neither are the English," Buckingham laughed. "Charles will not suffer a window to be open in his rooms... claims that all the ills of mankind, and indeed of womankind, reside in the night air."

"Who knows—he might be right."

"I have spent many a night out in the open," Buckingham answered, "and have not suffered from it."

A servant passed carrying a tray of beautiful long-stemmed glasses filled with white wine.

Lord Rich helped himself to two and gave one to Buckingham. "To the success of your mission," he toasted.

They touched glasses, and the duke asked him if Richelieu would attend the ball.

"It would be hard to know," Lord Rich replied, looking at several of the nearby guests. "Any one of them might be the cardinal." Then with a laugh he added, "But in truth, I do not think the cardinal is here. He prefers the more formal entertainments."

Buckingham did not respond. His interest was diverted to a woman in a Persian harem costume that hid none of her feminine charms.

She nodded to him.

Excusing himself to Lord Rich, the duke went to the woman.

"I have been trying to catch your eye for several minutes," she said.

He recognized the voice of Mme. de Chevreuse. "I was occupied with Lord Rich," he said.

"Anne will be dressed as a peasant girl from Provence," she told him.

"I do not know that costume," he admitted.

Mme. de Chevreuse shook her head. "There," she said, shifting her eyes to the left. "Anne is wearing the white lace collar."

Buckingham turned to look at her.

She smiled at him.

"Use my apartment," Mme. de Chevreuse told him.

"And what will you do?"

"Most likely make use of yours," she responded with a wicked laugh.

Buckingham looked at her breasts and said, "I should think you would have no difficulty finding someone to keep you company and provide sport."

"Ah, but there is sport and there is sport." She sighed. "Like everything else in life there are degrees of excellence in that too."

"I hope you find a man worthy of your needs," Buckingham answered with a low bow. "Now if you will excuse me, I must go to the one woman worthy of my needs."

"Be careful," Mme. de Chevreuse whispered. "The cardinal's spies are everywhere."

He nodded and, turning, began to thread his way toward Anne. Even through her half mask, he could see her eyes, and they never moved from him. He would have rushed to her, but such temerity would have attracted attention and perhaps revealed them to their enemies.

Buckingham slowed his pace as he came nearer to Anne. He wanted to savor her image. The costume she wore showed the lovely swell of her breasts and the womanly flare of her hips. Never, even if he lived to be a hundred, would he ever understand Louis' indifference toward this beautiful woman.

When he was directly in front of her, he bowed, extended his hand, and asked, "Madame, may I have this dance with you?"

"Yes, monsieur," she answered, giving him her hand.

Buckingham led her toward the dancers. For an instant, he imagined all eyes were following them. But when he looked earnestly at the guests they passed, he quickly realized that they were completely oblivious to the stupendous reality that after more than two years of separation, he was once again holding the hand of his beloved Anne.

Whenever they executed the promenade, he spoke in a whisper, telling her of the need that filled his body and the passion that ruled his heart.

"Your words," she said, at one point during the dance, "have quickened the beat of my heart."

"And knowing that," he hastily answered, "has made my longing for you almost unendurable."

The night wore on, and the great ballroom steamed with the heat of the many perspiring nobles. Several of the women sent their servants to fetch cones of perfumed wax which they skillfully inserted into their massive wigs.

Some of the older and fatter women fainted and were either hastily removed from the hall or quickly revived and then escorted out. Many of the guests had become drunk, and there were isolated arguments. But nothing serious came of them, because the participants were quickly drawn away by other guests.

By midnight the heat was unendurable, and several of the women bared their breasts, much to the delight of the men. The wine was affecting more and more of the guests. And soon couples began to move toward the walls, sink down on the floor, and unashamedly caress each other.

"It is time for us to go," Buckingham whispered to Anne.

She nodded.

He led her to the huge door, nodded to the servants, and then headed along the huge hallway that led to the portion of the Louvre where his apartment was located.

"It is cooler here," Anne said, fanning herself.

"Wine and sweltering rooms are not a good combination," the duke told her.

"Where are we going?" she asked.

"To where we can indulge ourselves in the ecstasy of our flesh," he answered.

"Wait!" she exclaimed.

Buckingham stopped. For a moment he wondered if he had blundered on that portion of the month which...

"Not to your rooms or my apartment," she told him. "Either place will be dangerous."

"We are going to Mme. de Chevreuse's rooms," he said with relief.

"Has ever a woman had a dearer and more loyal friend," Anne asked, "than I have in Marie?"

For several moments, Buckingham did not answer. During his last stay in Paris, he had taken the measure of Mme. de Chevreuse and found her lacking. She would act when she thought she could gain something from her actions, otherwise she would do nothing. But rather than deny Anne her illusion, he said, "We are both fortunate to have her as a friend and not a foe, for she would make as formidable an enemy as she does a good friend."

Anne did not question either the tone of his words or their implication, and he did not elaborate, since he saw nothing to be gained by wasting precious time discussing Mme. de Chevreuse's reasons for making possible a tryst that would mean her death if they were discovered. Anne, despite her life at court, was still too trusting. Long ago he had learned to inspire the belief and trust of others, while never really trusting anyone and believing very little that was told to him, unless he could verify it himself, or from several different sources.

Once they were inside Mme. de Chevreuse's apartment, he turned to Anne, took her in his arms, and kissed her passionately. All thoughts vanished. His brain was filled with her scent.

"Anne, Anne," he whispered. To say her name and know that she could hear his voice filled him with joy.

"Oh, George, I have waited so long for this," she told him. "I never thought I would ever see you again."

He placed his forefinger against her lips. "Now I am here," he said. "Nothing else matters." And sweeping her into his arms, he carried her into the bedroom. "I am like a thirsty man whose need is about to be slaked by the cold pure water of a deep spring." He set her down on her feet and kissed the bare top of each breast.

She trembled and said, "You cannot know how many times I dreamed of that, and so much more."

Buckingham snuffed out all the candles in the room, save one that he placed on a small table near the bed.

"I want to see you," he told her.

She nodded and began to disrobe, while he stood off and watched her. "I could not do this with any other man," she told him.

He did not answer. He knew she was telling the truth.

"There!" she exclaimed triumphantly as the peasant frock and the underskirts dropped to the floor and she stood proudly naked before him.

He could not speak. She was more beautiful in the

soft glow of the yellow candlelight than he had remembered.

Anne cupped her breasts and offered them to him. Her nipples were already hard with passion. "Come," she said with delightful wantonness, "cool the flame that makes me hot."

Buckingham rushed to her and pressed her naked body against him.

"I can feel you, hard and eager for love," she whispered.

"For your love," he answered, stepping away from her and quickly beginning to undress. By the time he was finished, Anne was already in bed. He settled down next to her and kissed her passionately on the lips, while his hand roamed over her firm breasts. When his tongue touched hers, Anne quivered. And then, almost ferociously, she sucked his tongue into her mouth. Moments later she said, "If you are that man dying of thirst, then I am a woman who is starving."

He kissed her breasts and sucked on her nipples until she moaned with delight.

Her hands caressed him and moved lightly over his penis.

Before he realized what she was doing, she had suddenly reversed her position and taken his erect phallus into her mouth.

For a moment she stopped moving her tongue over it and said, "I do this, George, because I love you and not because you ask. It is my way of giving you all I can."

He rolled slightly toward her, parted her naked thighs, and put his mouth to the warm moist lips of her sex.

She gasped and then moved closer to him. Delicious moments later she moved away and opened her arms and her thighs to him.

As Buckingham raised his body over hers, Anne reached down and gently guided him into her. She closed her eyes and sighed with pleasure.

Slowly Buckingham began to move, and at the same time he kissed her closed lids.

Anne made small throaty sounds of delight. She moved her head from side to side. "George," she gasped, "oh, George, I am yours and only yours, no matter what happens."

"And I am yours," he told her, quickening his pace. All too soon, he could feel his passion boil inside of him. This was an exquisite pleasure beyond anything he had hoped for.

Anne began to moan and heave herself wildly against him. "I am there, my love," she cried. "I am there!"

Within a moment Buckingham uttered a low, throaty growl of pleasure and fiercely clung to Anne. "I love you," he told her. "I love you."

She pressed his face against her breasts. "I will die without you," she said.

He silenced her with a passionate kiss, but he knew all too well what she meant. He knew individuals who seemed alive but were really dead inside where nothing other than moldering memories was left. To live like that would be a worse torment than hell. The thought of it happening to either one of them made him shudder.

NINE

For Anne, life had suddenly taken on a new and exciting dimension. She was filled with an exuberance that brought color to her cheeks and a brightness to her eyes.

To Mme. de Chevreuse, Anne came into possession of that particular demeanor often exhibited by young women who have experienced their first sexual encounter with a man and by their looks and actions silently tell all those who would listen: we have discovered a great and wonderful secret, something the rest of you have never known. Mme. de Chevreuse remembered having once thought that way herself. But that was a long time ago, when she was but a girl of fifteen and the man a youth of twenty.

Richelieu also noted the change in Anne, and it

simultaneously fueled his anger toward Buckingham and his passion for the queen. He absented himself from the court functions as much as possible, always sending word to the king at the last moment that the press of work forced him to remain at his desk. He did not even seek the company of Father Joseph but, like some caged and tormented beast, prowled the precincts of his own rooms, or sought relief from his anguish by galloping swiftly through the countryside that surrounded Paris.

And as for Buckingham, he was impatient for the night to come so he might hold his beloved Anne in his arms. Often during the day he would suddenly remember some particularly sweet or erotic happening of the previous night's encounter with Anne and for several moments he would relive the intensity of the experience. Several times during the days that followed he saw her in the company of the king, and it was exceedingly difficult for him to gaze at her without betraying his passion. But even more difficult was the reality that Anne legally belonged to Louis and not to him. Louis, if he were so inclined, could demand of her what she so freely gave to him. Thinking about that possibility was enough to put him in a doleful humor for several hours.

As the day of Henrietta's wedding drew closer, the activities in the court became more frenzied. All the regular political and social activities ceased. The king refused to grant an audience to any petitioner, and in honor of his sister's forthcoming wedding, he issued decrees that forbade any executions on the wedding day and granted freedom to several individuals who had been incarcerated in the Bastille for having written pamphlets in support of the Huguenots. He even issued orders to feed every prisoner more than his daily ration of food and to allow every galley slave a day of rest from his labor at the oar.

Louis' acts of generosity were greeted by a loud applause from the courtiers who were present when they were announced in the great hall.

And Louis, holding up his hands to quiet his people, told them, "We do these things to honor my sister and King Charles, her future husband, and to honor God. Since even a galley slave is, in His eyes, a man deserving of His forgiveness, then we can do no less than allow that man a day of rest."

Buckingham was present when these decrees were issued, and in a low voice, he said to Lord Gorden, a nobleman who had accompanied him from England, "A grudging gesture of magnanimity, if ever there was one."

"It is a large one for Louis, though," Lord Gorden answered. "He must have prayed mightily before some divine spark struck such dry tinder."

Suddenly Buckingham realized that the king's attention was directed toward him.

"My dear duke," Louis said, "we feel it incumbent on ourselves to grant you the privilege of petitioning our royal person for a worthy cause on behalf of your illustrious king and our soon-to-be brother-in-law."

Again an explosion of applause greeted the king's words.

Buckingham moved to where the king was standing and, bending his knee to him, said, "Your generosity does you honor. Since I am charged with speaking for my king and for myself, I find that by your consent to the marriage of your sister to my king, you have already given much more than I can ask, for by doing that you have served the worthy cause of peace between our two great countries."

The onlookers cheered.

"You must have something that you want," Louis pressed.

"Sire," the Duke answered, "I truly cannot think of anything . . . unless . . ."

"Yes? Please tell us what you would have us do."

"You have already done so much," Buckingham said, knowing exactly where he was leading the king.

"Yet if any man can do more, surely you can."

"But you have not told us what we can do," Louis said.

"Have peace throughout your land," Buckingham answered.

Louis' jaw went slack.

"Grant Frenchmen, no matter what their religious persuasion, the right to be Frenchmen and love their king."

A sudden, ominous silence filled the hall. Louis was very quiet. His lips trembled.

Buckingham looked straight at the king.

Louis started to speak and was forced to clear his throat before he said, "We will consider your request, and we thank you for asking nothing for yourself, or your king. We respect and honor your regard for the people of France."

Within moments the buzz of conversation picked up where it had some minutes before stopped, but now everyone was talking about the exchange that had just taken place between Louis and Buckingham.

Richelieu was in a fury when he heard what had happened between his king and Buckingham. He immediately dispatched a page to Louis with a note requesting a private audience. It was granted, and the two men met in the king's library.

The king was seated in a wing-backed chair near the window. He did not even bother to look at Richelieu and with a wave of his hand he said, "We are alone. There is no need for any of the courtly formalities."

The cardinal stood opposite the king and looked out at the garden. A great many flowers were in bloom, and many more were budding.

"Buckingham," the king said in a melancholy voice, "is a very brave man."

"He plays you, my lord!" Richelieu exclaimed in exasperation.

Louis looked up at the cardinal. "Play us or not," he answered, "only a man with great courage would have done what he did."

"Courage or bravado?"

"You do not like him," Louis said, "and have taken the wrong measure of the man. Were he Catholic you would see him in a different light."

"He is a rogue," Richelieu answered, "no matter what light is cast upon him."

"Would then that I were a rogue like him," Louis answered.

"God forbid."

"Men respect him," Louis said. "They follow him blindly. And women—"

"Do not speak about his virtues," Richelieu replied, interrupting the king. "He is your enemy. He is the enemy of France."

"It is difficult to hate someone you admire," Louis said. "God was more generous to Buckingham than He was to us. He gave him a body and spirit that were equally matched. No, Richelieu, I cannot hate him."

"Then you have no intentions of castigating him for interfering with the internal matters of France?"

Louis shook his head. "I already told you," he answered, "I think him a brave man."

"But—"

"Enough said about it," Louis said. "I do not want to discuss the matter any further."

"Yes, your highness," Richelieu responded, knowing that when the time came to reveal Buckingham's true nature to him, Louis would be relentless in his demand for revenge.

"Love me?" Anne whispered.

"More than the word could convey," Buckingham answered.

Naked they lay pressed against each other. Their lovemaking had been wildly intense, and now in the peaceful aftermath, they spoke softly to one another.

Anne knew about what had taken place between

Louis and Buckingham from Mme. de Chevreuse who had heard it from Chalais. And she was greatly perturbed by the duke's recklessness and told him as much.

"You must understand," he answered, "that I did not speak to irritate Louis but rather to indicate my king's concern about people whose religious persuasion is the same as his."

Anne ran her fingers on his hairy chest. "You should have waited until you were alone with Louis," she suggested.

"The words just came tumbling out." He laughed.

"Do not laugh," she said. "Can you imagine Richelieu's reaction to your request? I have heard him plead with Louis to take to the field and once and for all destroy the heretics."

"He too will have to understand that Charles will not stand by and have that happen," Buckingham answered.

"Is that true, or is it that the Duke of Buckingham will not stand by and let it happen?" Anne asked.

"An equal measure of both," he answered.

"Richelieu hates you."

"Because I am a Protestant?"

Anne suddenly began to tremble. She said, "Hold me tight, George, hold me tight."

He embraced her, kissing her passionately on her lips. He said, "I want you with me all the time, Anne, all the time."

"Oh my darling," she responded, "it can never be that way for us. When I leave you, I am but half a person."

Buckingham moved his hand over her breasts and rolled each nipple between his thumb and forefinger.

She reached down and fondled his manhood.

They made love again. This time they lingered at it, discovering and enjoying the nuances of pleasure made possible by the prolongation of their ecstasy. Together they experienced the moment of supreme delight, and when they again lay quietly in each other's embrace, Anne said, "I want your child, your son."

Buckingham touched her cheek with the tips of his fingers. "It might happen that way," he told her.

"I pray that it will. At least I will have something of you when you are gone, some living evidence of the man I love."

"We must find a way to be together," he said, cupping her naked breast with his hand. "You and I and our son... we must be together."

She turned to him and, burying her face in his chest, began to sob softly. "I have everything and nothing," she wept.

Gently he rubbed her back. "It is useless to weep," he said. "Tears do not change anything. We must think, and perhaps we will be able to find a way for us to be together."

"Your visit, my lord," M. Gerbier said with a low bow, "does my house honor." He was a slightly built man with wispy gray hair and sky-blue eyes.

Buckingham nodded approvingly at the man, who for the last two and a half years had conveyed his letters to Anne and hers to him through Lord Kensington. They had met the last time the duke had been in Paris.

"Shall we go into the library?" M. Gerbier suggested. "It is by far the most comfortable room in the house."

"It would be my pleasure," Buckingham responded. He motioned to Ed and told him to follow along and wait outside the door.

The library was indeed a splendid room, with a southern exposure that filled it with sunshine most of the day. Two large glass-paned doors opened onto a magnificent walled garden that contained not only flowers but three good-sized trees—a lovely gnarled chestnut, an apple, and a shade-giving maple.

The room itself was filled with books of every description. There was a huge globe in one corner,

and M. Gerbier's writing table was placed so tha[t]
during the day the light from the sun would b[e]
behind him.

"Please," M. Gerbier said, "sit down."

Buckingham chose a dark leather chair an[d]
settled into it. He gestured toward the chair opposit[e]
him and said, "I have been too much in your hands t[o]
stand on ceremony between us."

"It has been a pleasure to serve you," M. Gerbie[r]
responded as he sat down.

Buckingham removed a small pouch from insid[e]
his jacket. "I hope you will find this satisfactory," h[e]
said. "Should you require more, I will leave instruc[-]
tions to Lord Kensington to give you whatever sur[?]
you request." He set the pouch down on a small tabl[e]
that was within his reach.

"You know, my lord, that the house is bein[g]
watched and that I am followed wherever I go?"

"The cardinal's men?"

M. Gerbier nodded.

"Have you other people on whom you coul[d]
depend?" the duke asked.

"Yes. A man in my profession must work wit[h]
others."

"There are several things I want to know,"
Buckingham told him. "I want to know if there wer[e]
any survivors from the *Hermes* and anything abou[t]
how she happened to have been wrecked."

"I will do my best."

Buckingham leaned back and asked if Gerbie[r]
knew Dupris.

"I had occasion to travel with the man to L[a]
Rochelle," he answered.

"How would you account for his actions?"

"I could not," Gerbier replied. "He was an hones[t]
servant of those he served."

"That is still my opinion of him," Buckingha[m]
said. He removed another pouch from inside hi[s]
jacket. "I want you to go to Calais and give it to hi[m]

family. They will be in sore need of money."

"Shall I tell them who their benefactor is?"

"No need to," Buckingham said with a wave of his hand. "But I would appreciate knowing anything that might help me to better understand the man's actions."

"I will try to find out."

"Well, M. Gerbier," Buckingham said, "we have dispatched our business with a pleasant swiftness. Would that all my affairs were so easily resolved."

"Would your grace care for wine?"

"Yes, I would like that very much," Buckingham said.

M. Gerbier excused himself and left his visitor in the library.

The duke stood up and walked to where the doors opened on the garden. The afternoon sun was pleasantly warm, and several bees were hovering over a bush of small red roses. He took several deep breaths and then stepped back into the room. He went to the globe and slowly spun it on its axis. So much of the world was unknown.... Suddenly he was thinking about Anne and about a place where they might live out their lives together.

"But where?" he asked in a whisper. Finding no answer, he shook his head in despair. He walked back to the open door and looked out at the garden again.

Within a few minutes, M. Gerbier returned carrying a tray with a carafe of red wine and two glasses. He poured the wine and handed a glass to Buckingham.

"To your lordship's very good health," M. Gerbier toasted.

"And to yours," the duke responded.

They touched glasses, drank, and offered toasts to king and country before Buckingham shook Gerbier's hand and told him, "I will not visit you again unless the situation warrants it. But I will be in close touch with you while I am here in France."

"I am at your service," M. Gerbier replied, as he escorted his visitor to the front door and opened it. "Your visit here today will be reported by this evening to Richelieu."

"Is his man out there?"

"Not visible," M. Gerbier said. "But there nonetheless."

With a boisterous laugh, Buckingham made an obscene gesture.

Anne and Mme. de Chevreuse walked side by side along the bank of the river. Now and then Anne would point to a spot in the river and with girlish glee she would almost shout, "There...there...see the fish?"

And Mme. de Chevreuse would feign interest and an equal measure of excitement. But in truth she would not bother to look where Anne would point. She found Anne's behavior tedious and would have absented herself from the queen's company if she had not wanted to speak with her about a very important matter.

Ever since she had learned of Richelieu's savage attack on the Queen, Mme. de Chevreuse had given a great deal of thought to the possibilities that might arise from that stupid indiscretion. There was, of course, the most obvious: Anne could be pregnant with Richelieu's child. And if that was the case, then she would possess a mighty bludgeon which she could use against the cardinal for whatever purpose suited her.

But she sincerely doubted that such a rape child had been conceived by Anne, or if it had, it would stand little chance of surviving the hard jouncing given Anne by Buckingham for the last few nights.

The other possibility—which was a great deal more to her liking, despite the danger—revolved around eventually putting Monsieur on the throne and removing the cardinal from his place of power either at the same time that the new king was proclaimed or sometime before. Most preferably before—otherwise it would be impossible to depose Louis.

What Mme. de Chevreuse needed in order to pursue her scheme was Anne's participation, though she would readily accept her tacit approval. But the queen was too busy pointing out fish to care about anything else.

Mme. de Chevreuse saw the cardinal coming toward them and a quiver of apprehension raced down her back. It was almost as if he had somehow heard her thoughts. He was dressed in his gray cassock and red skullcap.

He came up to them, made his obeisance to the queen, and said, "Excuse me, your highness, but I have a matter to discuss with Mme. de Chevreuse."

Anne scarcely looked at him. With a nod, she said to her lady-in-waiting, "I will wait for you by the arbor at the far end of the garden."

"Yes, my lady," Mme. de Chevreuse answered with a curtsy.

Anne swept rapidly away.

Richelieu said, "Walk with me, madame."

"I would much prefer to stand here," she answered.

"You will walk," he said imperiously and started off in the opposite direction from the one taken by the queen.

Mme. de Chevreuse followed the cardinal and quickly fell in alongside of him.

"Despite what I said to you during our previous conversation," Richelieu commented, "you have taken it upon yourself to provide Buckingham and Anne with a place where they can indulge their illicit lusts."

"And I thought you wanted to discuss something of importance," she said sneeringly.

"Madame, you judge me wrong if—"

"I judge you, Armand, for what you are," she

answered just as harshly as she could without shouting at him. "You see, I know from my own experience with you about how much you really care about illicit lusts."

"You were not the queen," he said, coming to an abrupt halt and staring at her with undisguised malevolence.

"And you are not the king," she hurled at him, "though you may think you are."

He looked at her questioningly.

"Make of it what you will," she said. "But I think you know exactly what I mean."

Richelieu's eyes went to slits. His face flushed with rage. "You are playing a dangerous game, Marie," he said.

"No more dangerous than the one you play," she answered. "I at least have not violated anyone's person, nor has my lust gotten the better of my reason."

"If you were a man," Richelieu said in a flat deadly voice, "I would kill you!"

With a nod, Mme. de Chevreuse responded, "If I were a man, I would not talk about killing you—I would do it." Then she turned and started to walk to where Anne was waiting for her.

Richelieu hastily went after her. "Do not suppose," he told her, "that I will let our former relationship stand in the way of any punishment that might fall on you."

Mme. de Chevreuse stopped and, facing him, said, "Your arrogant self-righteousness forces me to tell you that as you would not have an English bastard as the heir to the throne of France, I would not have the bastard of an ecclesiastic."

They glared at each other for several moments.

"I will remember that," Richelieu said in a voice tight with fury. "I will indeed remember that." And turning away, he walked straight back up the pathway that led to the open doors of the palace.

Mme. de Chevreuse began to tremble. She had not only defied the most powerful man in France, she had declared war on him. And now that it was done, she was more than just slightly afraid. She was very frightened.

"What was that all about?" Anne asked as soon as Mme. de Chevreuse rejoined her.

"By the Holy Mother of God," the woman responded, "that man becomes more difficult with each passing day!"

"Louis says, 'He's my strong right hand,'" Anne said, mimicking her husband's voice.

Mme. de Chevreuse smiled.

"That is much better," Anne told her, and, patting a place on the bench next to her, she added, "Now come sit down."

"Thank you," Mme. de Chevreuse said. "But that man has a way of making me angry as no man ever had."

"He affects many people that way," Anne responded.

"I sometimes think France would be a better place without him," Mme. de Chevreuse said and realizing that she might have been too free with her words, her hand flew to cover her mouth.

"It is a thought that I am sure has crossed the minds of many Frenchmen," Anne replied.

Mme. de Chevreuse was quick to perceive the note of despair in the queen's voice and equally quick to sense that the moment she had earlier sought was suddenly at hand. "He is not without his weaknesses," she commented. "He can bleed and die like any other man."

Anne's jaw went slack.

"There are men who would be willing to do it," Mme. de Chevreuse said. "Men who see him as the real threat to France."

"I am afraid I have not heard you," Anne told her. "And please do not repeat what you had said."

"As you wish, my lady."

"I think I will go inside now," Anne said. "I feel a chill."

"But the sun is quite warm," Mme. de Chevreuse told her.

"The sun is indeed quite warm, but the thoughts that run through my brain are indeed chilling," Anne answered. "I have no wish to linger here any longer."

The two women walked back to the open doorway. Before they reached it, Anne said in a low voice, "If it can be done, do it—but I want no part of it. The risk is great."

"I know that, my lady," Mme. de Chevreuse answered with downcast eyes.

"Should you be found out, you know the punishment that would be meted out?"

"Yes."

"And you are still willing?"

"Yes, my lady," Mme. de Chevreuse said passionately. "I could do it a thousand times over for your happiness and for France."

TEN

The marriage of Henrietta Maria to King
Charles took place on a raised wooden platform
outside the great west door of Notre Dame, with the
Duc de Chevreuse standing in for the absent
Protestant king.

The fourteen-year-old princess was exquisitely
dressed in a bridal gown of gold and silver decorated
with gold fleurs-de-lis, and on her head was a
diamond crown that sparkled in the late-morning
sunlight.

The long ceremony was performed with punctili-
ous care by the Bishop of Paris, an old man with a
white beard.

Buckingham stood close enough to Anne to make
her aware of his presence. From time to time she

sought his eyes. In the privacy of her thoughts, she allowed herself to imagine that she and George were being married. It was impossible, she knew, but to be his wife was her most passionate wish.

Once, when their glances met, he winked at her, and she could feel the color rise in her cheeks. And closing her eyes for several moments, she recalled the wild ecstasy of their previous night's lovemaking. His fingers knew all her secret places . . . indeed, his lips and tongue knew them as well. . . .

Suddenly the great bells began to ring and everyone was shouting.

Anne opened her eyes. The bride and groom had been proclaimed man and wife. The wedding was over.

Added to the pealing of the bells, the blowing of the trumpets, and the shouting of thousands of people was the thunderous roaring of hundreds of guns being fired to honor the newly married couple.

Louis moved forward to embrace his sister, which he did without being able to hide the look of disdain on his face.

Anne too embraced Henrietta and wished the new bride well; then she fell back and waited until Buckingham was finished with his duty to the new Queen Consort of England.

"I thought the ceremony would never end," he said in a whisper as he took a place next to her.

"And I closed my eyes," she answered, "and imagined that we were being married."

"We are," he told her, "in the eyes of God, we are."

The royal party descended from the platform and boarded the several gold-and-silver-decorated coaches that would take them through the streets of Paris and finally back to the Louvre.

Buckingham's richly adorned coach followed immediately behind the three that held the members of Louis' immediate family. Lord Kensington and Lord Rich accompanied Buckingham, while Ed, dressed in splendid white livery with gold lace and buttons, rode behind on a fine white horse.

The people of Paris lined the sides of the streets and cheered their king, the new bride, and Buckingham with equal exuberance.

"From our own sources," Lord Kensington said, "we have learned that the captain and two officers from the *Hermes* are being held prisoner at Fort Mahon."

Buckingham stopped waving to the crowds. The smile left his face and his brow furrowed.

"Are you certain?" he asked.

"Absolutely," Lord Rich answered.

"They are being held on the cardinal's orders," Kensington explained, "though they have not been formally charged with having committed any crime."

Buckingham began to wave and smile to the crowds again as he said, "Then we shall have to have them released or free them ourselves. Can you procure a map of the area and accurate drawings of the fort?"

"I think so," Lord Rich answered.

"Excellent. Let me have them in, say, three days," Buckingham told him. "And for the time being say nothing about this to any of our visiting countrymen."

"Absolutely," Rich said.

Lord Kensington nodded.

"Were you able to discover how the *Hermes* happened to be wrecked?" Buckingham asked.

"No, my lord," Kensington replied. "But I will continue to try."

Buckingham made no mention of having asked M. Gerbier to procure the same information. It was not his habit to reveal anything about his own sources of information, though M. Gerbier was well known to both lords.

"There is one other matter that we believe should be brought to your immediate attention," Lord Kensington said.

"Yes, what is it?"

"There has been some talk about your liaison with

the queen," Kensington responded.

Buckingham looked at him and said, "I admire a man who comes straight to the point, because it enables me to do exactly the same thing. I will not hedge, or bluster, or even seek to explain. But I will say to you, you would not think to mention it if she were not Queen of France. Well, to me she is not the Queen of France. She is a woman. I trust that you, my lords, have the good sense to see her in that light."

"A most beautiful woman," Lord Rich said. "But she is also the Queen of France, and her station cannot be overlooked, or disregarded."

Buckingham glowered at them but said nothing.

"The whispers about the affair are growing louder. Sooner or later Louis will hear them, and then what will you do?" Kensington asked.

"Do? Do? I will do nothing and say nothing," Buckingham answered sharply, and he turned once more to waving and smiling at the crowds.

"We did not mean to anger you," Lord Rich said. "It was our intention to warn you—"

"Of what?" Buckingham asked fiercely, as he whirled around to face his two countrymen.

"Of the dangers attendant to your affair," Lord Kensington replied. "Each of us is here in the service of our king, you more than any of us."

"My duty will not be compromised by my relationship to the queen," Buckingham said.

"Not even if Louis is made aware of the affair?"

"He cares not a whit for her or, for that matter, for any woman."

"But he does value his honor," Lord Rich said.

Buckingham leaned back and said nothing more. The truth of his friends' warning was undeniable, but what did they expect him to do? Stop making love to Anne? He could not forgo the pleasure and the happiness she gave to him.

"There is also Richelieu to consider," Kensington said.

Buckingham raised his eyebrows.

"Suppose the queen bears your child?"

"There are ways to prevent conception," Buckingham answered.

"Has she used them?"

"Or more to the point," Lord Rich commented, "will she use them? The church strictly forbids a woman—"

"Fie! Fie! Fie!" Buckingham explained. "Have done with it. You have made your point and your duty to the king is done."

"We are sorry if we offended you," Lord Kensington said.

Buckingham waved him silent. He did not want to continue the conversation. But after a few moments, he whispered, "I will make sure that the heir to the French throne does not come from English loins, but as for ending my liaison with Anne, I will not do it while I live, and when I am dead it will no longer matter. You see, my lords, I love her."

"Then be less obvious about your love," Lord Kensington said.

"I am not ashamed of it, nor is she."

"Shame does not enter into the situation, but prudence does."

"If it will satisfy the two of you, I will be more prudent," Buckingham said.

"We have no choice but to be satisfied with it, my Lord," Rich answered.

"Then," Buckingham laughed, "I will be the most prudent of men. People will begin to call me Prudent Buckingham, or the Prudent Duke, or perhaps Buckingham, the prudent one."

Lord Kensington and Lord Rich smiled and then began to laugh along with the duke.

The wedding celebration was more magnificent than any previously held revel. Nobles from every court in Europe were there, even from the distant court of the Russian tsar.

The gardens surrounding the Louvre were lit with

171

hundreds of Chinese lanterns, and the royal guests were entertained by bands of strolling musicians.

Exactly at midnight the fireworks display started. And the dark, star-studded sky was suddenly ablaze with dozens of flaming colors that rose in great gothic arches over the river, or burst upward like huge flowers. The incandescent greens, reds, and oranges turned the black water of the river into a strange rainbow. Each burst of color brought exclamations of delight from the onlookers. There were special effects that created the illusion of water fountains suddenly gushing up from the river, and now and then huge blazing pinwheels whirled through the air to burn themselves out high over the streets of the city.

Louis was enormously pleased with the fireworks and told Buckingham he had employed two Venetians to arrange the spectacle.

"They are talented men," Buckingham answered. "I will recommend them to my king, should he want a similar display."

"Tell my new brother-in-law," Louis said, "that we are sure he will find them satisfactory."

"I will, your highness," Buckingham replied.

"Pyrotechnics has always been a passion of mine," Louis said.

Buckingham suddenly realized he was encountering a side of Louis that he had not previously seen, though Anne had told him that Louis was sometimes more child than man.

"Many, I am sure, hold a similar passion," the duke answered.

A huge white star burst over the garden, and Louis' face showed a pleasure so intense that Buckingham was almost certain that the king was experiencing something akin to sexual delight.

"Exquisite!" Louis exclaimed in a soft but passionate voice.

"Yes," Buckingham agreed, and after a moment

he added, "I have had similar feelings about certain sunsets I have seen, especially at sea."

"Sunsets?" Louis questioned.

"Yes, your grace, especially when the sun is low in the west and clouds—"

"We can admire sunsets," Louis said, "as God's work, but a display of fireworks is something altogether different."

"Yes, your highness," Buckingham responded, "you are quite right."

Louis nodded, obviously satisfied that he had made his point.

Buckingham waited for the opportune moment and then graciously took his leave. His brief conversation with Louis had created a strong need for drink. To think that the man had the lawful right to Anne's body was enough to make him furious with the laws that bound men and women together in holy matrimony until death took one of them. He thanked God that Henry VIII had had reason to do away with those damnable laws for Englishmen.

The duke went in search of something stronger than wine. Rum or gin would have satisfied him, but what he really wanted was whisky. He knew that Louis had provided several small barrels of it to accommodate his English visitors. He had not gone very far when he saw one of the servants carrying a gold tray with a dozen small glasses on it.

"Whisky?" he asked going to the man.

"Yes, your grace," the servant answered.

Buckingham quickly downed one.

The servant started away.

"Hold!" Buckingham exclaimed, and to the man's utter astonishment, he drank four more. Then, with a pleasant smile, he said, "It was all for medicinal purposes."

"Too much of such medicine, my lord, will surely make you much sicker than the illness which caused you to drink it."

"Sicker than frustrated love?"

"I could not say, my lord," the man answered. "I have been drunk on English whisky and know the ills that attend it, but I have never been frustrated with love."

"Lucky man!" Buckingham exclaimed, and thanking him for his conversation, he handed the servant several pieces of gold.

By the time the bells in the city tolled three, most of the guests were sprawled out in a drunken stupor. Some lay in the garden, but most found places indoors in the Great Hall, or in the various corridors of the palace. Many of the lords and ladies drunkenly embraced, giving way to concupiscence. The very air seemed to be charged with unbridled passion.

Buckingham sought out Anne. Louis had long since left for his apartment with one of his favorite young men, and Richelieu, realizing that the marriage celebration would soon turn into an orgy, had retired to his rooms.

Without speaking, Buckingham took hold of Anne's hand and quickly led her to Mme. de Chevreuse's apartment. Once they were in the bedroom, he said, "I could not spend what is left of the night without you." And embracing her, he kissed her passionately on her lips.

Each undressed the other. Still standing, their bodies warm with desire, they looked deeply into one another's eyes as they allowed their hands to touch, tease, and explore.

"Sometimes," Anne said, "when I look at you across a room, I think of holding you like this, and I feel myself become weak with passion."

Buckingham's reply was to press the palms of his hands against her breasts.

Anne eased herself down on her knees. Slowly, tantalizingly, she ran her moist pink tongue down the strong planes of his body until at last her lips closed lightly around his quivering rigidity.

Buckingham moved his fingers through her hair.

The pleasure she gave him was so intense that he shut his eyes and let the warmth from his groin spread throughout his body.

At last Anne looked up. "I am your slave," she told him.

He raised her up and carried her to the bed. Kneeling on the floor between her naked thighs, he placed his mouth hard against her sex.

"I am on fire!" she exclaimed in a throaty voice. "Oh, George, I burn...I burn for you, my love."

Using his tongue, he made her writhe with ecstasy until she lay back, abandoning herself to sensation.

"How am I going to live without you?" she suddenly cried out.

Buckingham moved up between her naked thighs. "I love you," he said, entering her.

She encircled his neck with her arms and brought his lips to hers. As her tongue found his, she moved her body to his rhythm—strong, insistent, throbbing.

"I can feel it deep inside me," she whispered. "It gathers together and knots...oh my love...my love...I am there!" Her voice trailed off, into a quavering moan of delight, as spasm after spasm of ecstasy shook her body.

An instant later Buckingham uttered a low growl of pleasure and kissed her fiercely on the lips. For several minutes they lay together, panting, satiated.

"How will I live without you?" she finally asked again.

"Come with me," he said. "Come back to England with me."

"What?"

"I will make you my wife," he said, kissing each of her bare nipples.

"But I am already married."

"Louis will divorce you, if you come with me. The church will allow him to divorce you."

"And what would happen to your wife?" she asked.

"I would divorce her," Buckingham said without hesitation.

Anne remained silent.

"Have we any other way open to us?" Buckingham asked. "Once I leave France—"

She put her hand against his mouth. "I know only too well what you are going to say," she told him. "I dread that day. Part of me will die when you leave."

"Come with me," he implored.

"And if I agreed," she responded, "do you really think I would be allowed to go?"

Buckingham raised himself on one elbow and placed his other hand on her breasts. "Who would stop you?" he asked. "Surely not Louis."

"Richelieu," she answered, her voice rising in pitch. "His men are everywhere. He would never let me leave France."

Buckingham spanned the distance between her nipples with his thumb and little finger. "The cardinal cannot stop you," he said. "He can be made to see—"

"He sees only what he wants to see. You do not know the man as I do."

"Say you will come with me," Buckingham told her, "and I will make sure that Richelieu does nothing to stop you."

"He will," she answered in a whisper. "He will. . . ."

Realizing that Anne's fears of Richelieu's power were greater than he could have imagined, Buckingham gathered her to him and once more began to make love to her.

"No," she said. "I would rather just remain quietly in your arms."

Buckingham held her close.

After a while her eyes closed and she was asleep.

He kissed her on the forehead. The strong possibility that he might never see her again after he left France was fast becoming an almost unbearable torment. When he had left France the last time, the idea that he would not see her again had never entered his mind. But now it was lodged there and he could not rid himself of it.

"We will have to find a way, my love." He sighed. "We will have to find a way to be together." And he moved his hand over her breast.

In her sleep, Anne murmured contentedly.

"I will not let anyone or anything keep us apart," he vowed, and then he closed his eyes and quickly drifted off to sleep.

Richelieu was drunk. He prowled from room to room in his apartment talking to God, telling Him his only mission in this life was to make France a great nation.

"I do not care if I must suffer in hell for ten thousand years," the cardinal said, "but here on earth France will be a nation other nations of the world bow before. But how, how can I achieve that when the queen is whore to an English heretic?"

He lurched toward the place near the hearth that opened to the secret passageway. "I do not lie," he said. "I will show you. You will see . . . You will see . . ." And he moved into the pitch blackness.

The cardinal made his way slowly, sometimes pausing to mumble a prayer and sometimes weeping softly to himself.

After a while, he became more resolute and quickened his step until he came to a place in the passageway where the wall would open into the room where Buckingham and Anne were accustomed to meet.

"They are beyond this wall," he said, tapping the adjacent rocks with his forefinger. "Come, I will show You." He pressed a place in the wall and a portion of it began to swing inward. A crack of light opened in the blackness and slowly became a wedge.

Richelieu stepped into the room. The window was already awash with the first gray light of dawn. The candles were burning low.

"Naked," he hissed, looking at the bed. "See, his hand is on her breast and her thigh is across his legs."

The wine left his head. Richelieu reached under his cassock for a dagger. To kill them in their shame would be fitting justice for their adultery. He started toward them.

Buckingham moved.

Richelieu stopped and hastily retreated back into the passageway.

Buckingham awoke with a start and quickly scanned the room. He had the most peculiar feeling that a third person had been in the room. Or had it been part of his dream?

He looked down at Anne.

She was still asleep.

He relaxed and decided he had dreamed about someone else being in the room. But the unpleasant feeling lingered.

The bells of the city began to toll the Angelus.

Buckingham closed his eyes and wondered why the residue of dreams was often more disturbing than the dreams themselves. But before he could think of an answer, he was again sleeping.

For ten days the celebrations at the French court continued and nothing of any importance was considered, much less acted upon. But even the most devoted reveler and the most avowed Sybarite wearied of the dancing, the gourmandizing, and the orgies. To add to the excesses, the weather suddenly turned hot and humid, making it impossible for anyone to remain either cool or in good temper for very long.

Louis too was in an ill humor. He would have much preferred to be out of Paris and in his summer residence at Auxerre, on the Loire River. During the day he remained in his apartment, and at night he made a brief appearance at the festivities.

Several afternoons in succession, huge black thunderclouds built up to the east and threatened to bring a deluge of rain. But nothing happened, except that the sky was soon ablaze with jagged flashes of lightning and the sound of thunder rolled over the countryside. The recurrence of all the aspects of a storm without the rain was considered an ill omen by everyone.

Richelieu saw it as God's displeasure over the marriage between Henrietta and Charles and subtly said as much to Louis, who, if he understood, preferred to ignore the matter.

"I tell you," the cardinal said to Father Joseph one afternoon when they were together in Richelieu's rooms and the thunder was so loud it seemed to shake the windows of the palace, "I tell you that we have made the wrong marriage, and since the bride has not yet slept with her husband, what was done can be undone."

"The king will not permit it," the monk said. "And you are powerless to do anything without his agreement."

"It will come to no good," Richelieu brooded, watching the lightning through the window.

"Have you had an official meeting with Buckingham yet?" the Capuchin asked.

"He has had the good sense to refrain from asking for an official audience," Richelieu answered.

"It must be granted when he asks," Father Joseph said.

The cardinal nodded.

"Be patient, Armand," Father Joseph counseled. "Sooner or later you will have Buckingham. Fortune hardly ever smiles on a person throughout his life. I have had word from Giroux. He has made the acquaintance of a man named John Felton, who has sufficient reason to kill Buckingham."

"And what reason would that be?"

"Buckingham killed his brother in a duel," the Capuchin answered.

Richelieu nodded.

"Fortune's smile might already be turning into an ugly grimace," Father Joseph commented.

Anne and Mme. de Chevreuse were alone in Anne's sitting room. Anne watched the great clouds turn the late afternoon into premature night, while at the same time great flashes of lightning leaped wildly across the sky and thunder hammered against the earth.

Marie was at her needlepoint. She had spent a wild night in the arms of Lord Rich, and every bone in her body ached. She found him to be a most acceptable lover.

"He has asked me to go to England with him," Anne suddenly said, turning from the window.

Marie stopped what she was doing. "And will you go?" she asked, forcing her voice not to betray any emotion.

"I want to with all my heart," Anne answered. "But how can I go?"

Marie stood up and pushed her needlepoint frame out of her path.

"He would divorce his wife and marry me," Anne said. "Yes, I know it is against our church, but not against his. If I could not get a special dispensation from the pope, I would renounce my faith and embrace his."

"Then you have decided to go?"

Anne shook her head.

"I do not understand. You just said—"

"Richelieu would never allow me to leave France," Anne said. "It would be so much easier if I were suddenly widowed, and then as queen I could rid myself of Richelieu."

Suddenly Marie saw the whole of the plan to put Monsieur on the throne of France and use Buckingham for her own benefit against the cardinal. "While the cardinal lives," she told Anne, "you will never be free. But if he should come to a premature end, then it might be possible for you to convince Louis to divorce you. If he should ask the pope for the divorce, I am sure it would be granted."

The two women moved closer to each other.

"I have already revealed there are those of us who are tired of the cardinal's iron-handed control."

Anne nodded.

"You said you would do nothing to hinder us," Marie reminded her.

"Yes," Anne answered.

"But will you help us, if such help is needed?"

Anne hesitated for several moments, but then she slowly nodded.

Marie embraced her and said, "Trust me and I will help you to become the wife of the Duke of Buckingham."

"I trust you," Anne answered, her heart pounding wildly. "I trust you, my dear Marie...."

ELEVEN

"*My king bade me speak to you on his*
behalf," Buckingham said, looking across the highly
polished table at Richelieu, who wore the vestments
of his princely rank in the hierarchy of the church.

The cardinal nodded. The vision of Buckingham
and Anne sleeping naked in each other's arms filled
the inside of his skull.

"You understand," Buckingham said, "that I
requested a private audience because of the delicate
nature of the subject."

Again the cardinal nodded.

Buckingham smiled. He realized that Richelieu's
silent nods were calculated to unnerve him. And
rather than allow the cardinal to labor under the
illusion that he was accomplishing his end, he said,

"Your eminence, I did not come here to waste your time or mine. I have a great deal of respect for your ability of statecraft, and whether or not you respect my ability is of no consequence to me. But be assured that it exists, and be assured that we are well matched."

The boldness of the man took Richelieu by surprise. He had expected a more subtle approach, yet in the openness there was a subtlety as potent as any he himself might employ.

"Shall we approach the matters I wish to bring before you as equals," Buckingham questioned, "or shall we attempt to impress one another with our roguery?"

Richelieu responded with a laugh. "This is the first time I have ever heard diplomacy referred to as roguery."

Buckingham leaned forward and placed his elbows on the table. "It is but a game," he said. "A game played by kings and other potentates for their pleasure."

"And what part do we play?"

"We are the rooks, the pawns, the knights, and the bishops."

"And here I have been told," Richelieu answered, "that many people believe I rule France and you rule England."

"We do indeed," Buckingham said. "But only because our respective kings permit us to. Should they for some reason deny us their permission, we would rule no more than our own garden patch, and even that can be taken away from us by our kings."

"I am ready to listen to you," Richelieu said, who was beginning to understand why Buckingham could hold sway over a variety of different types of men and women. Despite his own hatred for the man, he would have been less than truthful to himself and to God if he did not admit a degree of respect for his enemy on a diplomatic level.

Buckingham stood up and walked to the side of the room, where one wall was covered from floor to ceiling with a huge map of Europe that included a large section of Russia, a portion of North Africa, and the Holy Land.

"May I?" he asked, reaching for a silver pointer the length of a man's arm from shoulder to fingertips.

"By all means," Richelieu responded.

Buckingham touched the map at the Palatinate and said, "Spanish troops are here and here in the lowlands. Should they take more of the lowlands they will control the northern flank of France as well as a portion of its southern flank. King Charles would much prefer to see the Spanish forces out of the lowlands and the Palatinate. It is his view that it would be to France's interest to have her northern borders adjoining nations with less ambition than Spain has."

"It is indeed considerate of your king to worry about the borders of France," Richelieu commented. "But I do not think either of us in this room should lose sight of the fact that the deposed elector of the Palatinate happens to be brother-in-law to Charles and that England and Spain have not gotten on well for many years. And I think we should also note that the countries under Spanish domination are Protestant countries, while Spain and France, regardless of their political differences—and it would be foolish to try to minimize them—are nonetheless bound together in one faith, the one true church."

"Catholic countries have fought each other before," Buckingham answered, setting the pointer down and leaning on it.

"You would have France go to war with Spain?"

"For its own protection," Buckingham said, "to frustrate the wild ambitions of Philip. He will, if he can, devour all of Europe. Because of this danger, Charles asks France to unite with him against Spain."

"You make it sound so very simple," Richelieu

replied, as he stood up and moved toward the map. "But when you move the point as you did, you are talking about tens of thousands of men, thousands of leagues, and God alone knows how many ships." The cardinal reached up toward the Spanish peninsula with his hand. The tip of his forefinger touched the coast. "Spain sits here isolated from the rest of Europe by the mountains that stand between our two countries. She must transport her men and supplies by ship."

"That is exactly why she is vulnerable to a combined action—France against her on land," Buckingham said, raising the pointer to touch the northern border first and then the southern one, "here and here, while England attacks her at sea."

"It could be very effective," Richelieu answered. "But there is another problem."

"I see none if we move swiftly," Buckingham told him.

Though there was a smile on his lips, Richelieu's gray eyes became slits as he said, "Our queen is the sister of the Spanish king. To make war on her native country would be a disservice to her. She is well loved here and in her own country."

"We are not speaking of marriages that were made for political reasons," Buckingham answered. "Your queen is not a matter for our consideration."

"Since we are discussing such an important step as going to war, I would have thought that every aspect of the situation would come under discussion." Buckingham felt flushed.

"Now tell me, my lord," Richelieu asked, "what is your opinion of Charles' plan?"

"It has great merit," the duke answered. "And if successful, it would certainly put an end to the Spanish threat."

"But France does not feel threatened by Spain," Richelieu said. "I am truly sorry that England does.... But I will discuss your king's proposals with Louis."

Buckingham returned the pointer to the stand from which he had taken it and, looking straight at Richelieu, said, "Neither I nor my king would willingly do injury to your queen."

"I understand that," the cardinal answered. "But her allegiance would be sorely tested if France were to make war on her native country."

Buckingham agreed.

"Perhaps you should communicate with your king," Richelieu suggested, "and suggest that he withdraw the offer of a military alliance between our two nations against Spain. He might, after all, have cause to reconsider the adventure?"

"My instructions were explicit."

"Then perhaps when you return to London you might be able to convince him to change his mind?"

"He is determined to stop Spain," Buckingham answered.

"If determination alone could make things happen," the cardinal said with a smile, "then kings and other potentates would not need the pawns, rooks, knights, and bishops—in this case a cardinal and a duke—to provide the necessary means to accomplish what they are so determined to do."

The two men walked to the door and shook hands.

"Your eminence was most kind to meet with me," Buckingham said, knowing that Richelieu had already decided that France would not join England against Spain and that the decision was as much the result of the cardinal's jealousy as it was for political and religious reasons.

"We will talk again soon," Richelieu answered.

"We will indeed," Buckingham responded, and turning away, he walked down the long marble hallway.

Richelieu did not move. He watched Buckingham until the man was out of sight. His hatred for him was far greater now than it previously had been. He had to have him killed; but first he wanted to break him.

Buckingham studied the sketches of Fort Mahon that were spread out in front of him.

The fort was a square structure with a keep in the center. Guards patrolled the walls. But at night their number was reduced. There were two guards at the gate. The eastern wall looked out on a stretch of beach. There was a tunnel under the wall that led directly into the main courtyard. The quarters for the guards was located in the keep.

A late-afternoon sun flooded through the open window and poured over the table and his face. He looked up and, nodding to Lord Kensington, who was seated a short distance away, said, "I want you to choose a half dozen men from among the nobles with us—men who can be relied upon to fight and fight well should the situation warrant it. Tell them it is to carry out the king's business. Can you procure some eight Musketeer uniforms?"

"Yes."

"Excellent," Buckingham said, as he stood up and rubbed his hands. "I will make the necessary arrangements to have one of our sloops stand offshore. I want the members of my party to assemble six days from now in the morning at the town of Plage, which is but a short distance to the fort. Have them travel by twos. I will meet them there and we shall filch the captain and his two officers away from the French."

"It is dangerous," Lord Kensington commented. "And in my official capacity as ambassador to the French court, I must warn you against it. If you are caught—"

"We will be in and out of the prison before anyone knows that someone has been there."

"Your presence will be missed at court," Kensington said.

"Give out the story that I am ill with a fever," Buckingham told him. "I will be back at court as soon as possible."

Lord Kensington started to speak and then stopped himself.

"Say what you wanted to," Buckingham told him.

"How will you explain your absence to Anne?" he asked.

"Nature has conspired with me," Buckingham answered. "Anne will much prefer to sleep alone for the next few nights."

"And what about the days?" Kensington questioned. "If she hears you are ill, she will fly to your bedside."

Buckingham stood up and looked out at the garden through the open window. Despite the bright sunshine the air was dank. "Then I will tell her the truth," he said.

Kensington uttered a weary sigh.

"She will not betray me," Buckingham said. "She values my life more than she values her own."

Kensington did not answer. Planting his gold-knobbed walking stick to the floor in front of him, he used it to support his weight as he rose to his feet. "I will see that the men you require are in Plage at the appointed time," he said. "And God be with all of you."

Louis was in his aviary, feeding pieces of raw meat to his falcons. It gave him great pleasure to watch one of them snap the food while it was still in the air. He had a great love for birds, especially the predators.

Richelieu stood close to the king and said nothing. They had greeted each other informally, and now the cardinal was waiting for Louis to turn his attention from the birds to him. But the king was enjoying himself and obviously had no wish to come to grips with something considerably less enjoyable, which Richelieu knew he suspected the moment he saw him.

"The heat and the dankness have made them less active," Louis complained. "That gray one there in the corner usually fights with that black one on the perch for the meat."

The cardinal made no comment. He had no particular feeling for birds, other than to acknowledge that they too were God's creatures.

"Have you any idea," Louis questioned, "when our English guests will depart?"

"When Buckingham tells them to," the cardinal said.

Louis threw the last piece of meat into the huge cage and clapped when a pure-white falcon snatched it up before it touched the bottom of the cage. "If I could be a creature other than man," the King said, "I would choose to be a falcon. What would you choose, if you had the choice?"

"A cat of some sort," the cardinal answered.

"Then you would devour us," Louis said. "Unless, of course, you were small enough for us to tear apart."

"I would choose to be a large cat," Richelieu said, concealing a smile.

"I had no doubt that you would choose to be a large one, Armand," the king commented. "But if I were a very large falcon then we would be evenly matched."

"Yes, sire," Richelieu answered.

"And what type of creature do you suppose Buckingham would choose to be?" the King asked.

"A large dog," the cardinal answered without hesitation. "He has a great fondness for hunting dogs, I am told."

Louis nodded and said, "I have noticed your absence from our presence these past weeks."

"Matters of state need attention," Richelieu answered.

The king walked away from the cage of falcons and stopped in front of some brightly colored squawking parrots. "But now have the matters of state receded sufficiently to allow you to visit us?" he asked.

"Not exactly," the cardinal replied. "They have, if anything, grown more serious and require your attention."

Louis did not hide his dislike for the answer he had

received. The expression on his face showed his disdain, and he said, "I am never sure whether to look forward to seeing you or find some excuse to avoid you altogether."

"Nothing in statecraft goes away on its own accord," Richelieu answered.

"Tell us then what is so important as to require our attention and not your remedy for it."

"Buckingham, or rather Charles, your brother-in-law, has proposed an alliance against Spain. He suggests we attack on land while his ships sweep the seas of Spanish vessels."

"Is he serious?"

"Buckingham gave me his proposal yesterday," Richelieu said. "I wanted to think about it before presenting it to you."

"And what do you think about it?" Louis asked.

"It would gain France nothing to join England in such a venture," Richelieu answered.

"Then you turned it down?"

"No, sire, I wanted to discuss it with you before I—"

Louis put up his right hand and said, "We will play a bit with it. Do not give Buckingham an answer, but keep his hope alive. See what concessions we might gain from such an alliance, or the promise of one. Perhaps my brother-in-law would be willing to take our Huguenots for the promise of our assistance, or better still, if we help him fight his battles, he might help us fight ours against the Huguenots here in France."

"You mean you intend to take the field against them?"

"I have given it thought," the king answered, beginning to walk toward the door of the aviary.

"But what changed your mind, sire?"

"We would be interested in our brother-in-law's answer," the king said, ignoring Richelieu's question. "If he is truly bent on hobbling Spain, then he might agree to provide us with a few ships to hammer La Rochelle from the sea."

Richelieu smiled. There were times when Louis' ingenuity amazed him, and this was definitely one such time.

"Make the proposal to Buckingham," the king said, "and then come and tell me what effect it had on him."

"I will, sire," Richelieu answered. "I most certainly will."

"And now," Louis said, "we have practiced enough statecraft for one afternoon and crave something by way of relaxation."

"May I suggest a visit to the queen?" Richelieu said.

The king shook his head. "We would prefer not to," Louis responded. "It is much too hard and sweaty work to beget an heir on such a hot and dank day."

"Fool," Richelieu silently shouted, while nodding at the king. "Stupid fool!"

Mme. de Chevreuse held a pink parasol to keep the blaze of the afternoon sun off her fair skin. She wore a white gown, cut low across the tops of her breasts, and simple white slippers. She walked through the gardens near the river, where there was a chance of being cooled by a stray breeze.

Monsieur accompanied her. Ever since the arrival of Buckingham, she had noticed a certain sullenness in the young man's demeanor. He seemed to have lost his capacity to laugh and seldom even smiled. Determined to discover the cause of Monsieur's gloomy mood, she had invited him for a walk in the garden. And more important, at least as far as she was concerned, she intended to sound Gaston out again about his willingness to participate in her scheme to remove Richelieu and eventually unseat the king. But if Monsieur gained the throne through her efforts, she wanted to be sure she would have a great deal to say in matters at court and that she would be richly rewarded with lands.

They stopped to watch a small skiff tack its way upriver.

"There is hardly a breath of wind," Gaston said.

"M. Courrant, a well-recommended astrologer says the heat is the result of three planets that are in conjunction with each other and with the earth. He says the summer will be very, very hot."

"Yes," Gaston answered. "Chalais puts a great deal of store in what Courrant says."

"Many at court do," Mme. de Chevreuse answered already deciding how to broach the subject. "Perhaps the conjunction of the three planets has had an affect on you?"

He shrugged and said, "My brother has an affect on me."

"As king, he most certainly affects all of us," she said, moving the parasol from her right hand to her left.

Gaston remained silent.

She began to walk again, knowing he would follow along.

"Once Buckingham leaves," Monsieur told her, as they walked, "I will leave too. I find that I no longer feel welcome at court."

"You, the brother of the king, not welcome at court? Why, that is absurd, Gaston. Absolutely absurd!" she exclaimed, coming to an abrupt halt and facing him.

Gaston shook his head.

The expression on his face was so melancholy that Mme. de Chevreuse was sorely tempted to embrace him and offer the softness of her breasts for comfort. He was, after all, a stunningly handsome man, and his reputation as a lover was sufficient to interest any woman of spirit. And she was but a few years older than he.

"My brother," he said haltingly, "rebuked me on the day of our sister's wedding in Buckingham's presence."

Mme. de Chevreuse looked horror-stricken.

Gaston proceeded to relate the entire incident ending by saying, "Nothing I do pleases him. He would be satisfied only if I devoted the rest of my life to the church. Better than reap his rebuke, I will remove myself from his sight."

"And where will you go?" she asked, again shifting the parasol to her right hand.

"South...perhaps to Italy, or Spain," Gaston answered, his voice cracking with emotion.

Mme. de Chevreuse slowly twirled her parasol in one direction and then in the other. She looked at the boat in the river; it seemed to be in the same place as it had been before.

"If I were you," she said in a soft voice, "I would not run away. I would try to discover what I might do to remedy my situation." And before he could speak, she continued, "Not too long ago you and Chalais were in my apartment and we spoke of certain things."

Gaston nodded and said, "I have not forgotten them. But Anne and Buckingham are—"

"Certain information has come my way since we spoke," she told him, "that has cast everything in a better light for you. I have been waiting for several days to speak to you about it."

"For the love of God, tell me and ease my anguish," he implored, coming to an abrupt halt and turning to her.

Mme. de Chevreuse extended her free hand and lightly tapped Gaston on the chest as she said, "Let us continue to walk, or those who see us will think that we are either arguing or in earnest discussion. Either one would arouse the interest of the cardinal's spies."

"That man," Monsieur said through his teeth, as he resumed walking, "would have us all be churchmen."

Mme. de Chevreuse laughed lightly.

"Can he be gotten rid of?" Gaston asked.

"Yes," Mme. de Chevreuse answered nonchalantly. "In order to put you on the throne, he must be done away with."

"Madame!" Monsieur exclaimed, losing his footing. But immediately regaining it, he said, "I will do everything in my power to help."

"And what will you do once you are King of France?"

"All you wish."

"Your promise must be put in writing to me," she said.

"It will be done. But tell me how—"

"A way must be found to murder Richelieu," she said in a whisper, "and perhaps even to make it seem that Buckingham was the author of the crime."

"But what reason would he have?"

"Reason enough," Mme. de Chevreuse said, nodding her head. "Do not concern yourself with that. Certain letters will be left that point to the duke and give the reason by implication."

"And who will kill him?"

"For a price most men will do anything. You will supply the gold that will steady the hand."

"And what of Anne, when Louis leaves the throne?"

"She will be given the opportunity to join Buckingham, which will be but more evidence of the duke's involvement in the murder of the cardinal. She will take it."

"And if she does not?"

"If you want her, she will be your queen," Mme. de Chevreuse answered.

"But Louis—"

"He will be dead," she answered without faltering.

After a long pause, Monsieur said, "If we fail, we will be dead."

"We will not fail," she answered him. "I must find the right assassin to kill Richelieu. He must be someone who would be able to do it and make it seem as if it were a regrettable accident. I will think more about it."

"And what about Chalais?" Monsieur asked. "He

194

is as close to my brother as any man could be, other than his favorite boy."

"We will need his help," Mme. de Chevreuse said. "Tell him what we are about. Now that I think of it, he would be a most excellent person to find the kind of assassin we need. No one would suspect him."

"And when will this take place?" Gaston asked gleefully.

"Soon, very soon," she answered.

"I am indebted to you," Monsieur said with passion in his voice.

They had entered a bosky area sheltered somewhat from observation. Suddenly Mme. de Chevreuse took hold of his hand and pressed it against her breast.

Gaston's eyes went wide with surprise.

"If you sat on the throne," she said in a low throaty whisper, "and I sat beside you, we would rule France together." The thoughts and the words formed at the same instant. "I am not without a certain proficiency in the arts of love, and should you ever feel the need to experience pleasure with some other woman, I would not stand in your way, as long as you accorded me the same right."

"Your husband—"

"To kill three men would be as easy as to kill two," she answered, smiling at him as his hand fondled a breast he had bared.

The inn in Plage was a crude place with an earthen floor, several rough-hewn tables, benches to match, and only candles for light.

Buckingham and the men with him had met there early in the morning of the appointed day. All of them were dressed as musketeers, complete with sword and pistol.

Just before Buckingham had left Paris, he had received a message from M. Gerbier, informing him that Dupris' family had been dispersed. The sons had been sent to the galleys and the mother to the Bastille, and the daughter had been handed over to the crew of a galley for their pleasure. M. Gerbier had hazarded the guess that Dupris had fallen into Richelieu's hands. And when Buckingham had read what had happened to the unfortunate man's family he had silently agreed with M. Gerbier's guess.

The duke spoke in a low voice to those with him and told them what he expected each of them to do. "We must be quick about it," he said. "In and out in a trice, or we will have a fight on our hands we can ill afford. The *Ajax* is standing offshore. She will come in close tonight, and we will meet her just before midnight. Have you gentlemen any questions?"

"Do we take prisoners?"

"No," Buckingham answered.

The men looked at each other, and then one said, "That means we must kill every man we see, or who sees us."

"Yes," Buckingham replied and added, "Pray for their souls when next you go to church, but do not forget that they will try to kill you. All you have is the element of surprise and your skill. They have their skill and numbers. It is only the element of surprise that makes it at all possible to do what we have come to do."

Buckingham and his men spent the better part of the day going over the plans for their operation. In the evening the men ate well, drank a great deal of local red wine, and slept.

Buckingham and Ed remained awake, talking in low tones about everything from Ed's life as a wherryman to the duke's unhappy experience with Prince Charles in the Spanish court.

Despite Ed's lack of education, Buckingham found him far wiser than a great many nobles who were university-trained. In the short time that he had been in the duke's service, the man's speech had improved and he had learned enough French to speak the language tolerably well, albeit with a London street accent.

"Are you frightened?" Buckingham asked.

"I'd be a fool if'n I weren't," Ed answered. "But once the fightin' starts and the blood is up then the fear goes until afterward."

"And how would you know that?" the duke asked.

"My lord," Ed answered, "from all the street brawlin' I've done."

Buckingham laughed and affectionately slapped his servant on the back. Then he settled down in a corner, closed his eyes, and drifted into a restful sleep.

It was twilight when the men awoke. Outside the wind had picked up and the sky was a leaden gray. Buckingham stood in the doorway of the inn and looked toward the sea. Already the waves were building to such heights that spume was blowing off their white crests.

"To bring a ship close inshore will be hard," Ed commented, as he came up behind the duke and looked to the sea.

Buckingham nodded but said nothing.

A short while later the duke and the men with him were riding toward Fort Mahon, some ten leagues distant. Despite the summer heat of only a few hours before, the wind chilled them. They rode along the beach, keeping well away from the breaking surf.

The leaden sky quickened the coming of darkness, and with it came a pelting rain. The men wrapped their cloaks more securely around their bodies and bent low against the necks of their mounts.

After several hours of riding, they saw in the distance the dark outline of the fort looming up above them. It was a massive structure with the high keep in its center. The entire edifice had been built on solid rock, above the beach.

"Are you sure there is a tunnel from the beach to the courtyard?" one of the noblemen asked Buckingham.

"The drawing shows it," the duke answered. "We must assume it is there."

When they were very close to the fort, they

dismounted and tethered their horses in the woods behind the beach. Then they freed their swords and made their way on foot, along the base of the cliff on which the fort stood.

"Do not use your pistols unless you must," Buckingham cautioned them. "We must do our killing silently." Suddenly a man seemed to step out of the face of the cliff.

"The tunnel," Buckingham whispered. He motioned to the two men whose task it was to open the way for the others. "Wait until he steps back in.... Now!" he exclaimed.

The two men sprang forward and ran to where the man had been. Within moments they signaled the others to join them.

Buckingham rushed into the tunnel and leaped over the bodies of the two guards that had been killed. The men followed him. At the other end he made his way across the rain-drenched courtyard to the keep. He sent two men scurrying up the wooden stairway to the parapet that faced the sea. They dispatched the guards swiftly and returned to the main body of men.

"We are going in," Buckingham told his men. He pushed the door in and immediately came face to face with several French soldiers.

The fight was on. Buckingham lunged at the first man he saw, driving his sword through the man's stomach.

The men with him fought the other soldiers, who were quickly overwhelmed but not before one of them had managed to fire a pistol. The ball stuck the far wall and, ricocheting, caught Buckingham in the left shoulder. The hammerlike blow knocked him off his feet, and the seering pain that immediately followed forced him to clench his jaws together, lest he cry out in pain.

Ed was at his side, ready to offer him support.

The wound bled profusely.

"Hurry," Buckingham gasped. "The keys to the cell...they are on the wall."

One of the noblemen grabbed them, and Buckingham led his band of men up into the tower where the three officers were imprisoned.

"Are you strong enough to move?" Buckingham asked, speaking English to the hollow-cheeked men.

"Yes," one of them answered.

"Then we must hurry," the duke told them.

"Who in God's name are you?" another asked.

"No time for questions now," a nobleman answered. "We must be gone."

They clattered down the steps and ran from the keep. Already lights were moving on the far side of the courtyard.

"If we run for the tunnel," a lord said, "they will see us."

"No choice," Buckingham answered, tying a handkerchief around his wounded arm to stanch the flow of blood. "We must go. They will not be able to fire their muskets in this rain." And he began to run.

"There! There! There!" A French soldier cried out.

Buckingham raced into the tunnel. The others were close behind. As soon as they emerged, they found themselves waist-high in water. They made their way through it, listening to the shouts of the French soldiers that rose above the sound of the wind and the rain.

"They're followin' us!" Ed exclaimed, between gasps.

Buckingham did not answer. He plunged forward. There was fire in his left arm. His eyes were blurred by the rain, and the wind cut like a knife.

Once they were clear of the water, they ran along the sandy beach and finally into the woods where they had left their horses.

"Mount up," Buckingham ordered, reaching down and taking one of the ship's officers up into the saddle with him. Ed took another, and one of the lords took the third. "Now away," Buckingham shouted, putting the spur to his animal. "Away before we are caught."

They galloped along the beach and then across the fields, away from the sea. Buckingham realized it would be impossible for him to put them aboard a ship.

The men followed him without question.

They rode hard, and when they paused briefly to rest their overheated mounts, Buckingham gathered his men together and told the prisoners who he was and that his original intention was to place them aboard the *Ajax* but the weather had made that impossible.

"The only thing we can do," Buckingham said, "is to take you back to Paris with us. There we will provide you with the necessary papers and you will travel back to England on an ordinary Channel boat."

The three officers were too overwhelmed to speak, other than to profusely thank Buckingham and those with him for rescuing them.

They remounted, and rode the rest of the night and all of the next day, stopping only to rest the horses and let them drink. The rain stopped the next afternoon, and when the sun came out, its heat was as fierce as previously.

Buckingham was in pain and feverish. By the time they entered Paris, he was slumped low in the saddle. Each man went his own way.

Buckingham directed Ed to Lord Kensington's house. "I am afraid," he told his servant, "I will not be able to walk to the door . . . Would you be so kind as to assist me?" And he dropped to his knees with the world going black in front of him.

Some time later he opened his eyes and saw the face of a strange man close to him.

"Do not worry," the man told him, "I am a physician."

Then he heard Lord Kensington say, "He has been tending you these past two days."

"Two days!" Buckingham exclaimed, trying to rise. He lacked the strength and dropped back on to the pillow, panting for breath and wet with perspiration.

"You will be up and around in no time at all," the physician assured him.

Buckingham touched his wounded arm and winced with pain.

TWELVE

Richelieu sat behind his large writing table, glaring at the young lieutenant who had just finished relating what had taken place at Fort Mahon the previous night. Too angry to speak, he took several ragged breaths before he could think clearly. For two days now, Buckingham and his man Ed had not been seen at court, and several other English noblemen had also been absent. The connection between the incident at the fort and the missing Buckingham was all too obvious. And it was reinforced by his previous intelligence about M. Gerbier's inquiries as to the possibility of survivors from the *Hermes*.

The cardinal leaned against the back of his chair and, lacing his long fingers together, said, "Tell your commanding officer—"

"Excuse me, your eminence, he was killed as soon as the door to the keep was thrown open," the lieutenant said.

Richelieu winced.

"How many dead?"

"Ten, your eminence, and another five wounded," the lieutenant said in a low, unsteady voice.

Richelieu dismissed the officer and hurriedly went to Father Joseph, whom he met in the lower corridor of the palace.

"I was on my way to see you," Father Joseph told him.

"And I was coming to see you," Richelieu responded. "I think it best that we speak where there are no walls."

The Capuchin nodded, and the two found their way into the garden, where they strolled toward a copse of young willow trees near the riverbank.

Richelieu related what had happened at Fort Mahon and finished by saying, "I am sure it was Buckingham's work."

"It was," Father Joseph said. "A certain physician I know was summoned by Lord Kensington and removed a ball from the duke's left arm. It seems Buckingham was struck by a ricochet. I suspect that he should return to court looking somewhat paler than usual within a day or so."

"And the three officers?" Richelieu questioned.

"On their way to England, I would guess."

They reached the willows and stopped.

"Bide your time," Father Joseph said. "In this instance we can take no action against Buckingham, since the officers were held without Louis' knowledge. To reveal what Buckingham did would also necessitate telling the king about the officers. I think he would have difficulty understanding our reasons for imprisoning them."

"What about those with Buckingham?"

"I am sure they will keep silent about their

success," the Capuchin said. "They do not want to cause any trouble for themselves."

"And our soldiers in the fort?"

"I suggest you arrange to have them transferred," Father Joseph said. "No two to the same garrison."

"I will attend to it," Richelieu responded.

For a while the two men stood and looked out across the river. Then, without a word spoken, they returned to the palace, each going to his own apartment.

When Richelieu was at his writing table again, he could not settle down to work. The shear audacity of Buckingham's actions made him both angry and envious at the same time. He could not conceive of himself leading a similar foray. To give the orders to kill was one thing, to be able to do it himself was quite another.

The cardinal picked up his quill and tried to force himself to sign the documents that required his signature. But he could not do even that. In a pique, he threw the quill on the table and stood up. The very walls of the room seemed to close down on him. He began to pace.

Suddenly he left his office and hurried into his private rooms. He needed to be free of Buckingham, the king, of everything connected with the palace, at least for a few hours. With extraordinary swiftness, he removed his churchly vestments and dressed in clothing befitting a man of means.

Despite the danger of plague, which daily took its toll in the city, Richelieu was anxious to roam through the streets of the city, take drink and food in a café, and somewhere find a woman who would drain him of the passion that seethed in his groin and brought torment to his soul.

He stood at his window and watched the shadows lengthen. When it was quite dark, he left his room and, by means of the secret passageway, emerged into a small abandoned house several streets away from the main gate of the palace.

A short time later, he crossed the Pont Neuf and entered the first inn he came to. He was thirsty and immensely pleased with himself. He had the rest of the night to enjoy whatever pleasures came his way, and in his mind he imagined them in extraordinary detail.

Hours later Richelieu lay next to a naked woman. She smelled of sweat and wine. But he was too exhausted to care.

Buckingham knew he was dreaming but was curious about what would happen. He saw himself on a street. Nearby were some ships. He could see their masts but nothing else. There was a great deal of fog. He was going somewhere . . . and then he was inside an inn. The place looked familiar, but he could not identify it.

He sat down at a table and was given food and drink. A man suggested he go up to one of the rooms and avail himself of the pleasure one of the house women was willing to give him. He declined the offer.

The man became very angry, picked up a cudgel, and tried to strike him. They fought. And Buckingham killed him. Then he sat down to finish the food he had/ started to eat.

A hag came into the inn. She called his name.

He turned.

She told him that she had something to tell him.

He laughed.

She crabbed her way across the floor to where he was seated.

The more he looked at her, the more hideous she became. Bits of her flesh seemed to be torn away from her body. Her eyes were nothing but holes. He tried to turn away but could not move.

She took hold of his hand and bent close to it.

He cursed and pulled his hand from hers.

She cackled and shaked a bony finger at him, then used it to trace a line in the air. "Here it ends," she told him. "Here, not a minute longer. You will die here, love. Not three years from now you will be a dead man."

He studied his palm as if by staring at it he might see how his end would come.

"It is there," the hag assured him. "It will come with suddenness."

"How?" he asked.

The crone shook her head and, cackling with glee, crabbed her way to the door.

Buckingham awoke. The dream was fresh in his mind. He did not want to be afraid, but he could not stop his heart from pounding, or the terrible feeling that death would soon take him.

"I only ask," he said aloud, "that when it comes, it comes swiftly. Dear God, grant me that boon, I beseech you!"

He turned toward the window. The darkness that covered it seemed less deep. Most of the night had passed and dawn was on its way.

Lord Kensington let it be known that Buckingham had suffered a slight accident while hunting, and when he returned to the Louvre, everyone, including Louis, was most solicitous about his well-being.

"We trust," Louis said, the first time he saw Buckingham, "that you are well?"

The duke smiled and thanked the king for his concern.

Despite the outward acceptance of Kensington's story, there was much whispering about what really had happened to Buckingham. It was clear to everyone that for some of the time that the duke had been gone, so were six other English noblemen.

Mme. de Chevreuse tried to question Lord Rich, but he claimed to be totally ignorant of any information other than that the duke had been injured while hunting.

The first night that Buckingham and Anne were together again, she wept when she saw the bandage around his left arm.

"If you had been killed," she told him, "I would have taken my own life."

He silenced her with a passionate kiss. His hands caressed her naked body, and he drew pleasure from the touch of her warm silken skin.

"I love you," she told him, as she moved his hand between her naked thighs.

"This time," he said, "you must be astride me."

She laughed and quickly positioned herself over him. "You are deep in me," she whispered.

He reached up and fondled her softly rounded breasts as she sat upright.

Anne leaned slightly forward and began to rotate her hips. He raised his head and kissed her budlike nipples.

As their movements became more and more wild, he could feel her body become tense.

"Oh George ... George ... George," she moaned. "I will wither and die without you!"

Despite the pain in his left arm, he hugged her fiercely to him. And each of them reached the ultimate moment of ecstasy at the same instant....

Afterward, Anne lay astride him. He held the rounded cheeks of her buttocks in his hands, allowing his fingers to caress her lightly. "Come with me to England," he whispered. "Come with me, Anne!"

"Perhaps," she answered. "Perhaps, my love."

In the days that followed Buckingham's return, he and Richelieu played cat and mouse with each other. Each took his turn at being the mouse, though not willingly.

Buckingham quickly realized that Richelieu knew he had led the assault against Fort Mahon, and he also guessed that the cardinal was powerless to exact any sort of retribution because of it.

Buckingham pressed for an answer to King Charles' proposed alliance between England and France against Spain.

Richelieu was always evasive. Sometimes he claimed that Louis, because of his sister's marriage, was not inclined to discuss warlike matters. Other times he said, "If the alliance were more attractive, I think the king would be more disposed toward it." But he never mentioned exactly what terms would make it more attractive to Louis.

Buckingham chaffed under the delay. He was being pressed with more and more urgency by Charles' letters to bring the political business to a successful conclusion and return home with the new queen.

Then one day, when the clouds threatened rain and the air was heavy with moisture, Buckingham was determined to have a definite answer from Richelieu to communicate to Charles. He sat across from the cardinal, who was dressed in his gray cassock and red skullcap.

"My king grows impatient," Buckingham said. "He begs you to realize that France would gain all of the territory she wrests from Spain."

Richelieu nodded, knowing that Buckingham was perspiring profusely. It pleased him to know that though he could not lead an assault as the duke had done, he could, given the time, bend that man of iron to his will.

"War is an enterprise that requires much preparation, and—"

"We would gladly join England," Richelieu said with a hint of a smile, "if England would help us with our war with the Huguenots. They are here in our midst and not on our borders."

Buckingham was so surprised that he was rendered speechless.

"If you agree to help us with our war against the Huguenots," Richelieu said, "we would be honor-bound to help you with yours against Spain."

Buckingham shook his head. "It cannot be," he answered.

Richelieu smiled.

"I will send your offer to my king," Buckingham said, still finding it difficult to speak.

"That is your duty," the cardinal answered.

There was nothing left to discuss, and Richelieu brought the meeting to an end by suggesting they meet again after Charles replied to Louis' proposal.

Buckingham stood up, shook the cardinal's hand, and left his office.

As soon as he was alone, Richelieu howled with laughter. "I bested you, Buckingham," he shouted toward the door. And he poured himself a glass of wine to celebrate his victory. "Richelieu," he said, lifting his glass, "I salute you!" Then he drank, until nothing was left of the wine.

The inn was on the rue St. Agnes, in the heart of the notorious section of Paris known euphemistically as the Thieves' Market. In reality it was a very old section of the city that stood between the Cathedral of Notre Dame and the university. The streets here were extremely narrow and twisting; many of them led into cul-de-sacs, where all too often unwary strangers were waylaid by bands of cutthroats to be beaten, robbed, and frequently killed. Poverty, wretchedness, and disease made the streets common roadways for three of the four horsemen of the Apocalypse. The houses rose above the streets, blocking out the sun, and filth was everywhere.

The inn, like most of them in the Thieves' Market, was nameless. Its proprietor, a one-eyed former privateer, with an ugly scar on the right side of his face, was simply known as M. Shark. He sat across the wooden table from Chalais, who had come to the inn to meet M. Shark and discuss the business of hiring an assassin.

Chalais was dressed in clothing befitting his rank, and though the room was bathed in the wavering light of smoky torches, he was more conspicuous than he would have liked to be. Everyone else in the room was in rags that barely deserved to be called clothing. Even M. Shark's attire was torn and filthy.

Though he was half frightened to death by the men around him and more particularly by M. Shark, whose one good eye seemed to be concentrated on the gold chain he wore around his neck, Chalais was determined to have his discussion. He had already dispensed several gold pieces to various low-bred individuals, including one young whore, to meet someone like M. Shark. The whore, as it turned out, was a cousin to the innkeeper and brought him there after he had given twice what he had paid to have her spread her thighs for him.

"Jeanette," M. Shark said, referring to his niece, "says that you have a situation that needs taking care of."

Chalais nodded.

M. Shark called one of the bar maids to the table and told her to bring wine. As he spoke to her, he moved his hand under her gown. She stood there and spread her legs for him.

Fascinated, Chalais watched. He often preferred a woman to a man. When he had been Louis' favorite, he often had satisfied the king and then had found one of the servant women to satisfy himself. But now the king had taken to M. de Barras, a country bumpkin with a mop of blond hair. And he, Chalais, was denied certain privileges he had previously enjoyed. He was angry with Louis for rejecting him, so angry that he would be happy to see the king dethroned, or, as Monsieur had indicated, if it came to it, to see him dead.

"She's better than Jeanette," Shark told him with a twisted smile. "Her tongue and lips are perhaps the best in all of Paris to give pleasure."

"Perhaps I will try her later," Chalais replied.

The Shark laughed and withdrew his hand, and the barmaid went off to fetch the wine. "Now tell me what you need," he said, leaning halfway across the width of the table.

"A man who will kill another," Chalais answered in a low voice.

The Shark made a broad gesture and said, "Any man here will do that. Some for one price, some for another. Like whores, they will take what the traffic will bear."

The barmaid returned with a large pitcher of wine and two mugs. She smiled at Chalais.

He smiled back.

"My name is Jou-Jou," she said.

"Be off with you," the Shark roared. "You'll be called when you're wanted."

Jou-Jou flounced away.

"It's not hard to have a man killed," the Shark said.

"This is a very special man," Chalais explained.

"How special?"

"He will be guarded."

The Shark rubbed his unshaven jaw, making a scratching sound. "Guarded by how many?" he asked.

"One never knows," Chalais responded with a shrug. "Sometimes it seems as if no one is guarding him, but you can be sure that someone is."

"Then not only will a killer be needed but some sort of sideplay to draw the guards from him," the Shark said.

Chalais smiled. "Yes, a diversionary action...excellent!"

"A thousand gold pieces," the Shark said, striking the palm of his hand on the table. "A thousand pieces of eight and your man is as good as dead. Five hundred before and five hundred after the deed is done."

"I agree," Chalais answered. "I will pay you and you will pay—"

"Leave everything to me," the Shark told him. "Bring me five hundred pieces of eight and I will take care of everything. Now tell me, who is the victim?"

"His eminence Cardinal Richelieu."

The Shark made a soft whistling sound. "Had I known who it was beforehand, I would have asked for two thousand pieces of gold."

"I will give you three," Chalais told him, "if it is done and done to make it seem as though it were an accident."

"It's that important to you?"

"And to several others whose positions are higher than my own," Chalais answered.

The Shark offered his hand to seal the agreement and then called for Jou-Jou. "I want you to entertain my friend in every way you can," he told her with a broad wink. "He has very special tastes."

Jou-Jou quickly opened the front of her bodice and, stroking her breasts, she said, "Come, monsieur, come help me play with them." Taking Chalais' hand, she placed it on her breast. As soon as it was there, she backed away. Chalais followed her up a flight of steps and into a small room.

"Here," she told him, taking off all of her clothing, "we will enjoy ourselves."

Chalais undressed quickly and lay down on the bed so that Jou-Jou could show the talents of her wonderful tongue and lips. He closed his eyes and gave himself up to the complete voluptuousness of the experience....

Within an hour Jou-Jou had exhausted Chalais and he was soundly asleep. She dressed, opened the door, taking care to be very quiet, and hastened downstairs, where M. Shark was waiting with two men. One of them was Cahusac, one of the cardinal's men.

"He will sleep for a while," Jou-Jou said, coming up to the table.

"How much did you take from him?" the Shark asked.

"My usual price," she answered with a toss of her head.

In an instant the Shark was on his feet. He

grabbed hold of her, dug his hand inside her bodice, and pulled out a pouch of gold coins and Chalais' golden chain. With one swift movement, he struck Jou-Jou across the face with the back of his hand.

Blood spurted from her nose.

"Now get out of here before I knock your teeth out," he told her.

She ran from him.

The Shark sat down at the table again and threw the purse and chain between him and Cahusac. "I claim those as part of my fee," he said.

"In matters like this," Cahusac said, "you'll find the cardinal a very generous man. Are you absolutely sure he said that people higher than himself are interested in having the cardinal killed?"

"His words were: 'And to several others whose positions are higher than my own.' That was his answer when I asked if it was very important to have his eminence killed."

Cahusac nodded and, looking toward the steps, said to the man with him, "It is time we went for the Comte de Chalais and brought him to the Bastille for questioning."

The coach with Chalais, Cahusac, and another of the cardinal's men pounded through the streets of Paris toward the Bastille.

Chalais wept, pleaded, and promised thousands in gold if his captors would free him.

"I promise," he cried, "that I will disavow myself from—"

"Gag him," Cahusac ordered.

A handkerchief was forced into Chalais' mouth, and to hold it in place another was tied over it.

The coach rumbled on.

Chalais was so frightened he passed water and began to weep.

Neither Cahusac nor the other man made any comment. Soon the coach slowed down and stopped in front of the dark stone fortress.

Chalais was roughly pushed out of the coach. He tried to fight them by twisting away. The man without a name struck him across the face.

"Walk," he said, "or you will be dragged."

Chalais walked. He moved between Cahusac and the other man. They descended the narrow flight of stone steps that led to the torture chamber. Their footfalls and his own shallow breathing were the only sounds Chalais could hear.

Then suddenly they were there.

He tried to scream, but the gag stopped him. The torturers, stripped to the waist and wearing half masks, came toward him.

He was pushed at them.

They grabbed him by the arms.

Again he passed water. His feet refused to move.

"Have pen and ink ready," Cahusac said. "I will summon M. Sequir."

Chalais' eyes went wide with horror. He shook his head violently.

"Keep him gagged until I return," Cahusac ordered. "Let him sit down, or stand—whatever he chooses. After all, he is a count."

Tears streamed from Chalais' eyes. He knew that he would betray everyone to save himself and that he would do it without first having any pain inflicted on his person. He moved toward the chair and sat down. He was not the stuff that heroes were made of; he was born to be gently treated, to be loved by a woman, or a man.

His head drooped; he slept, knowing he would escape the pain of torture and possibly death, at least for the time being....

It was midmorning when M. Sequir presented himself to Father Joseph with Chalais' signed confession. He stood in front of the Capuchin and said, "This was taken down last night in the Bastille."

Father Joseph spread the sheaves of paper out on

his table. As soon as he saw the name, he looked questioningly up at M. Sequir.

"We did not have to torture him," M. Sequir said. 'He was all too willing to speak, as soon as I arrived and the gag was removed from his mouth."

The monk gave his attention once more to the confession. Soon he began to utter low exclamations of surprise. When he had finished reading the document, he gathered up the papers and, nodding to M. Sequir, he asked, "How much does this M. Shark know?"

"Only that some very important people wanted to have the cardinal killed," Sequir answered.

"I think M. Shark should do his swimming in the Bastille until we know more about this matter," Father Joseph said.

"He will be there before the sun goes down," Sequir answered. "But what shall we do with the Comte de Chalais?"

"Keep him," the Capuchin answered. "I need time to think about all this and then present it to his eminence the cardinal. He too will need time to study it."

"The comte is well known at court," Sequir said. 'He will be quickly missed. Perhaps even the king will have reason to ask for him?"

"The story will get out that he was last seen in the Thieves' Market," Father Joseph said. "Each day, more will be said until it seems to everyone that he was murdered. When we need him, it will be easy enough to bring him back to life."

Sequir smiled.

Father Joseph stood up. "You and Cahusac have done the cardinal a very great service," he said. "I am sure he will remember it at an opportune time in the near future." And he walked to the door with Sequir. "How many people have heard this confession?"

"Myself and the scribe who took it down," Sequir answered.

"And the scribe, can he be trusted to say nothing about it?"

"Most certainly!"

Father Joseph made the sign of the cross over the man as he bid him good day and saw him out of his office. Alone, the monk sat down and reread Chalais' confession. It certainly opened up some very interesting possibilities for Richelieu to expand his power.

THIRTEEN

    Father Joseph did not bring Chalais' confession to the immediate attention of Richelieu; he did not even mention it to the cardinal. But that very afternoon, he did send written orders to Sequir and Cahusac to remain absolutely silent about the entire matter. He also instructed them to place the former favorite of the king in a cell worthy of his rank and well removed from the rest of the prisoners. He enjoined them to treat the young count with courtesy and keep him well fed. Then he notified his network of palace spies to report any suspicious movements of the individuals mentioned in Chalais' signed confession. And the last thing he did was to increase the guards around Richelieu.

Having done those things which he thought required immediate action, Father Joseph sat back and reread the confession several more times until he had committed the entire document to memory. By then, the afternoon had slipped into the long twilight of late spring. The Capuchin left his writing table and in his own bedroom he knelt to pray and ask for divine guidance in the difficult days that he knew lay ahead of him.

After eating a frugal repast of cheese, black bread, and wine, the monk took a walk around the palace gardens, pausing now and then to admire a particular bed of flowers or watch the western sky as it changed color from the setting of the sun.

Father Joseph did not dwell on the Chalais matter. He allowed what thoughts he had to come and go without making any strenuous effort to detain any one of them. He knew from experience that it would be useless for him to try to force himself to think about a plan of action, though he fully recognized that one would be needed. Yet he had absolute confidence that sooner or later God would help him determine what should be done.

Halfway through his second circuit of the garden, Father Joseph decided to pay a visit to Chalais, hoping that he might not only offer some spiritual solace to the man but also gain some further insight into the depth of the conspiracy against the cardinal and the king. He completed his walk before he departed for the Bastille by coach.

Night had already fallen when the monk reached the towering mass of the prison. He was immediately allowed to enter and a short time later found himself in the higher reaches of the building.

"The young man occupies the northeast tower cell," the warder told him, as he opened the cell.

Father Joseph nodded and said, "I will call you when I want to leave."

The warder nodded.

A moment later the Capuchin entered Chalais' cell.

Terrified, the count stood with his back against the wall.

Father Joseph waited until the door was closed and locked before he moved farther into the cell. His eyes swept the small room. A single candle stood in an iron holder on a table. There was a bench near the table and a wooden pallet against one wall. The place smelled of urine and excrement. The food that had been brought to the count remained uneaten on a pewter plate.

"If you do not eat it," Father Joseph said, pointing to the food, "then you can be sure that the rats will."

"They have already been at it," Chalais answered in a quavering voice. "I have been standing here watching them."

The monk said nothing, but he understood the young man's fear. The Bastille's rats were infamous. Their voraciousness often led them to attack the prisoners.

"I thought we might talk," Father Joseph said, after moving away from the door to the small window, from which he was able to see a portion of the city. "This is a most difficult situation for you."

Chalais uttered a low moan but did not move.

"Perhaps you would tell me those things that burden your conscience," the monk suggested. "I will try to comfort you and—"

Chalais sank to the stone floor and began to weep.

"I am sure God accepts your tears," Father Joseph said, sitting down on the small bench near the table.

"I have confessed all." Chalais sobbed. "What more do you want me to say?"

"Only that which is true."

"I have done that."

"You named Monsieur, the queen, Mme. de Chevreuse, and—"

"The ducs Eperon, La Vatitte, and Vendôme and the Comte de Soissons," Chalais tearfully sobbed. "I know of no others."

"Are you absolutely certain?" the Capuchin questioned.

Chalais nodded; then he said, "Monsieur mentioned that certain papers would be left to make it seem as if the Duke of Buckingham might be responsible for the crime."

Father Joseph's heart began to race. "Do you know if the queen knew about that aspect of the plot?" he questioned.

"I do not know what the queen knew," Chalais answered. "I never spoke to her. She was never kindly disposed toward me. She was jealous of my relationship with her husband."

The remark sent a shiver of disgust through the monk. That the king was less than wholesome in his sexual needs had always revolted the Capuchin.

"I have given orders that you be supplied with whatever you require," he said.

"Will you notify my mother?" Chalais asked.

"Not immediately," the monk answered. "But you have my word that she will be told as soon as it becomes appropriate."

Neither man had anything more to say to the other, and Father Joseph summoned the warder. He left Chalais' cell, but not before saying a prayer for the unfortunate man and making the sign of the cross over him.

"Buckingham," he repeated aloud in the coach on the way back to the palace. And then he smiled, secure in the knowledge that God works in mysterious ways for those who work for Him.

The first day of Chalais' absence from court attracted no attention at all. But by the third day he was missed, and there were ugly rumors about his disappearance circulating among the courtiers.

Some said he was dying of the plague. Others claimed he was so despondent over the king's recent rejection that he had hanged himself, and his family was even now trying to have him buried in holy ground. And there was a third group who somehow got hold of the story that Chalais had paid a visit to the Thieves' Market and had become involved first with a whore and through her in a fight with her pimp.

But of all he people in the court, only Monsieur knew that Chalais had indeed paid a visit to the Thieves' Market to make arrangements to hire an assassin. Chalais had not told him precisely where he was going. He had preferred to keep certain of his dealings secret. But when the story of Chalais' misadventure reached him, he immediately found an excuse to visit Mme. de Chevreuse in her apartment.

She too had heard the various rumors and was very upset by them. Pacing back and forth in the privacy of her sitting room, she said, "We would be better off if he were dead."

Monsieur suggested that he might be.

"We do not know," Mme. de Chevreuse answered, "and until we do know, we must not make another move. I cannot believe he was fool enough to become involved with a whore and then fight with her pimp."

With a shrug, Monsieur commented, "After too much wine, it could have happened."

"You should have made him tell you who he was going to see," she said.

"He considered it his affair," Monsieur responded, somewhat annoyed with the rebuke. "I would not presume to interfere."

Mme. de Chevreuse knew that for her to follow that line of argument would be useless. The future King of France could be as stupidly stubborn as the present one.

"Is there any way you might be able to find out what happened?" she asked.

"I will try," he replied.

"Let me know as soon as you have any information."

"I will," he said, stepping up to her and putting his hand on her bare shoulders.

Though she was too agitated to feel any sexual need, she allowed him to take her into the bedroom, where they spent the next two hours in her bed. Before they were finished, Monsieur had aroused her to such a pitch of sexual ecstasy that she had promised to be his slave in and out of bed. Once she had regained her composure, she knew that out of bed he would do what she asked, but in bed, she would most willingly let him be her master.

Buckingham too heard the various rumors about Chalais but did not pay much attention to them, even though Anne mentioned the young count's disappearance to him. He was too involved with his own problems to devote any thought to what he considered a French problem. Besides, having met Chalais several times, he did not care for him.

But during a conference with Lord Kensington, the ambassador brought to the fore an interesting point that Buckingham could not overlook when he said, "The Thieves' Market is a strange place for someone like Chalais to go without another person."

Buckingham agreed.

"He was not a very brave man," Kensington commented, lighting his long-stemmed pipe. "I have been told that he weeps as easily as any woman. Perhaps easier than most women...Louis often made him weep."

"Are you suggesting that he did not go to the Thieves' Market?" the duke asked.

"I am only suggesting that if he did go, it was strange he went alone," Kensington answered.

Buckingham agreed but did not pursue the subject. He turned the conversation between him and Kensington toward Richelieu's absurd proposal and his need to meet with the Duc de Rohan, the commander of the Huguenot forces at La Rochelle.

"Time grows short," Buckingham said. "The meeting must be soon."

"He is already on his way to Paris," Lord Kensington answered. "But he must travel a somewhat circuitous route to the city."

"I understand," Buckingham said.

By the fourth day of Chalais' disappearance, Louis had heard the story of his former favorite's visit to the Thieves' Market and was in a rage for not having been told about it earlier. He immediately summoned Richelieu and demanded to know whether the story was true or false.

"I am sorry, your majesty," the cardinal answered, "but I have been busy in my rooms for the past few days and did not know that the Comte de Chalais had disappeared."

"I expect you to know," Louis said angrily. "I expect you to know all that goes on in France. I want you to find out if Chalais visited the Thieves' Market and if he came to any harm there. I want the culprits punished. Do you understand me?"

"Yes, sire," Richelieu answered. Hastily retreating from the royal presence, he went straight to Father Joseph's rooms, where he found the monk poring over various documents.

The cardinal was furious with the way Louis had treated him. Quivering with suppressed anger, he dropped into a chair in front of the monk's writing table. "Now," he complained, "I am to spend my time trying to find the Comte de Chalais. You know, of course, that he has been missing some four days?"

"He is not missing," Father Joseph said quietly.

"But—"

"He is a guest in the Bastille," the monk explained. "He occupies the cell in the northeast tower."

Richelieu's anger faded. It was replaced by fear of what the king would do to his friend when he learned where Chalais had spent the last four days.

Father Joseph stood up, went to a wooden cabinet, and unlocked one of the drawers. "I have something I want you to read," he said, returning with several sheets of paper.

Richelieu leaned forward and repositioned one of the candles to shed more light on the papers before him. He began to read, though now and then he glanced up at Father Joseph, who was seated directly across from him.

"Now do you understand why the Comte de Chalais is a guest at the Bastille?" the monk asked, when he saw that Richelieu had finished reading.

"Yes."

"And why I choose to keep it a secret?"

"Yes."

"Here is some additional material which I am sure will interest you," Father Joseph said. "It concerns Monsieur's visit to Mme. de Chevreuse and Buckingham's strange involvement in the plot—this time as an innocent dupe, though without too much effort, it could be turned the other way."

Under the best of circumstances Richelieu was an insomniac. When he would finally manage to drift off to sleep, it was always closer to wakefulness than to a deep and tranquil slumber. But now with his brain teeming with knowledge of the conspiracy against his life and possibly the king's, sleep was impossible, though he dearly longed for it.

"Armand," he told himself aloud, "she hates you enough to risk her own life to have yours taken from you." Uttering a deep sigh, he left his bed and went to the table, where the light from a small oil lamp cast its yellow glow over Chalais' confession. He looked down at the neat writing of the scribe who had taken down the comte's words and shook his head with disbelief.

The cardinal turned away and poured himself a glass of wine, knowing full well that no matter how much he drank, he would find neither sleep nor drunkenness and that he would experience no more than a sour stomach in the morning. He moved to the open window, still holding the glass of wine in his hand.

The night sky was ineffably beautiful, and the air thrummed from the sounds of crickets and other insects. Now and then a night bird called to its mate, or the hoot of an owl came from the eaves.

It was the kind of night when country lovers find a hay rick for their bed and let the stars look down on the exercise of their passion.

Richelieu realized how much he envied those men who were not burdened as he was; whose lives were more their own than his would ever be and who could experience the love of a woman without guilt and remorse.

He finished the wine and returned to the table to pour another glass. But instead of lifting it to his lips, he let it remain on the table while he began to pace.

Several times since he had first learned of the plot to kill him and then the king, he thought about bringing the entire matter before Louis and suggesting that Buckingham might have had a role in it. But that would most certainly bring England and France into an armed conflict, which France could not tolerate at the present. And Buckingham might be exonerated if the others involved testified that he had no knowledge of the conspiracy. There was also the risk that Buckingham's affair with the queen would be brought to Louis' attention, though Richelieu found it difficult to see how the king could not be aware of it unless he chose not to be, which was a definite possibility.

The cardinal stopped at the table and sipped a bit of wine before commencing to pace again.

His plan to destroy Buckingham had already been formed. He wanted to bring him low in the eyes of the queen and the rest of the world and then have him killed. He had a quantity of information that would damn him in Anne's eyes, not the least of which was his plan to make war against her native country. But he also knew about his forthcoming meeting with the Duc de Rohan, and when his spies furnished him with a report about what was discussed at that meeting, he would be ready to show Anne the perfidiousness of her lover—a man who would make love to her while thinking nothing of making war against her native country and the country of which she was queen.

Richelieu was determined to affect a break between Buckingham and the queen. He already had other people working on his behalf in England to bring about the duke's fall and eventually his death.

Felton was most anxious to avenge the death of his brother, and Giroux was carefully laying plans to allow the young man to do what so many before him had failed to do.

The cardinal went back to the table, drank more of the wine, and went to the window again. He looked across to Mme. de Chevreuse's windows; they were quite dark. He wondered if Monsieur was with her. With a shrug, he went back to his bed and dropped down on it. One of Louis' greatest fears was that he would meet the same fate as his father, who had been assassinated when Louis was still a child. The possibility that he would meet his maker without having had the opportunity to be given the last rites was something that truly haunted the king. To tell him about the plot would seal the fate of all those involved.

"I will have to find another way," Richelieu said aloud. Though he knew Chalais was as good as dead now, he would do everything in his power to save Anne. "As for the others, the queen mother will protect Monsieur and Mme. de Chevreuse will find a way to protect herself. The other noblemen will live or die according to the vagaries of the court. The most important question that I must answer is: when do I tell the king?" Toward the end of what he was saying, his words became slurred and there were long pauses between them.

Richelieu lay in a restive sleep that was filled with mutilated men hanging from strange crosses. He moaned a great deal and several times called out for mercy.

Then suddenly he was awake.

Dawn had long since passed; a new day was at hand. He left his bed and saw through the window that the sun was shining.

As he went through his morning prayers and ablutions, Richelieu made the decision to withhold Chalais' confession from the king until Buckingham and his entourage were back in England. Then Louis would be less embarrassed by the scandal that would sweep the court, which would touch not only on his brother but also on his queen. For now he would wait, keeping Chalais in the Bastille and at the same time playing a game of nerves with Monsieur and Mme. de Chevreuse which they could not hope to win, because they would not even be aware that they were players.

Even before he had his breakfast, Richelieu hurried to Father Joseph's rooms to tell the monk what he had decided about what he now had labeled the Chalais Affair.

FOURTEEN

It had rained all through the night, starting the previous evening with a series of savage thunderstorms and a cold north wind that brought relief from the heat. Now in the predawn grayness the mists swirled and undulated across the fields and woods that lay beyond the city gates.

Buckingham had been loath to leave Anne's bed, but his rendezvous with the Duc de Rohan had been set for early that morning. The meeting place had already been changed three different times, since it had been learned that Richelieu had somehow become aware of the forthcoming meeting.

Lord Kensington and Lord Rich rode alongside Buckingham, followed by several of the men who had been with the duke at Fort Mahon. Everyone in the party was armed with a pistol and a sword.

"Will you be returning to England soon?" Lord Kensington asked, knowing that the meeting with the Duc de Rohan would bring to an end all of Buckingham's business in France.

"I have already given word to the various lords to make preparations for the return trip. The king is anxious for his bride."

"And are you not anxious to return home as well?" Lord Rich questioned.

"I am weary of France, if that is what you mean," Buckingham answered. "But once I am home I will be in the thick of it again." He said nothing of his hope to take Anne with him when he left, or of the possibility of her joining him at some future time. Recently she had given him more hope than ever that she would be willing to leave France and go to England to be with him. He had never believed it would be possible for him to love a woman as he loved her.

"By the way," Kensington said, "I heard something very strange the other day. I meant to tell you, but with the various changes attending this meeting, I forgot about it until a moment ago. Mind you now, I have no reason to suspect there is any truth in it, but one of my men—an Englishman, whom I employ as a groom, or at least that is what he appears to be, though he renders more important services in other ways—found himself with a whore in the Thieves' Market. She took him to an inn, where he overheard some very strange conversation. It seems the owner of the inn is a man called the Shark. He appears to have disappeared, taken away by two men, one of whom fits the description of Cahusac, the cardinal's chief henchman."

"Why should that interest me?" Buckingham asked.

"No reason," Kensington answered. "But I thought it interesting because the Shark was taken the morning after Chalais was in the same inn and spent time with the same whore that serviced my man."

"Are you inferring that...that the Shark killed Chalais?" the duke asked.

"No," Kensington said with a shake of his head. "If that were the case, we would know about it. But I warrant you, there is some other connection there, though I could not begin to guess what it might be."

Buckingham shrugged. He had already lost interest in the matter and was too occupied with his own thoughts to be concerned about the connection between some Frenchman with the ridiculous name of Shark and the Comte de Chalais. It was obvious that Richelieu and Louis had no intentions of forming an alliance with England against Spain. He had already communicated the results of his conversations with the cardinal to Charles and had received instructions to assure the Duc de Rohan of England's backing in all the Huguenots' endeavors to keep themselves free of Louis' control. Buckingham saw in this message more of Charles' spiteful anger than good statecraft. But he was duty-bound to deliver the message.

They walked their horses across a narrow wooden bridge that spanned a rocky, swiftly flowing stream. The mists had thickened, making it necessary for them to remain even closer together than they previously had been. Everything dripped with moisture and their clothing was sodden. Water ran down their faces and into their beards.

"How much longer?" Lord Rich asked.

"A few leagues yet," Kensington answered. "We will be met by some of the duc's men."

After a few minutes they broke out of the wood and moved onto a broad expanse of field, where they followed a stone wall. The mist over the open field was considerably less dense than it had been in the woods, and already the first rays of the rising sun were beginning to dispel the ground fog. Whole patches of countryside were suddenly revealed and just as swiftly concealed by the rapid movement of the mist.

Sun touched them briefly, and Buckingham remarked, "How good its warmth feels."

"Aye," Kensington agreed. "But when all of this is burned off, we will pray for a bit of cool."

And he was right. As soon as the sky was clear, the sun was fierce and the air was filled with swarms of small insects. Buckingham began to gallop, and the rest followed suit. Then quite suddenly he reined in and pointing off to the right, he said, "Riders. Let us hope they are the duc's." He removed the pistol from his belt, cocked it, and pointed it toward the oncoming riders. The rest of his party flanked him and pointed their weapons at the strangers.

The horsemen stopped within hailing distance, and their leader called out for Lord Kensington.

"Yes," Kensington answered.

"Have your men follow us!" the man shouted, wheeling around and galloping off with his men behind him.

The meeting between Buckingham and the Duc de Rohan took place in what once had been a farmhouse but now was only an empty shell with a burned-off roof and one of the walls partially down.

The Duc de Rohan was as tall and broad as Buckingham. He was several years older than the duke, but he also possessed a commanding presence. Neither of them wasted time on formalities. With a vigorous handshake, they walked away from the rest of the group and, leaning against a sun-drenched wall, immediately began their discussion.

Buckingham delivered Charles' token of support to the leader of the Huguenots, who accepted the ring with a nod and said, "Your sovereign's gift is most appreciated. But it is not gifts or words we need. We need food...we need weapons and we need men to fight for our cause."

Buckingham reached down and picked up a rock,

not because he wanted the stone but rather because he needed a brief interval of time to think of a reply. The duc was certainly frank, and he had to be as straightforward in what he would say.

"I cannot make commitments to satisfy any of your needs," he said. "We are not prepared to go to war with France over the religious question at this time. Charles has just taken a Catholic wife. He has made many concessions to the Catholics in England, and he hopes to persuade his brother-in-law, Louis, to accord the Protestants of France the same rights that other Frenchmen have."

"Richelieu will never permit him to do it," the Duc de Rohan replied without any hesitation. "The cardinal wants to see us destroyed, and we will be soon if England does not come to our aid." Suddenly there was a tone of great sadness in his voice and a weary look on his face. "We will not survive another assault against us."

"How bad is the situation at La Rochelle?"

"More than half the garrison is ill, and we are all hungry."

Buckingham pulled gently on his beard and in a low voice he said, "I will present your plight to the king. The decision is his as to what will or will not be done."

"But you have the power to sway him," the duc said. "I implore you to sway him to support our cause."

"I will state your situation as honestly as I can, but—"

"You can recommend."

"Yes," Buckingham replied. "But I will not if it is not in England's best interests."

"Then we have nothing more to say to one another," the Duc de Rohan said. Turning away, he immediately rejoined the others, leaving Buckingham standing at the wall.

Buckingham waited until the Huguenots had ridden away before he walked to where the members of his party were waiting. He said nothing and mounted his horse. He was not angry at the Duc de Rohan; he understood the man's disappointment.

After they had recrossed the fields and entered the woods again, he said to Kensington, "The Huguenots need much more than moral support at this time."

"And will England provide it?"

"I think not," Buckingham said, ducking to avoid a low branch.

With a silent nod, Kensington agreed.

Buckingham said nothing more all the way back to Paris. That he had not been able to be more help to the Huguenots' cause bothered him. He understood Richelieu's desire—nay, need—to destroy them. Perhaps if England's navy had been in a better state of readiness, he might have considered suggesting to the king that one or two squadrons of ships be assigned to aid the Huguenots at La Rochelle, but the navy had barely that many squadrons fit for sea now. Still, if there was ever a cause he would support, it would most definitely be that of the Huguenots.

When they reached the city, Buckingham and the other nobles rode straight for the palace, stopping now and then when the press of traffic was too great for them to move through. The day had indeed turned out to be very hot. But it was not nearly as humid as it had been.

As soon as Buckingham reached the stables, he dismounted and hurried to his rooms, where he intended to bathe and dress before going down to the Great Hall. But as soon as he reached the hallway that led to his apartment, he saw Mme. de Chevreuse and called to her.

She did not stop, though he was certain she heard him.

He called again, this time in a much louder voice.

But Mme. de Chevreuse continued to hurry down the long corridor and finally made a turn that took her out of sight.

Buckingham pulled on his beard, wondered why

she had not stopped, and then with a shrug of his shoulders entered his apartment. The early ride and his brief meeting with the Duc de Rohan had tried him much more than he had realized.

He went through his apartment calling for Ed. Then he found him lying on the floor and sweating profusely. The former wherryman was sick with the plague.

Buckingham stayed with Ed, doing all he could to make the sick man more comfortable. But there was little he could do other than apply wet compresses to soothe Ed's fevered brow.

Several times the wherryman tried to speak, but his tongue was too swollen for him to make anything more than unintelligible sounds.

Now and then Buckingham took some wine, but he had nothing in the way of food. As soon as he could, he sent a servant with a message to Anne, telling her of Ed's illness and explaining that he intended to remain with his servant until the fever broke or the man died. But from the signs he was almost certain death would claim the unfortunate man.

The day drifted on, and Ed's body showed signs of the dark buboes that accompanied the disease. Ed was in pain and tears came often to his eyes, but he neither cried out nor whimpered. Twice Buckingham tried to give him water, but because of his swollen tongue, he could not swallow.

Buckingham stood by the window and wondered if he too would come down with the dreaded disease. If he did, he did not imagine that too many people would be willing to tend him, and though Anne might, he supposed that she would be prevented, if not by members of the royal family, then by Richelieu. Without really understanding why he juxtaposed the cardinal and Anne, he suddenly realized that Richelieu was in love with the queen, in love with her the way he himself was. He wondered if Anne knew.

A low moan from Ed turned his attention to the servant. He left the window and went to the bed.

Ed was coughing up blood.

Buckingham wiped the man's face and put another compress across his forehead. Then he sat down next to the bed. If he was right about Richelieu, then it would be more difficult for her to leave France than he had previously thought. The cardinal would not let her go.

Buckingham looked at Ed.

The man's head lolled off to one side; he was dead. Buckingham closed the wherryman's eyes, and with the aid of another servant he carried the body out of the room and down into the lower reaches of the palace. Before the evening was over, the duke had Ed buried in a decent grave at the base of a small hill that overlooked the river.

When Buckingham returned to the Louvre, he ordered all of Ed's personal belongings burned along with the bedding and the clothes he himself had worn while tending the man. Then he finally had his bath.

The loss of Ed bothered Buckingham; he considered it an ill omen for the future. And much later, when he was with Anne, he said to her, "I had planned to make a valet out of Ed. He was quick to learn and would have eventually done well for himself. But that, like many of my other plans, never came to fruition. They are stillborn." And she comforted him in the only way she knew how: with her love and with her softly yielding body.

Mme. de Chevreuse had heard Buckingham call to her, but just a short while before she had received an urgent message from Monsieur asking her to meet him in his apartment. That the request had come so early in the morning was an indication of one of two possibilities: his passion for her made it imperative that he be with her, or some serious development had occurred that he thought she should be made aware of.

The moment she entered his sitting room and saw him standing under a large painting of Zeus, she knew the nature of the meeting had nothing at all to do with passion.

Monsieur gestured to one of the chairs and bade her sit down.

"I would rather stand," she told him.

"Wine?" he asked.

"If you please," she answered, quickly aware of his formality.

He handed her a glass of Burgundy and said, "I have heard some disturbing rumors about Chalais."

"Indeed," she answered, sipping her wine. Chalais' name brought a sudden flutter to her heart. But she remained outwardly composed.

"He is being held in the Bastille," Monsieur said.

"What?" She asked. Her fingers opened. The glass she held dropped to the floor and shattered. Now her heart was racing. "Where did you hear that? Or better still, from whom did you hear it?"

Monsieur gestured to a small couch.

This time she accepted. Her legs felt as if they would give way under her.

Monsieur took hold of her hand and guided her to the couch. When they were both seated, he said, "My inquiries have led me to an inn located in the Thieves' Market. It is owned by a one-eyed cutthroat named the Shark. He too is in the Bastille."

"I still do not understand," Mme. de Chevreuse admitted. She was perspiring profusely, and to prevent her hands from shaking, she held them clasped together.

"Chalais was seen talking to the Shark. Later he went upstairs with a whore. During the time he was upstairs, the Shark went out. No one ever saw Chalais come down, but the Shark returned with two men, one of whom fits Cahusac's description."

"Holy Mother of God protect us!" Marie exclaimed, crossing herself.

"If Chalais is in the Bastille," Monsieur said, "Richelieu must have his signed confession."

With a slow nod, she agreed. She whispered, "We must now fight for our lives. Treason is punishable by death, to say nothing of the torture that would precede it."

"If the cardinal has a signed confession," Monsieur asked, leaning forward to rest his elbows on his knees, "why has he not used it against us?"

"He has reasons," Marie said. "You can be sure that he does nothing without having a reason."

Monsieur moved to the empty hearth. Standing with his hand braced against the mantel, he told her, "I for one do not intend to answer to the cardinal. I will speak with my mother, and she in turn will discuss the entire matter with Louis. I am sure my brother will allow himself to be persuaded by our mother."

Mme. de Chevreuse said quietly, "You are deluding yourself, Gaston, if you think your mother holds more power over your brother than the cardinal does."

"Then what would you suggest I do?" he asked, his voice rising in pitch.

"Nothing. Because nothing will be done to you, at least nothing serious. Louis does not have an heir. You must be there to take the throne if anything should happen to him. Once Louis learns of Anne's complicity, he will avoid her bed completely. You are safe in that you are a male and next in line for the throne."

Monsieur moved away from the hearth. His hand went to his beard several times before he said, "You understand that now there can be nothing between us. What I mean is that it would be best if we did not indulge ourselves with—"

"Yes," Mme. de Chevreuse said, forcing herself to stand, "you are quite right." Then with a tight smile she added, "It was—" She could not finish, and with a shake of her head she went straight to the door and left Monsieur's apartment. Her grand scheme had failed. Now she would have to bargain with Richelieu for her life, and though she knew he could be tender and giving, she also knew that once his ire was inflamed, he could be completely intractable.

Richelieu was walking in the garden, enjoying the cool of the evening and watching the colors change in the western sky. Though a totally pragmatic man, he had a keen appreciation of beauty and sometimes thought that if he had the time to dabble he would very much like to paint trees and women. The shape of each was far more beautiful than anything else that he could think of, though the sea held a special appeal for him as well. The western sky was a deep vermilion edged with mauve. He nodded appreciatively and walked to a marble bench overlooking the river.

Suddenly he realized that someone was approaching him. He turned and, seeing Mme. de Chevreuse, stood up.

"Your eminence," she began to say as she approached him.

"No need for that now," Richelieu told her with a wave of his hand. "I am just here to enjoy a few minutes of relaxation."

She nodded understandingly.

"Would you care to walk?" he asked.

"I would like that very much," she told him. "The court is still agog over Buckingham's gesture to his dying servant."

Richelieu did not respond immediately. When he had first heard of what Buckingham had done he thought him a fool. But upon some reflection, he realized that whatever else the duke was, he was incredibly loyal to those who served him and to those he served in turn.

"He is a brave man," Richelieu said. "It is easy to see why men follow him, even if he leads them blindly into hell."

Mme. de Chevreuse was not prepared to hear Buckingham praised by Richelieu, of all men. "So he has gained your love too," she mocked. "I never thought that would happen."

"Respect," Richelieu corrected, turning toward the river at the very moment two large fish leaped free of the water and dropped back into it with a sharp slapping sound. "I find that it is always wiser to respect my enemies than to undervalue their abilities and achievements."

They continued to walk in silence.

"The king will be going to his summer residence," Richelieu said, "and our English guests will be returning home, taking their new queen with them."

"When?"

"Within a few days," the cardinal answered. "Five at the very most."

"Perhaps then life at court will return to a more normal condition," Mme. de Chevreuse commented.

"Oh, I doubt that," Richelieu answered. "There are always things that upset the tranquillity of the court."

"I suppose you are right," Mme. de Chevreuse said, wondering if she should take her leave or stay and have the discussion that sooner or later she must have with him. Had she not seen him alone in the garden, she would have never ventured to approach him in such an informal setting. She would have asked to speak with him in his office.

Richelieu turned toward the west again. The sky, no longer red and mauve, had become considerably darker. Night was almost on them.

"We must talk, Armand," Mme. de Chevreuse said, using his given name to emphasize the urgency of her demand.

Richelieu stopped. He had not suspected that she might have had an ulterior motive for walking with him, and it had not occurred to him that she might have discovered what had been done with Chalais.

"You are not in a position to say what we must do,"

he answered in an ordinary tone of voice. "But I know what I must do, and when the time is right I will do it."

"That is your duty," she answered.

"Then I do not see what you think we must talk about," he told her, starting to walk again.

She reached out and, catching hold of his arm, stayed his movement. "Anne," she said softly. "We must talk about Anne."

With a swift motion, Richelieu brushed her hand away. His blood pounded in his ears.

"My life and property," she told him, "in exchange for your life and honor."

He was livid.

"Anne told me," she said, nodding her head. "I would be forced to make her discredit you."

"Bitch!" he exclaimed in a tight voice. "Bitch! You would have had me killed and then—"

"My life and property," she repeated, "in exchange for your life and honor."

They glared at each other for several moments. Neither of them flinched or turned away.

"I can promise nothing," Richelieu told her.

"Then you will protect me?"

"Yes," Richelieu said with a nod. "I will protect you." And turning, he hurriedly left the garden. He had never expected Anne to reveal what he had done to her. He had never expected to protect himself at the expense of his duty. Angrier now than he had been in a long time, he was determined to hurt Anne as much as she had hurt him, and he knew exactly how he would do it.

FIFTEEN

Anne felt besieged. She did not know how to cope with her own feelings. She had trusted Buckingham with her love so completely that even to think he had abused that trust was enough to bring tears to her eyes. To think she had been on the verge of telling him that she had decided to return to England with him!

She paced back and forth in her bedroom, wondering how to broach the subject of his perfidy to him. Was he using her for naught but his own pleasure, as Richelieu had claimed, or did he really love her as he had sworn a thousand times over?

Anne paused and looked toward the canopied bed. How many times had she lain there with him, savoring the feel of his lips on her throat, his hands on her breasts, as they'd made love?

"And yet," she whispered, "he would make war on my native country and aid those who fight against France."

Anne had always taken it for granted that there was a difference between the love of a man for a woman and that of a woman for a man. Yet when she had been in Buckingham's arms, her lust had matched his and his tenderness had matched hers. There did not seem to have been any difference in their love for one another.

Dressed for bed, Anne waited impatiently for Buckingham to come to her. She had to know the truth.

Anne dropped down on the bed. She leaned back into the pillows. With a loud sigh, she closed her eyes. She hated Richelieu with as much passion as she loved Buckingham, and though she did not trust the cardinal, she knew he would not have challenged her to discover the truth for herself if his accusations were not valid.

"Oh George," Anne whispered aloud, "what am I to do?"

A moment later she crossed her arms over her breasts. She could feel her nipples through the thinness of her nightdress.

"Do I let him make love to me first," she asked, "or do I first confront him with what I was told?"

Tears welled up in her eyes, and she placed the back of her hand across her mouth to stifle a sob that made her throat ache with pain. That she might never again feel the press of his body on hers or know the deliciousness of his kiss brought her to a pitch of almost unendurable agony. But even with that strange ineffable pain that made her cold one moment and hot the next, she could not stop herself from saying aloud, "I am the daughter of a king and a queen in my own right. I must demand a reckoning; I must be answered. If I have been ill used, then he must know I know. He must weep. Even as I am weeping I will make him weep. By all that is holy in this world and the next, I will make him weep for abusing my love. But he must not find me weeping; he must find me resolute."

Buckingham was very tired. He had spent most of the afternoon and evening with members of his retinue organizing the return journey to Calais. There were just as many problems attending the order of march now as there were when they had left London. But somehow he had manged either to solve them with a viable suggestion, or to suggest with a laugh that the problem was more imagined than real.

He was looking forward to being with Anne. Time—their time together—was rapidly dwindling. That he would soon leave her weighed heavily on him, and though he tried not to think about their parting, it hovered in his thoughts like some dark cloud that promised a gray sky and chilling rain.

But when he greeted her near the empty hearth of her drawing room, he was faced with another problem.

"I put the question to you again," Anne said, looking at him from across the room. "Did you attempt to draw France into an alliance with your country to make war on Spain?" Though she spoke with a tremor in her voice, her words were precise.

"What I did or did not do," he answered, "has no relationship to my love for you."

"I am the daughter of the King of Spain. What about my love for my father?"

"I am not challenging that," Buckingham said. "What I did was a matter of statecraft. That you should even suggest that it had any bearing on my feelings for you is absolutely absurd."

"It is absurd that you come to my bed at night and during the day seek to destroy my father's kingdom. That is what is absurd."

Buckingham did not ask who had told her about his request. He said, "I do not know what Richelieu intends to gain by setting you against me, but by all that I hold sacred, I love you, Anne. What I do in the way of statecraft, I do for my king. I am his instrument."

"And as his instrument did you also plot with the Huguenots against me?"

"Not against you," he said, advancing toward her. "Surely you cannot believe that?"

She stayed his movement with a swift backward motion of her hand. "I am the Queen of France," Anne responded. "Those who plot against France also plot against me."

"Are those Richelieu's words?" he asked, his voice hard with anger. "He loves you, Anne. It is only recently that I came to understand that. He will stop at nothing to keep you from loving me. See how he has already made trouble between us. Would I have asked you to come to England if my feelings for you were not true?"

"You are the original author of the trouble between us," she told him.

Seeing that he would not be able to reason with her, Buckingham said, "I will not plead for your bed this night, or any other night. I love you, Anne. If you do not know and believe that, you know and believe nothing. All that you accuse me of, I have done for my king, but my love for you is my own. It is, perhaps, all I have that is my own."

Turning her head away, Anne did not answer. She had hoped he would plead more passionately for her forgiveness, but he had never mentioned the word. All he had asked was that she understand he had acted in the service of his king.

Despite the acrimony, Buckingham could not help but feel the need to hold her in his arms. He crossed the few paces between them to take her to him.

"No," she said, struggling against his embrace. "You have practiced your statecraft while plowing my field. It was perfidious to do that. Perfidious in the extreme."

Buckingham stepped back. She had never before refused his embrace. "It did not occur to me that we would ever part in any way but what we were to each other. But since it is your will for us not to be lovers, I must abide by it." And with a swift bow, he left her bedroom and stalked back to his own apartment.

He was so full of rage that he would have sought Richelieu out and challenged him to a duel if the man had not been a member of the church. He poured himself a glass of wine and drank it swiftly. Couldn't Anne see what Richelieu had done? Buckingham thought she should have shown more understanding.

He did not see how she could have become so confused. "England's war would be war against Spain," he said aloud. "It would not be mine, though I would have to take part in it. She must understand that!" He struck the palm of his left hand with the balled fist of his right. "Damn her to hell, she does not realize I am lackey to the king whenever it suits him to be the king."

He drank more wine and decided it would be best if he left Paris with the vanguard rather than traveling with the main body of the column. That way he would not give Anne additional insult by being so close to her and yet so distant.

He drank a great deal of wine. And staggering to his bed, he dropped his sword along the way.

"It was all a beautiful dream," he said aloud. "And all beautiful dreams, like life itself, must come to an end. But this ending was sad, very sad indeed." Turning his face into a huge soft pillow, he fought the threatening tears.

And when he finally slept the old hag came to him again.

"When?" he asked. "Tell me, when?"

"After the wars," she answered.

"Perhaps sooner?"

"After the wars," she cackled. "After the wars."

Buckingham smiled in his sleep.

By midmorning the following day, Buckingham had left Paris. He traveled with the vanguard, taking with him the men who had been on the raid of Fort Mahon.

He had left the palace without any fanfare. Shortly before leaving, he had sent word to Anne through Mme. de Chevreuse that he had wanted to say goodbye to her. But she had claimed to be indisposed. He had accepted the answer with a silent nod and had gone off to take his leave of the king.

Though all the amenities of the situation had been observed between them, neither one had pretended to be the least bit sorry that the time for leavetaking had arrived. Louis had bade him to take care of his sister, and he had promised that he would. Buckingham had shaken the king's hand, and the king had kissed Buckingham on each cheek. Richelieu had not been present, and Buckingham had made no effort to see him.

The line of march would take them through the city of Amiens and finally to Calais, where they would board the ships already waiting to take them across the Channel. Buckingham intended to reach England at least three days before the main body of the cortege. He wanted to see Charles and explain France's position to him with regard to the alliance against Spain, but even more important, he wanted to discuss England's stance toward the Huguenots. The French Protestants were more of a thorn in Richelieu's side than they were in Louis', and he would have liked to twist the thorn just enough to make the cardinal bleed a bit.

Though the day was bright with sunshine, a strong breeze kept the riders cool and made their flags flap with a martial air. Buckingham was grimly silent and rebuffed any attempt made to speak with him. Several times the duke looked back over his shoulder, hoping to see a rider bearing a message from Anne. None came, and he knew none would come.

Despite the fact that all through his life Buckingham had been surrounded by people, he had often been a lonely man. But never had he felt his loneliness as intensely as he did now.

He shook his head, spurred his mount, and galloped the animal until he and the horse were wet with sweat and breathing hard. But his loneliness was not assuaged, and his rage, if anything, was more inflamed than ever.

Toward evening, Buckingham noticed how few people they saw during the day and commented as much to one of the lords close by.

"The plague, my lord, has frightened them away," the courtier answered. "They have even left the fields unplowed. This winter will see much hunger in France."

Buckingham nodded. He was more determined than ever to convince Charles to help the Huguenots. First with food, then with arms. Perhaps he could make Richelieu bleed a great deal. Perhaps he could bring him low.

Father Joseph paced back and forth, stopping now and then to look at Richelieu, who was seated behind the writing table, his slender face awash with the fading light of late afternoon. Until a few minutes before, he had had no idea that Richelieu had told the queen about Buckingham's attempt to bring England and France together against Spain and about his meeting with the duc de Rohan—the import of which, though they did not have any direct report, had to be against the king, since the Huguenots were in open rebellion against the crown. Nor had he known that Buckingham was already on his way to Calais. The monk frowned and shook his head.

"Say what you must," Richelieu told him.

"It was foolish to bring the queen into state matters."

Richelieu stood up and said, "I had information

that she intended to leave France with Buckingham, and if not that, then to join him later."

Father Joseph shook his head. "You let your own feeling get in the way of your logic, Armand," the Capuchin commented. "You have given Buckingham a reason to destroy you, or at least to try to destroy you. Until now he had no idea that you were trying to have him killed. But now, even if he had suspicions because of Dupris, those suspicions would be confirmed. Even more to the point, he suspects your passion for the queen."

Richelieu flushed but did not attempt to argue with the monk.

"Buckingham must not be allowed to leave France alive," Father Joseph said. "Take the matter to the king. Tell him all you know about Buckingham's activities and about Buckingham's affair with Anne, though I am sure he knows but refuses to admit it. Tell him that Buckingham must be brought back to Paris in chains and charged with spying, and high crimes against the state, and that the famous duke must be put to death, regardless of the consequences."

Richelieu was on his feet. He had never known the Capuchin to speak with such passion in his voice. And he answered, "I will send several of my men after Buckingham."

"You must tell the king what really took place at Fort Mahon," Father Joseph said. "Make him understand that he has been host to a viper."

"And what about the business of Chalais?"

"Let us take care of Buckingham while we can," Father Joseph said. "Chalais is not going to leave the Bastille. Besides, if you hand Louis two problems that need immediate solutions he is more than likely to do nothing about either one. Stop Buckingham now!"

"I will go to the king immediately," Richelieu replied.

"Do nothing, Armand, until the king orders it. You already have much to answer for, and by taking matters into your own hands, you might exacerbate the situation. You must tread very carefully."

Louis remained absolutely motionless in his chair as he listened to Richelieu's account of Buckingham's activities. The color rose in his otherwise pale cheeks, and his breathing quickened.

He had known about the duke and Anne but had chosen to overlook the affair, suspecting that others in his court would do the same. In a very real sense Buckingham's passion for Anne had relieved him of the odious duty of having to go to her bed. He had in odd moments even hoped that she would become pregnant. Though the heir would in truth have been Buckingham's, he could have claimed it and no one would have disputed him.

He was livid when he heard about the raid on Fort Mahon and demanded to be told why he had not been informed about the English officers who were being kept there and the assault that freed them.

"Sire," Richelieu explained, "it was my intention to tell you, but events moved too swiftly."

Louis was on his feet. He did not want to know what events the cardinal was talking about. He was being forced, pressured to making a decision that could plunge France into a war with England and deny his sister her groom.

He shouted for a servant and ordered him to fetch the queen. "We will wait until she arrives," he growled at the cardinal, "before we continue this discussion."

"As you wish, your majesty," Richelieu answered, knowing that Louis was once again procrastinating. "But every delay puts Buckingham farther away from us."

Louis pretended not to hear. He walked to the window and stared out at his garden. He was more chagrined by the daring Buckingham had exhibited in the raid on Fort Mahon than by the duke's affair with Anne, though he knew he must react to that as a oint of honor.

He turned toward Richelieu. "Why were you holding three English officers captive when we are not at war with England?"

"Sire, their ship carried—"

"If anyone else had done that," Louis said, "I would have him thrown in the Bastille. Count yourself lucky that you are a man of the church."

Richelieu flushed. His impulse was to leave the room and abandon Louis to his own fate, but more than Louis was involved. He could abandon Louis, but he could not leave France's fate in the hands of someone like Louis.

Suddenly the door opened and Anne was announced.

She entered the room, her coal-black eyes moving from Louis to Richelieu and back to her husband.

She tried not to show her fear, but she was very frightened. Not five minutes before Louis had summoned her she had been told by Mme. de Chevreuse that their scheme to undo Richelieu had gone awry, and there was every reason to believe that the cardinal had her name as well as those of the other conspirators.

And she had asked, "Do you think he will press the matter?"

"When it suits his purpose," Marie had answered.

She had not had the opportunity to say anything more before the king's servant had arrived.

Anne waited until the door closed behind her before she asked why she was sent for. It was a great effort for her to keep her voice steady, and to speak in a tone that simulated if not anger, then most surely annoyance.

"I have been told," Louis said, "that you have cuckolded me with Buckingham."

Anne flushed. Her heart quickened.

"True or not true?" Louis demanded, his voice rising in anger.

Anne looked at Richelieu. She hated him more than she believed possible.

"I am waiting for an answer," Louis shouted.

"If you did not favor your young men, I would not have been forced to—"

"Silence!" he screamed. "Richelieu, arrest Buckingham. I want him back here in Paris. As for you, strumpet, whore, I will attend to you later. Go to your rooms." And turning to Richelieu, he said, "I will have him publicly drawn and quartered. By all that is holy, I will punish that man."

Anne flung open the door and rushed from the room. Once she was back in her own apartment, she quickly penned a note to Buckingham, warning him of the danger. Now full of remorse for having sent him from her, she ended her brief message with: "I have never loved another man, nor will I. My love for you is all I have, and I will keep it until the day that I die. I do not know what the future holds for me, but whatever it is, it will always be lacking if you are not there to share it with me." She signed it, "Your beloved Anne." Then she dispatched it with Mme. de Chevreuse to Lord Kensington with instructions to send her message to Buckingham without delay, since the duke's life might well depend on how rapidly he received it.

As soon as she was alone, Anne knelt and prayed to the Virgin Mary, asking her to intercede on her behalf. "I cannot deny that I am an adulteress, nor can I deny that I delighted in the pleasures of the flesh. But the sin is mine and not George's. If I were more steadfast in my faith, I would not have gone to his bed. I am the guilty one and not he. I beg you to keep him safe. Protect him and I will renounce all worldly pleasures. I will devote my entire life to the church, and if it should please you, I offer my life for his." She could say no more and began to sob.

Suddenly she felt another presence in the room. She raised her head and saw Richelieu. She stood up.

"Get out," she hissed. "Get out. Crawl through the walls like the loathsome creature you are."

"I entered by way of the doorway," he answered, ruffled by her anger.

"Then leave the same way."

Richelieu did not move. And in a low voice, he said, "I did not come here to be sent away."

She turned her back to him.

"That only removes me from your sight," he told her, "but changes nothing else."

She wheeled around. "If I were a man," she said, "I would kill you."

"I know that too," he answered in the same low tone and with his eyes going to slits.

"Since you know that," she said in an icy voice, "I should think you would also know that I have nothing to say to you."

"Ah, but I have something to say to you," he told her, moving toward her and stopping when he was slightly less than an arm's length from her.

"Say it then and be gone!"

"I will give you Buckingham's life for what you will give me," he said calmly.

"What? How dare you—"

"I want a simple yes or no," Richelieu told her in that same low voice. "I heard you praying. Think of me as God's instrument...God's justice."

For an instant the room seemed to be spinning around her. She closed her eyes. "My body," she whispered, looking at Richelieu, "for George's freedom?"

"Your body and your solemn vow never to see Buckingham again. I will not ask you to stop communications with him, but I demand that you never allow yourself to be alone with him. Those are my terms, nothing more and certainly nothing less."

"Give me time to think."

He shook his head. "A yes or no is all I require," he told her.

Anne slowly nodded.

Richelieu turned and left her sitting room. He had won the queen after all.

Buckingham stood on the windswept stern of the sloop *Aries* and watched the coast of France dr away. Anne had saved his life, but, more important, she still loved him. Knowing that would be enough to sustain him in the difficult times that lay ahead.

Several seagulls circled the ship and cried noisily to each other.

He had once heard it said that gulls choose a mate for life and that some will pine away and die should they lose their mate.

He vowed that he would not lose Anne. Even if he had to return to France at the head of an army, he would come back to claim the woman he loved.

"I mean to have her," he said to sea and sky. "As God is my judge, I mean to have her back."

The ship went over on a different tack, and Buckingham moved to the side of the vessel. France lay off in the distance, and after a while, when the coast became no more than a dark blur, Buckingham went below to his cabin.

He sat down over a huge map of France and studied the area around La Rochelle, where the Duc de Rohan's forces still held a position off the coast. There was little doubt in his mind that by helping the Huguenots' cause, he would be helping his own. It would take time to convince Charles to send an army to La Rochelle, but he intended to let not one day pass without reminding the king of his obligation to defend men and women of the Protestant faith wherever and whenever they were threatened by the Catholic Church. He would be like Cato the Elder, who always ended his speeches in the Roman Senate with the words *Delenda est Carthago*—Carthage must be destroyed. He would vary those words in that he would say, "The Huguenots must be saved," to which he always would silently add, "And Anne must be mine...."

MASTER NOVELISTS

CHESAPEAKE   CB 24163 $3.95
by James A. Michener

An enthralling historical saga. It gives the account of different generations and races of American families who struggled, invented, endured and triumphed on Maryland's Chesapeake Bay. It is the first work of fiction in ten years to make its debut as #1 on *The New York Times Best Seller List*.

THE BEST PLACE TO BE   PB 04024 $2.50
by Helen Van Slyke

Sheila Callaghan's husband suddenly died, her children are grown, independent and troubled, the men she meets expect an easy kind of woman. Is there a place of comfort? A place for strength against an aching void? A novel for every woman who has ever loved.

ONE FEARFUL YELLOW EYE   GB 14146 $1.95
by John D. MacDonald

Dr. Fortner Geis relinquishes $600,000 to someone that no one knows. Who knows his reasons? There is a history of threats which Travis McGee exposes. But why does the full explanation live behind the eerie yellow eye of a mutilated corpse?

8002

GREAT ROMANTIC NOVELS

SISTERS AND STRANGERS PB 04445 $2.50
by Helen Van Slyke

Three women—three sisters each grown into an independent lifestyle—now are three strangers who reunite to find that their intimate feelings and perilous fates are entwined.

THE SUMMER OF THE SPANISH WOMAN
CB 23809 $2.50
by Catherine Gaskin

A young, fervent Irish beauty is alone. The only man she ever loved is lost as is the ancient family estate. She flees to Spain. There she unexpectedly discovers the simmering secrets of her wretched past... meets the Spanish Woman... and plots revenge.

THE CURSE OF THE KINGS CB 23284 $1.95
by Victoria Holt

This is Victoria Holt's most exotic novel! It is a story of romance when Judith marries Tybalt, the young archeologist, and they set out to explore the Pharaoh's tombs on their honeymoon. But the tombs are cursed... two archeologists have already died mysteriously.

8000